WITCHING BONES

A Wild Hunt Novel, Book 8

YASMINE GALENORN

D1714274

A Nightqueen Enterprises LLC Publication

Published by Yasmine Galenorn

PO Box 2037, Kirkland WA 98083-2037

WITCHING BONES

An Ante-Fae Adventure

A Wild Hunt Novel

Copyright © 2019 by Yasmine Galenorn

First Electronic Printing: 2019 Nightqueen Enterprises LLC

First Print Edition: 2019 Nightqueen Enterprises

Cover Art & Design: Ravven

Art Copyright: Yasmine Galenorn

Editor: Elizabeth Flynn

A Nightqueen Enterprises LLC Publication

Published in the United States of America

ACKNOWLEDGMENTS

Welcome back into the world of the Wild Hunt. Once again, I'm diving back into a world that has grabbed me by the heart and dragged me into its realm. Raven has led me a merry pace this book, and while she's so different than Ember, I truly adore her.

Thanks to my usual crew: Samwise, my husband, Andria and Jennifer—without their help, I'd be swamped. To the women who have helped me find my way in indie, you're all great and thank you to everyone. To my wonderful cover artist, Ravven, for the beautiful work she's done.

Also, my love to my furbles, who keep me happy. My most reverent devotion to Mielikki, Tapio, Ukko, Rauni, and Brighid, my spiritual guardians and guides. My love and reverence to Herne, and Cernunnos, and to the Fae, who still rule the wild places of this world. And a nod to the Wild Hunt, which runs deep in my magick, as well as in my fiction.

If you wish to reach me, you can find me through my

website at Galenorn.com and be sure to sign up for my newsletter to keep updated on all my latest releases! If you liked this book, I'd be grateful if you'd leave a review—it helps more than you can think.

Brightest Blessings,
~The Painted Panther~
~Yasmine Galenorn~

WELCOME TO WITCHING BONES

When you dance with Death, you have to be willing to roll the bones...

Raven BoneTalker, the Daughter of Bones, has her plate full. Not only is her neighbor still driving her nuts, but she's in a new relationship with Kipa, the Lord of the Wolves, and neither one is ready for everything that entails. But life takes a sinister turn when a spirit begins siphoning off the life force of one of Kipa's wolf shifters.

Gunnar, a member of the SuVahta—the pack of divine wolf shifters bound to the Lord of Wolves—is dying, and nobody can figure out why. Gunnar blames himself for the death of his beloved wife, and he believes she is haunting him.

When Kipa asks Raven to examine the wolf shifter, she finds a far deadlier spirit has latched on. And the only way Raven can help is to first agree to a deadly alliance with one of the ancient Ante-Fae—Arachana, the Web Weaver. But Arachana's price is far steeper than Raven can afford to pay, and the fallout threatens to shake the very core of Raven's life.

Reading Order for the Wild Hunt Series (For Series Timeline, see Table of Contents).

- Book 1: The Silver Stag
- Book 2: Oak & Thorns
- Book 3: Iron Bones
- Book 4: A Shadow of Crows
- Book 5: The Hallowed Hunt
- Book 6: The Silver Mist
- Book 7: Witching Hour
- Book 8: Witching Bones
- Book 9: A Sacred Magic (forthcoming)

CHAPTER ONE

I stared in horror at the shambles that was my kitchen. Skirting the edge of the room, I made my way toward the half-naked man who was standing in front of my stove. It wasn't that he was wearing an apron and nothing else that bothered me. Kipa was gorgeous and I happily feasted my gaze on his body. But the counters were a disaster. Pancake batter oozed off the counter, dripping on the floor where Raj was licking it up. It looked as though the bowl had exploded, but it was just tipped on its side. A pan of bacon sizzled enticingly, but on the other side of the counter, the jug of syrup had been knocked over, and it, too, was drizzling over the edge to form sticky puddles on the floor.

"What the fuck? Dude, you're making a mess! Clean it up, would you?" I pointed toward the cleanup items. "Those are what you call *paper towels*. The sponge is on the edge of the sink, and that shiny thing? It's called a faucet, and you can get water from there. The soap is right next to it. It's not rocket science, I promise you."

This wasn't the first time Kipa had left a trail of chaos in his wake. Either he was used to others following him around to clean up his messes, or he just didn't care. I hadn't figured out which yet. We'd only been together—and I used that word loosely—for a couple weeks.

He blinked, staring at me with a hurt look on his face. "I'm making you pancakes, woman!"

"What you're making is a mess." I shook my head. "I'm happy you wanted to fix me pancakes, but Kipa, look at what you've done." I restrained myself from grabbing a towel. It was his mess and I wasn't his maid. "Raj, quit eating pancake batter. It's not good for you."

The gargoyle gave me a guilty look, but said nothing. Raj's verdict on Kipa was still out, but he was never one to turn down free food, even if it did give him a stomachache. He slowly backed away, then lumbered over to the giant dog bed I'd bought for him and snuggled down in it. With a huff, he rested his head on the pillow and closed his eyes.

Kipa laughed. "Don't yell at him if you're mad at me. He was just taking advantage of the situation."

"I'm not. The batter will give him a tummy ache." I glared at him.

"I promise, I'll clean up after I'm done. Now get back to bed, woman, and I'll bring you breakfast in bed." He winked at me and my knees went weak.

I tried to summon up a little more outrage, but the way his gaze lingered on my body chased away all thoughts of the spilled batter and syrup. I cleared my throat, then stuck out my tongue.

"You'd better clean up, and dude, you'd better have lots

of sweet treats for me." Wiggling my ass at him, I headed back to the bedroom. I stripped off my robe, pulled on a plum-colored bustier that lifted my boobs till they almost fell out, pulled on a matching thong, and then jumped under the covers. Sometimes, waking up early was worth it.

WHEN KIPA APPEARED IN MY BEDROOM DOORWAY, HE WAS holding a tray with a large coffee cup on it, as well as a rose. He was also fully naked. I felt an immediate ache as I stared at him. His skin was somewhere between golden and brown and his muscles gleamed under the smooth flesh. Scars here and there only strengthened his roguish look. His dark brown hair flowed down past his shoulders. A full beard curved around his chin, and a tidy mustache barely covered the top of his full and inviting lips.

I shuddered, remembering the feel of them as they traced their way down my body, the cool metal of his dolphin bite piercing chilling my skin.

"How about dessert first?" he said.

I slowly threw back the covers, rising to my knees, and let out a little growl.

Kipa silently set the tray on the dresser, his eyes dark as coal. He swept his gaze over me, lingering long enough to set me on fire. I jumped to a crouching position, hand on the mattress to brace myself.

"Come get me," I said. "I dare you." I sprang off the bed, leaping for the door.

Kipa let out a loud howl, launching himself in front of

me. "You're not going anywhere, beautiful." His voice was throaty, raw and hungry.

"Make me want to stay." I pressed my hands against his chest, pushing him back so I could look at him. His muscles rippled under my fingers, the fierce strength tensing as I leaned forward and slowly ran my tongue down his chest. He was salty, the silken sweat beading on my tongue. I could taste the feral magic in him, like sweet wild strawberries on a summer evening. I fluttered my tongue over his nipples and he let out a husky groan, his eyes gleaming as I looked up to lock his gaze with mine.

Breathing hard, he focused on my face. I could feel his longing. It saturated the room, his pheromones thick, hanging in the air like droplets of moisture.

"Raven."

His whisper cut through the silence as he gathered me up, pulling me to him. He kissed me, insistent, and I opened my lips to welcome him in. As our lips met, Kipa slid his hands under my butt and I wrapped my legs around his waist, my arms draped around his shoulders. I could feel him pressing against me, his arousal long and thick, hard as rock, hot as a shaft of fire. My breath quickened as he carried me over to the bed and, with my legs still around his waist, laid me down on the sheets.

As I lowered my feet on the bed, bending my knees, Kipa hooked his fingers around the sides of my panties and yanked them down, moving so he could pull them off my feet. I spread my legs, letting him watch as I dropped my hand between my thighs and leisurely stroked myself, teasing him with my smile. I let out a long, shuddering breath and closed my eyes. With my other hand, I slowly trailed my fingers over my breast, over the jacquard of the bustier. I was on fire, so hungry for him that I felt like I might burst. I shivered, brushing my mound with my fingers. Every nerve quivered, every inch of my body aflame. I felt like one giant erogenous zone.

"Look at me," Kipa ordered.

I opened my eyes as Kipa knelt by the edge of the bed, lowering himself to his knees. I propped myself up on my elbows just enough to watch as he brought his head between my thighs. With two fingers, he spread my labia and lowered his lips, spreading me wide so he could reach me with his tongue. I let out another moan, my breath quickening, as he reached his target. As he lightly fluttered quick strokes against me, I moaned again.

I caught my breath, forcing myself to hold still, but I wanted more so I quickly unzipped the bustier, letting it fall open, and began to stroke my nipples, circling them between my fingers as he drove me closer to the edge.

"Don't stop," I pleaded.

I had missed this so much. Ulstair and I had been hot and heavy, and I was used to regular sex—a lot of it. But his death had put an end to that. I missed him, but when I met Kipa, our chemistry had combusted. We couldn't keep our hands off each other, and he had been the gasoline to my wildfire.

Kipa shifted his position, increasing the pressure. I could barely control my breath, and I began to whimper, little cries escaping from my throat as he began to swirl his tongue faster. I could hear the howling of wolves from the astral. They felt the passion of their master and were adding their voices to our union.

Then the wave swept over me, an undulation of golden light, and I gave in, coming so hard that I felt like I was going to pass out. All through it, those brilliant dark eyes of his burned deep in my soul.

As I fell back against the bed, every muscle in my body relaxing, arm crossed over my head, Kipa joined me on the bed.

He laughed a deep, throaty laugh. "I'm not done with you yet, woman."

Leaning down, he took one of my nipples in his mouth, curling his tongue around it, and then swung up over me, slipping between my legs. I wrapped my legs around his waist again, pulling him down into me, and he slid in deep and hard. He began to thrust, pressing against me, crushing my breasts against his chest.

The fire began to build again as my pulse quickened. I wrapped my arms around him and rolled him over, with him still deep inside me. I rose up, riding him hard, and he cupped my breasts as I set a new pace, one I controlled. Smiling triumphantly, I ground against him, swiveling my hips against his pelvis, so full with his girth that it felt like he filled every nook and cranny of my body. I was slick with hunger, and he dropped his hands to my waist as the passion intensified, holding me as I picked up the pace. I dropped my head back, my hair streaming down my back, and began to rub my breasts as he watched from beneath me.

His eyes were almost black now, and his breath sharp. "I'm close," he whispered.

"Hold on, just a little longer," I ordered as my own desire quickened again.

He slid one hand down between my legs, fingering me as I rode him, and that was all it took to bring me to climax again, the world exploding in one giant orgasm as

Kipa let out a long cry, coming too. I stiffened against him, shaking, as he thrust again, and then once more, and then, one last time.

WE WERE SNUGGLED DEEP BENEATH THE COVERS. KIPA stroked my face with one hand, his other arm wrapped around me. I lay quietly against his shoulder, feeling both drained and energized. It was as though every drop of tension had fled from my body and left behind a warm glow that buoyed me up.

"That was amazing." He kissed my forehead.

"Yeah, it was. I'm still basking." I peeked over him at the clock on the table. It was nearly eight-thirty. "But Raj needs his breakfast, and the ferrets, and I need to eat." I paused, thinking of the mess in the kitchen. "I think I'll duck out to buy us breakfast while you clean up the kitchen."

"Give me a break, woman. I was making *pancakes* for you!" He laughed. "Don't I get points for that?"

I snickered, rolling over atop him, straddling his hips. "You would have, if they had turned out and you hadn't left my kitchen in a wreck. Nope, but you get points for the bedplay. That, you definitely have mastered." I gave him a quick kiss.

"Another go?" he asked, his eyes twinkling.

The fire in my belly rose again, but I let out a sigh. "No, I need to jump in the shower and get the day started. Will you feed Raj? I'll take care of the ferrets when I get back. I'll call and put in an order at Deanne's Diner, so it will be ready once I get there. What do you want?"

"Pancakes?" He laughed as I hit him with a pillow. "And bacon, sausage, eggs. Coffee. Maybe a doughnut as well."

"In other words, you want everything on the menu." I hopped out of bed and dashed into the bathroom through the chill air. It had snowed a little the night before, though it was slated to turn to sleet later today. But sleet or not, it was cold. The high was only forecast for forty-one today, and a humid, wet forty-one at that.

I had washed my hair the night before, so I gathered it into a ponytail to keep it from getting wet before climbing into the shower, where I lathered up with a spicy amber bath gel. As I washed over my curves and the tattoos spread across my body, my thoughts lingered on Kipa's hands and on his lips. I still didn't know what to make of the relationship—it wasn't something I had been prepared for, and I had the feeling he felt the same way. We got along well, I liked him a lot, but we had only been together a few weeks and most of that time had been spent in bed. Whether this was a wonderful, passionate fling, or whether it would lead to something deeper, I had no clue. And I wasn't in a hurry to rush it.

As I stepped out of the shower onto the heated floor— I had radiant heating—I wrapped a fluffy bath sheet around me and settled myself at the vanity, peering into the mirror. I had no real insecurities about my looks, even though I wasn't the conventional beauty in terms of human standards. I still wasn't sure about how I handled the social niceties that went with society, though. At least Kipa was a god. With him, I didn't have to sort out how I acted, at least not as much as I did—among people, especially humans.

As for me, I was one of the Ante-Fae, the predecessors to the Fae races. We were *all* a little squirrelly, and we each had unique abilities. While I was cautious with Kipa —the god thing was a double-edged sword—I also felt I could hold my own with him, for the most part. Perhaps it was false courage on my part, but it worked.

I dried off, then put on my makeup. I was a makeup junkie, especially with eyeliner, and I tended to run on the Goth girl side. It was my style, as natural to me as breathing. I applied retro wings to the sides of my eyes, then mascara on my top lashes. As I powdered the foundation down, I realized I was almost out of my favorite color of lip color. I spread the liquid lip lacquer around my bow lips, the deep blackberry shade vivid against my pale skin. Then, shaking my hair out of the ponytail, I brushed the tangle of curls that fell mid-back. With a shake of the head, I gave myself one last look, feeling ready for the day.

As I returned to my bedroom to dress, I could hear Kipa in the kitchen. It sounded like he was cleaning, and I smiled softly. He'd get his props for pancakes when he made them correctly and didn't dirty up every dish in the kitchen. And when he kept the batter in the pan instead of on the counter, he'd get a few more.

I slipped on a pair of fishnet tights, then chose a black lace dress that fell four inches above my knees in front, and down to my calves in back. It had a sweetheart neckline and lace sleeves, and the overlay of black lace over nude fabric made it look almost see-through. I buckled a purple corset belt around my waist, and then slid my feet into a pair of chunky heeled boots that came up to my knees. They were black leather, with chains on the sides and studs down the front where they laced up. A hidden zipper made them easy to take off and on.

As I headed toward the kitchen, I peeked in the ferrets' room. Elise stood up against the cage, staring at me.

"I'll be back in a little bit to clean your cages and feed you. I just need to run out and get some food first."

She gave me a long look, and then a soft whisper touched my thoughts. *Thank you. We'll be fine until then. I wanted to talk to you about Gordon when you have a moment.*

I nodded. "We'll talk when I'm cleaning your cage. Is everything all right?"

I think so, came the soft thought. *I'm just a little concerned, but I don't think he's sick.*

I shut the door behind me, worried. The ferrets had been with me for over twenty years. I'd found them as spirits up on Mount Rainier, when they were trapped inside a tree stump portal. They were actually spirits of people who had been murdered up on the mountain and then cursed. I had attempted to free them, but in a comedy of errors, had simply transferred their spirits into ferret form. Now they were stuck. But at least they weren't trapped in the tree trunk anymore, and I could communicate with them while I researched how to break the curse, to free them to go on in their journey.

As I entered the kitchen, I saw Kipa had made good time on cleaning up. The sink was still full of dishes, and there was still batter trailing down a couple of the cupboards, but the floor was clean.

He glanced up at me. "I was about to feed Raj."

"I'll do it." I scooted over to one side and pulled out a dish for Raj. I give him a can of cat food. It was quick, easy, and he liked it. As I spooned the food into the dish,

Raj came up behind me, nudging me. I glanced down at him and he gave me a plaintive look. Stroking his head, I realized what was wrong. Kipa had been here for nearly twenty-four hours. Raj and I hadn't had time to talk. Raj didn't like speaking in front of other people. In fact, almost no one knew that he could talk besides me. I set the dish down for him, and turned to Kipa.

"Why don't we just go out for breakfast? I'll clean the rest of this up later. I have a busy day scheduled, and need to get moving." I didn't want to just send him on his way abruptly, but I wasn't going to betray Raj's secret. And Raj was having a rough-enough time adjusting to Kipa's presence. I suspected that the gargoyle was jealous of all the time I was spending with Kipa.

Kipa frowned. "Are you sure? I thought we were going to spend the morning together."

We hadn't talked about it, so this was news to me. But I had discovered early on that Kipa assumed that if he liked something, everybody else should as well. And if he had made plans, everybody should be accommodating. It wasn't rudeness on his part, he was just used to being the leader of the pack, so to speak.

And he was, in his own world. Ember, a good friend of mine, and I had seen just how well he played with others when he and his cousin Herne had gotten embroiled in an argument that ended up with Ember and me down in a pit, facing a deadly foe. The two men hadn't even noticed we disappeared. Luckily, girl power had seen us through before they found us.

"You never mentioned wanting to spend the morning together." I stared at him. "This is the first I've heard of it."

He let out an exasperated sigh. "I didn't know you had anything going on this morning. I just assumed—"

"You just assumed that I'd be available. Well, today's my day to read cards down at the Sun & Moon Apothecary, so I don't have the morning to give you. I have to take care of the ferrets, then head down to the shop to meet Llew." I bit my lip, trying to decide just how bitchy to get. We'd had a wonderful morning, but I wasn't about to let Kipa start taking me for granted.

"What is it? I can tell something's wrong." Kipa crossed his arms, leaning one hip against the counter. It didn't help that he was so damn sexy.

"Here's the thing. Obviously, I like you a lot or we wouldn't be thrashing around in bed so much. And I'd like this—*us*—to continue. At least until we find out where *we're* going. But this relationship won't work if you keep planning out my days without consulting me. Newsflash: you aren't the center of my universe. I know it must be hard to hear that, given you're one of the gods. But I don't notice Herne doing that with Ember."

His eyes narrowed and I had a feeling I'd hit a sore spot. In fact, I knew I had.

"Comparing me to *Herne*, are you?"

"Don't get your Speedos in a wad. I'm not saying that you need to be like Herne. But it wouldn't hurt you to be a little more considerate of other people and their feelings, or their time."

He looked so hurt that I felt a pang of guilt, but it was for his own good. If I didn't tell him, somebody else might and they wouldn't do so out of caring about him.

"Listen, dude. You're fantastic, Kipa. And I know you

care about people. You wouldn't be allowed in my house if you didn't, god or not. But this is just one example of something I've noticed during the past few weeks. You assumed that I would have the time because *you* have the time. You didn't bother asking *me*—and *that's* the problem. Understand?" I rested my hand on the counter as I continued to stare at him. I wasn't going to look away, or let him cow me.

"All right. I'll try to do better," he muttered. "I'm sorry. I'm used to being—"

"In charge. I get it. I truly do. But you're not my boss, you're not my owner, and you're not my parent. You're my *lover*. And that gives you certain rights, but running my life and organizing my schedule isn't one of them." I searched his face, wondering if he would be able to handle me as I asserted my boundaries. It would be a deal breaker if he couldn't.

He paused for a moment before a crooked smile spread across his face. He held out his hands to me. "Okay, I promise. I will pay more attention to the way I act. I *like* that you're not afraid of me. I *like* that you stand up for yourself. It may take me some time to get used to, but I think I'm going to enjoy being with a strong woman who knows what she wants and isn't afraid to stand up for herself." He leaned down, pressing his lips against mine. "Don't worry about breakfast. I'll grab something on the way back to my apartment. When can I see you again?"

A wave of relief washed over me. I pulled out my calendar.

"Why don't you come over for dinner tomorrow night? I've got a lot of errands to do tomorrow, but we can have dinner, and then watch a movie. Or not watch a movie, as the case may be." I blew him a kiss, winking.

I knew very well that even if we started watching a movie, we wouldn't end up finishing it. The flames burned strong between us. Even now, I found it hard to keep my hands to myself. I wanted to run them up and down his chest. I reached up, smoothing his hair back.

"You are so fucking sexy. If you don't get out of here, I may throw the day away and drag you back to bed and I really shouldn't do that." I caught my breath, shuddering.

Laughing, Kipa stroked my face and, in a husky voice, said, "I'd better get out of here. Or neither one of us will get anything done." With another kiss, he grabbed his leather jacket, turned, and headed out the door.

CHAPTER TWO

I returned to the kitchen after locking the door behind him. I didn't trust my neighbors enough to leave it unlocked. I'd been on a campaign to drum them out of the neighborhood, but they'd been stubborn so far.

Raj was sitting in the kitchen, staring at the drying batter that had dripped over the edge of the counters.

"Does Raven like Kipa better than Raj?"

I groaned. "No. Raven does *not* like Kipa better than Raj. Raven loves Raj. Raven likes Kipa in an entirely different way than she likes Raj." I knelt beside the gargoyle, holding him by the sides of the head so that he was staring into my eyes. "No matter what happens, nobody will ever replace Raj. Raj will *always* be in Raven's life. Remember, Ulstair and Raven loved each other, but Raven and Raj still had a wonderful relationship."

Raj let out a deep sigh. He was about as big as a rottweiler, with a sloped back. He actually walked on his knuckles. His front legs were actually his arms, but they

15

were as thick as his back legs, and even though gargoyles could walk upright, most of them chose to walk like a dog. Raj was also missing his wings, and that affected his gait. A demon had cut them off of him when he was young, and I had won the gargoyle in a poker game, determined to give him a better life. I made sure that he didn't remember his life before me, wiping away the pain with a spell I had bummed off of a powerful witch.

"Raj misses Ulstair. Does Raven miss Ulstair?"

I blinked. I hadn't expected that particular question. And then it dawned on me. Raj wasn't just jealous of me spending time with Kipa. He was angry at *Kipa*, whom he saw as taking Ulstair's place.

"Raven misses Ulstair every day. Raven will never forget him. Raven loved Ulstair, but Ulstair is dead now, and even though it's hard, Raven and Raj have to move on. We don't want to bind Ulstair's spirit here, and missing him too much—holding onto the past—can do that. Raven is a bone witch, she knows these things. Do you understand?"

A light gleamed in Raj's eyes. He paused, then nodded.

"Raj thinks he understands. Raj will try to let Ulstair rest. It's hard for Raj but he will try." A tear trickled down his cheek.

I leaned down and kissed the tear away, then stroked his head and rubbed his back the way he liked it.

"I know it's hard. Raven knows it's hard. It's difficult for Raven, too. Raven and Raj are here for each other, though. And nothing—no one—will ever come between us. Remember that. Raven will always be here for Raj." I kissed him on the head, and he made the little murphing sound that he did when he was content.

"Raj eat breakfast now. Raj loves Raven."

"And Raven loves Raj." I patted him on the back as he turned and walked over to his dish and began to eat his breakfast. Then, grabbing a sponge, I made quick work of the remaining mess that Kipa had left in the kitchen. I had forgotten how difficult it was dealing with another person on such an intimate level. Ulstair had died in September, and by November, I had started to get used to being alone again. We hadn't lived together, so it was easier for me than some people. I wasn't sure I had liked it, but I was getting used to relying on myself for everything. Now all of a sudden I was having to adapt to compromising with another person again.

With a sigh, I tossed the sponge in the sink and wiped down the cupboards with a paper towel to dry them. Then I pulled out a carton of yogurt for breakfast and ate it on my way to the ferrets' room.

After cleaning out the cages, feeding the ferrets, and changing their water bottles, I let them out to play for twenty minutes or so. Gordon and Templeton raced around the room, playing with their toys and generally causing havoc. Elise squirmed up on my lap, and I set her on the table.

"So, what's going on?"

Elise trembled, then snuggled into my arms as I stroked her soft sable fur. Over the years I had grown extremely fond of the ferrets, although Templeton and Gordon were beginning to forget they had ever been human. I hoped to find a way to break the curse on them before they totally lost themselves in the world of ferretness. I wasn't sure it was possible, but I was giving it my best shot.

Gordon hardly answers me anymore. At least not like this. He doesn't remember his life before, I think. And his forgetfulness is progressing quickly. Almost like some sort of dementia. He's happy enough, but it hurts me to see my brother losing himself. I know how easy it is, and how tempting it is at times to just let go and allow the animal nature take over. Templeton is managing to resist, though he slips more than I do. But Gordon? Gordon has given up, I think.

I glanced over at the cage. Templeton, who was jet black, was watching Elise and me from one of the perches. He had gotten the zoomies out of him, and now he was listening to our conversation. But Gordon was still dashing around the room, playing with a squeak toy. I set Elise down, and sat on the floor beside Gordon.

"Gordon? Gordon, can you hear me? I'd like to talk to you." I scooped him up in my arms, scratching behind his ears. "Gordon, I know you're in there. I know behind those beautiful ferret eyes of yours, you can still hear me. Please answer."

As I gazed into his eyes, I felt a spark rise up. It was almost as though the question hung between us. After a moment, I petted his head again, gazing deep into his eyes. "Gordon? Elise is worried about you. She thinks that you're losing yourself. Please talk to me."

Very slowly, as if from a great distance, a whisper-soft *Hello* touched my thoughts.

"Gordon? Was that you?"

There was another pause as he searched my face, quivering in my arms. And then, again so soft I almost didn't catch it, a whisper touched my thoughts.

It's so hard to keep focused. It's very difficult, Raven. I don't know how long I can hold onto myself. I've never been the strong one. Elise has always been the strongest. And Templeton is stronger than me. I'm weak.

"No, Gordon. You're not weak. You really aren't. You're just in a very difficult situation. I'm still working to find a way to free you, so hold onto yourself as long as you can. Talk to Elise, talk to Templeton. Let them remind you of your life before here. Let them help you bring back the memories. Hold on, please. For all of us?"

He blinked, one long, slow blink of those brilliant eyes, and then let out a little sigh.

I'll try. But I don't know if I can manage. Please don't be angry if I fail.

"Of course we won't be angry. We all care about you. Elise and Templeton love you so much, and I'm so very fond of you. But try as long as you can. I'll step up my search for a way to break the curse."

I want to thank you. Without you we'd be stuck in that tree, lost forever. At least we have a life now, and it's a good life.

The whispers were waning, and I could tell he was getting distracted again. I gently set him down on the floor and gave him another stroke down his back. But his eyes caught sight of his toy again, and he was off to play with it once more. Feeling helpless, I stood and returned to the table, where Elise was watching Gordon with sorrowful eyes.

"I'm doing what I can, Elise. I promise you that. I'm trying. Did you catch what he said?"

She ducked her head in a nod.

I heard. I'll try to keep him connected, I'll tell him more stories of when we were children. I'll tell both of them because I think Templeton is getting closer to that stage.

She paused, then snuggled against me with a sound that almost sounded like a cry.

If it happens to all of us, it will be okay. But I don't want to forget. I don't want to forget who I am.

Almost in tears, I kissed her forehead. "You hold on, Elise. I'll try harder."

I know you are, Raven. I know you're trying. Maybe there isn't a way. Maybe there's no hope to lift this curse. And if there isn't, this isn't a bad life. Will you promise to watch over us as long as we need, if we all forget?

"I promise you, as long as you are in this form, and as long as you need me, I will be here for you. And I take my oaths with absolute seriousness." I stood, feeling incredibly sad. I loved the ferrets, but I wanted them to be free, to be on their way to the afterlife that they deserved.

As I left the room, after shutting them back in their cage, I decided to approach Llew again. I had asked him a couple years ago if he knew of any way to take care of this curse. At the time he hadn't, but both his experience and his knowledge had grown since then. It was worth a shot.

I MADE SURE RAJ WAS COMFORTABLE WITH THE TV AND HIS cartoons. I used to leave him out in his doghouse when I wasn't home, but given the state of my feud with the neighbors, I didn't trust Buck to not try to hurt him. I tossed a couple apples in my bag, made sure I had everything I needed, and locked the door securely behind me.

As I headed to my car, I glanced across the street. Sure enough, it looked like Buck Smith and his cronies were hosting another meeting of the Human Liberation Army.

I recognized several of the cars, and the fact that they had anti-SubCult stickers on their bumpers didn't help. Although they didn't use that term for those who weren't human. Instead, their slogans bandied around terms like *coontie*—a vulgar term for Crypto women that referred to their genitals, and *softrocks*—a similar label for Crypto men, as well as other, worse idioms.

I considered tossing a fireball down one of their gas tanks, but that would only make things worse. And while I knew Herne, who ran the Wild Hunt agency, and he could probably step in for me if need be, I didn't want to press our friendship.

With a sigh, I settled for giving Buck and his house the finger as I pulled out the cul-de-sac and headed for downtown Redmond.

CHAPTER THREE

I was still hungry. The yogurt had barely touched my appetite, so I stopped in at A Taste of Latte, which was next door to the Sun and Moon Apothecary. Jordan Roberts owned the coffee shop, and he was Llew's husband. Llew was one of my best friends, and Jordan, who had been rather standoffish before, had quickly become a close friend as well. We had endured a run-in with a creepy-assed doll bent on making Jordan's life miserable. The freakshow toy had threatened both of their lives until I helped them destroy it. Now we were all copacetic.

As the shop bells jangled, Jordan waved to me from behind the counter. I glanced around. The coffee shop wasn't empty, but it looked as though the morning rush was over, and the lunch rush had yet to begin.

"Hey, Raven! I assume you want a mocha. How many shots?" He grinned at me. He had me pegged, all right.

"Quad shot today. And I'm hungry. Give me a sausage breakfast sandwich and a couple of the apple hand-pies to go, please. I'm due next door in a few minutes."

Jordan fixed my mocha, handing me the cup with a stopper in it. After popping the sandwich into the toaster oven to warm it, he bagged my pastries.

"That will be $14.54, please."

I gave him three fives and motioned for him to put the change in the tip jar. Jordan handed me my pastries, and then the breakfast sandwich wrapped in a leakproof bag.

"What's going on with you today? You're glowing, but you look a little sad." Jordan was a tiger shifter, and he was good at sensing nuances in emotions and mood.

"New boyfriend, so great sex. But I've got a situation that I'm trying to figure out how to solve. Totally unrelated. The situation's a magical issue." Nobody knew about the ferrets except Llew, and I had only told him because I needed his help to find out a solution to the curse. He had promised to keep the matter silent and I trusted him. Llew was first, and foremost, a man of his word.

"Congrats on the new boytoy. If I can do anything to help with the other problem, please—just ask. I still feel like I owe you one." He shrugged, grinning.

"You and Llew took me out to dinner. That squared us up. I know you don't believe it, but getting rid of ghosts and their cronies *is* my business. I don't run the Witching Hour just to make friends. What I do *is* dangerous, but it's a danger I choose. It's a danger I was born to." I winked at him. "Besides, Llew already paid me back in spell components, remember?" Another customer approached the counter and I took my leave, waving good-bye to Jordan from the door.

Next door, Llew was setting out a new display of essential oils. I glanced at the blends. It looked like he had found a new supplier. Energy emanated off of the bottles in waves.

"Whoever made those is a strong witch," I said.

"You don't have to tell me that. She came in last week to show me samples. I could tell right away they were the real deal, and that she's got more experience than just about anybody I've met." He paused, then added, "She's a good sort too. I felt an instant camaraderie with her."

I set my food on the table that I used for readings, then slipped out of my jacket, hanging it on a hook near my station. "Just don't replace me," I said, laughing.

"Nobody could ever replace you, Raven." Llew slung his arm around my shoulder, pulling me in for a hug. He paused, then lifted my hair back away from my neck. "I can see somebody got a pearl necklace this morning. Kipa's keeping you busy, isn't he?" Llew winked. "He any good?"

"You're talking about a *god*, dude. And yes, he's keeping me plenty busy, and yes, he's *very* good. So good I'm sore." I stuck my tongue out at him, then took a swig of the mocha.

"Careful with where you aim that tongue. I don't know where it's been." Llew wiggled his eyebrows.

I almost spit out my coffee. Setting down the cup, I crossed my arms and shook my head. "Oh, dude. You are *so* asking for it. But yes, Kipa's more than a match for me. Trouble is, I need to socialize him a bit. He's self-centered, with an ego to match."

"That doesn't sound good. He's not hurting you, is he?"

Llew asked, tilting his head just enough that I knew he was listening to the undertones of my words.

I shook my head. "No. You know me, Llew. I wouldn't be with him if he was. Let's just say, I brought the issue to his notice and he's working on it." I sorted out my things, spreading my cloth on the table. I pulled out my portable crystal ball that I kept in my traveling bag and my deck of cards and set them up. Llew handed me the candle we kept at the shop for my use. It was a beautiful black pillar candle on a dragon pedestal.

"Okay, what else is going on? I can tell something's wrong, and it's not boyfriend trouble. What's shaking?" Llew sat down on the opposite side of the table. "By now, I know that look."

I frowned. "Yeah, so, you're right. It's about the ferrets."

He blinked. "Are they okay? Is one of them sick?"

I shook my head. "No, not really. But the curse is taking its toll on Gordon. He's forgetting who he is, and Elise is scared for him. I know they enjoy the life they have now, but they should be off roaming the Aether, out in the Netherworld. You know—moving on. The curse is preventing that, and I haven't been able to break it. I promised Elise I'd renew my efforts, but I've run out of options. I've read every book on hex-breaking that I can find. I've talked to so many of the magic-born that I could start my own club. And Arawn and Cerridwen aren't being much help on this."

"And you feel guilty." Llew straightened the cloth on his side for me.

"I feel...oh," I said, frustrated and not finding the right words. "It isn't guilt, per se. I feel like anybody else does when a friend is hurting and you can't do anything to help. I promised I'd do my best, and lately I haven't been keeping that promise."

"Why?"

"I've run out of ideas on which direction to look in next. Which brings me to a favor I want to ask. I know you looked into this for me a few years ago without success, but…if there's *any* chance, could you look again?" I shuffled my cards, warming them up, then set them to one side. As I opened the sausage muffin, the warm, yeasty scent of bread, cheese, and sausage wafted out. I was so hungry, my stomach rumbled.

Llew laughed. "Eat that before you get heartburn from being so hungry. And yes, I'll start researching tonight. I can reach out to some of the people I know now. People I didn't know back then. Maybe one of them will have some ideas."

I jumped up, dashing around the table, to give him a hug and a kiss. "Thank you. I know that it might be futile, but I *have* to try."

Llew pointed to my food. "Finish eating. I booked appointments for you starting at noon, so your first client will be coming in soon. Moira has more questions about her sister."

I laughed, shaking my head. "She'll never rest, will she?"

Moira Ness was a wonderful little old lady who came to me for advice. Every month like clockwork, she scheduled an appointment to ask about her twin sister, who died thirty-five years ago in a house fire. And every month I told her the truth. Her sister had moved on, and there was nothing I could do.

During each reading, she would try slanting her questions in a new way, hoping for a different answer. She missed her twin so much that I had actually entertained the thought of lying to her, of telling her what she wanted to hear. But that went against my ethics.

So, every single month, I would gently let her down, steering her to talking about her memories. She would forget about her questions and tell me stories about their lives together. I never charged her full price—I knew she was on a fixed income—and I always took extra time to listen. I had a feeling I was her only social outlet, and if she wanted to come and pay me to chat about her sister, I didn't mind.

I finished my breakfast sandwich, then ate the apple pies. As I was throwing out my trash and finishing my mocha, Moira entered the shop. She was dressed in a faded Chanel suit. I let out a long breath, mentally shifted gears, and went to greet her and guide her to my table. The day was officially on.

AFTER I FINISHED MY LAST READING, IT WAS FOUR-THIRTY and dark as sin outside. I waved to Llew, then forged my way through the evening hustle. The wind had picked up, and the temperature had dropped. The scent of ozone hung in the air, a prediction of more snow to come. I glanced at the sky. Sure enough, while it was dark, there was a strong silver glint to the clouds. I shivered, pulling my jacket closer. My phone buzzed as I headed to my car and I pulled it out of my bra, where I kept it tucked away. I glanced at the screen. It was Ember.

HEY, YOU UP FOR COMPANY TONIGHT? ANGEL AND I'LL BE ON THE EASTSIDE AND WE THOUGHT WE MIGHT DROP OVER FOR A FEW.

I smiled. Even though I had put Kipa off till tomorrow night, I really didn't have plans for the evening. I didn't want to be too available. SURE. WHAT TIME?

WE'LL BE THERE AT SEVEN. WE'LL BRING DINNER, SINCE YOU TREATED LAST TIME. WE'LL BRING A TREAT FOR RAJ TOO.

SEE YOU THEN.

I tucked my phone away as I approached my car—a Toyota Camry—and pulled out my keys, unlocking the door. I'd rigged it so that the moment I unlocked the car, the overhead light turned on. It was a safety measure. By the time I was tucked inside, doors locked and heater running, the first few flakes of sleet began to appear. As the temperature dropped, the sleet would turn to snow. But sleet meant for a dicey drive home. Grateful I didn't live too far away, I eased out from the curb and headed back to my house.

CHAPTER FOUR

*E*ven though Ember and Angel promised they were bringing over dinner, I decided to make a batch of cookies. First, though, I fixed Raj a steak. He'd been so good around Kipa the past few weeks, and I wanted to make sure he knew how much I appreciated it. While he was happily gnawing on the porterhouse bone, I told him that Ember and Angel were coming over.

"Raj like Ember and Angel," Raj said.

I sat down beside him on the floor, eating chocolate chips out of the bag. "Does Raj think he might ever want to talk to Ember or Angel?" I kept my voice light, trying not to stress him out.

He stopped eating for a moment, cocking his head. Then he looked back at his food, as if contemplating what that would mean. After a moment, he let out an odd noise, then said, "Maybe. Someday, Raj say hello to them. Raj eat now?"

"Raj eat now." I stroked his leathery head. "Doodlebug knows Raven loves him, right?"

"Doodlebug" was my nickname for him. I didn't use it often, mostly when I wanted to reassure him how much I loved him.

"Doodlebug knows." He smiled then—a gargoyle smiling was almost more frightening than one with a grim expression—and went back to his food.

By the time I finished making the cookies, it was almost time for Ember and Angel to arrive. I set out a bottle of wine and three goblets. The doorbell rang and I dashed to get it.

"Hey, Raven." Ember's jacket was covered with a dusting of snow. I peered beyond her to see that several inches had piled up on the sidewalk since I'd gotten home.

"Snowing much?" I blinked, not expecting to see the blanket of white.

They stomped their boots before they crowded in.

Angel shivered as she unwound the scarf from around her neck. "The weatherman said the storm took a detour and we're right in the convergence zone—Seattle and the Eastside. We're supposed to get at least five to eight inches tonight. Ember and I didn't realize it was going to be this bad before we decided to make a trip over to Serena's Day Spa."

"Day spa, huh? Sounds like fun." Actually, it didn't. I loved massages and getting my nails and hair done, but I wasn't into the whole bathhouse, sit-in-mud, hot-tub experience. But I knew Angel was, and I thought Ember might be, and I wasn't going to rain on their parade.

"I needed that," Ember said, glowing. "It was a belated birthday present from my bestie, here." She leaned her head against Angel's arm. "By the way, thank you so much for showing up at my party. I love the conch shell!"

I had attended Ember's birthday party earlier in the week. Since I knew she was part Leannan Sidhe—and pledged to Morgana—I had traded a reading for a sea shell that had come from a siren's collection. It was highly polished with the residue of the ocean's energy clinging to it. It felt like just the right thing, and Ember seemed happy with it.

"I'm glad." I hung their coats on the coat rack as they took off their boots, then led them into the dining room. Raj meandered over to the door and looked at me, so I let him out, chaining him up by his doghouse. Raj had a propensity for taking off on walks by himself and it wasn't safe. At least, I didn't *think* it was safe. Not with the Bucks of the world out there.

When I returned to the dining room, Ember was opening the wine, while Angel was arranging the takeout containers. Apparently we were eating Chinese tonight, and the smells of egg rolls and pot stickers filled the air.

"So what's shaking?" I asked, getting plates from the kitchen. "Any news on the front with the Tuathan Brotherhood?" Ember and the Wild Hunt were chasing down a ruthless hate group purporting to be Fae in nature. They had already caused massive political unrest, including getting the Fae Courts suspended from the United Coalition, an act that had far-reaching ramifications in a number of quarters.

Ember shook her head. "No, but we're trying to track down Nuanda. Unfortunately, there wasn't much left of the compound, so we don't have a lot of leads at the moment." She looked tired.

"You're dragging butt, girl. What's going on?"

Angel sighed. "Tell her. Maybe Raven will have some insight on what's going down in your dreams."

I perked up. "Dreams?" I was always interested in discussing dreams. The Dreamtime was close to the Aetheric realm, and sometimes I went dreamwalking in my sleep.

"Nightmares is more like it," Ember said, frowning. "I've been having recurring dreams that scare the hell out of me, and I'm not sure why. They don't seem like they should be so frightening, but they are."

"What are they about?" I asked, pouring the wine. Ember handed me the carton of egg rolls and I took two of them, putting them on my plate. Angel was spooning chicken fried rice onto her plate, and Ember had hold of the orange chicken.

Ember took a deep breath, then sat back, staring at her plate. "I keep dreaming of a tall man—I can't see his face, but he's as tall as a giant. He's in silhouette against the sun, which is rising behind a mountain. He holds a spear over one shoulder, and behind him stands an army of soldiers, ready for battle. I can't see them distinctly, but I can feel they're hungry to be on the battlefield, spilling blood. The next moment, a flaming golden arrow soars through the air. I'm not sure from where it's coming from, though I know it isn't the man with the spear. It lands directly in front of my feet. The fire clinging to it feels clean and fierce. As I look down at the arrow, I'm compelled to take hold of it, and it turns into a sword in my hand. I pull the sword from the ground, and find that it was actually caught in a low well, and the blade's dripping with water and moss. The man with the spear lets out a war cry, and in the distance, a horn sounds. As his army begins to

32

move forward, I realize that I'm directly in their path. Then I wake up."

I blinked. "That's a pretty specific dream. You say it's the same every time? How many times have you dreamed it?"

She bit her lip, thinking. After a moment, she said, "About five times. It started right after we took down the compound over on the Olympic Peninsula. And yes, it's the same every time. I know it has something to do with the brotherhood. I've asked Morgana, but she's been pretty tight-lipped lately. I have a weird feeling that there's a great deal going on behind the scenes that we're not allowed to know yet, and I'm almost afraid of when Cernunnos and Morgana decide it's time to fill us in."

"Has Herne said anything?"

She shook her head. "He's in the dark as much as I am."

I wasn't so sure I believed that, given Herne was the son of Cernunnos and Morgana, and he ran the Wild Hunt for them, but Ember seemed sure so I didn't question her.

"What do you think?" I turned to Angel. "About the dream?"

She blinked, her eyes luminous against the glow of her dark skin. She easily could have been a model—she was tall enough and lean enough, and she had a striking look to her. But she had opted to go a vastly different route.

"Ember's right that it's connected to the Tuathan Brotherhood, that much I can sense. But I don't know how. And it also has something to do with a promise Ember made." She gazed pointedly at Ember. "*You* know what I'm talking about. The bow?"

"Don't remind me." Ember ducked her head, staring at

33

her plate. "I just… I don't want to do this, Angel. I don't. But I told Morgana I would, and she's pushing on it."

"Pushing you about what? Is it private, or can you tell me?" The last thing I wanted to do was force secrets out of her that she wasn't allowed to discuss. I knew that a lot of the cases that went on at the Wild Hunt were classified, under an NDA. But she seemed so distressed that I wanted to help if I could.

"Yes, I can tell you," she said. "After we wrapped up the mess over on the peninsula, Morgana told me that I had to go to both TirNaNog and Navane. In TirNaNog, I'm to contact my great-uncle—my grandfather's brother. Apparently he has a bow that's mine, by right of inheritance. And in Navane, my great-grandmother has a crown that belongs to me. I'm to retrieve both." The look in her eyes told me just how much those visits would cost her.

Ember's parents had been from the opposing Courts. Her mother had been Light Fae, her father Dark Fae. Their love had cost them their lives, and almost cost Ember hers.

When her family—her paternal grandfather, to be specific—had reached out to her, he had attempted to strip her of her Light Fae heritage. When that didn't work, he tried to kill her. She had ended up killing him first, which cost her an emotional fortune. Queen Saílle had made reparations to keep the whole incident quiet, but the impact had been a lasting one.

I frowned. "Given Morgana told you to do that, then you have no choice, I'm assuming?"

Ember held my gaze for a moment. "This is one of the only times I've been tempted to defy her. But there's no getting around it. It's something I have to do, even though I'm dreading it."

I turned to Angel. "Are you going with her?"

Angel shook her head. "I would, but neither Court would allow me in, given I'm human."

I suspected that Angel had a touch of the magic-born in her, given her empathic abilities, but even if she did, the Fae Queens wouldn't open their gates to her.

"What about Herne?"

Again, Ember shook her head. "No. Because he runs the Wild Hunt, Morgana thinks it's best if he stay away from the Courts unless he's on official business. And this is personal. I really don't want to go in there alone. I was hoping Rafé could go with me to TirNaNog, but he's still healing up." She paused, and I could practically hear the wheels turning in her head. "You wouldn't be up for a trip, would you?"

I gave her a skeptical grin. "You do realize that I'm more likely to be a liability than a help, don't you?"

"You're one of the Ante-Fae, though. They *have* to respect you."

That made me laugh. I leaned back in my chair, shaking my head.

"It's true that my people are the predecessors to both the Light and the Dark Fae. However, neither race wants to admit it. They prefer to think they jumped full-blown into this world, like Venus on the clamshell, or Athena springing out of Zeus's head. Anything or anyone reminding them that they were birthed from the same stock drives them into a frenzy."

"That's stupid." Angel blushed when Ember looked at

her. "You know I love you, *chica*, but your people are wacked sometimes."

"That's the truth," Ember said.

"Angel's right," I said. "I know that you come from *both* sides, Ember, but the truth is—the Fae—both Light and Dark—are entirely too arrogant. That's a weakness that will be their downfall one of these days. I'm amazed that the two Courts haven't killed each other off yet. The war between them has been going on since the beginning of time, or at least since the beginning of *their* time. If *I* go waltzing in there with you, it will just antagonize them against you even more, because *I'm* a reminder that they aren't quite so powerful as they like to believe."

Ember shook her head, a stubborn look on her face. "I don't care. As long as there isn't a rule against it, and as long as you don't mind, I'd feel more comfortable having you by my side."

I tried to suppress a smile, but after a moment, my shoulders shook with laughter. "I'll go with you. Let me know when. If anyone bothers us, they'll learn exactly why the Ante-Fae consider them no better than toddlers."

That settled, I turned to Angel as we started to eat. "So how is Rafé? You said he's still healing up?"

She nodded, biting into a pot sticker, then wiped her lips with a napkin.

"He should be getting out of his casts soon. His arm is almost healed up, and his leg is better. He'll be walking with a cane for a while. His ribs have healed as well, though Ferosyn has forbidden him to do anything strenuous for a long while. He'll need physical therapy, considering just how badly his bones were shattered. I'm just grateful that Cernunnos brought in his personal healer. I don't think Rafé would be so far along if he had stuck with the doctor that he usually goes to."

"How is he emotionally?" I asked, finishing my wine and pouring another glass. "That stint must have taken a terrible emotional toll on him." I had gone with the Wild Hunt on their trip over to the peninsula, and I had seen just how horribly Rafé had been treated. He had been tortured and beaten to within an inch of his life.

"He has flashbacks now and then," she said. "I worry that he's angry at Herne over what happened to him. He hasn't said anything, but there seems to be this…*darkness*…inside him, ever since we rescued him." She paused, then added, "Let's change the subject, please. I don't like thinking about what went on. I was wondering —I have some material that a friend gave me. It's right up your alley. Black velvet with an embossed purple pattern on it—and woven with gold metallic threads. It would make a gorgeous dress, but it's not my style, or Ember's."

"Sure, drop it by. I can find a tailor to make me something fabulous—" I paused as a noise sounded from outside. Like a crash, followed by a loud yelp that I recognized as Raj's cry.

I was on my feet immediately, tipping my chair over as I raced toward the door, with Ember and Angel right behind me. I yanked open the door, screaming when I saw Buck and two other men crowding around Raj, hitting him with sticks.

I launched myself toward them, conjuring up a ball of fire in my hand. Snarling, I slammed the flame against Buck's chest. He shrieked as the fire bit into his clothes and began to smolder. As he stumbled back, I backhanded him so hard that he went flying across the sidewalk, sprawling down the concrete steps that led up to my porch. There were only two steps, but the way he shouted made it sound as though he had fallen down an entire flight.

Ember was shouting something, and I glanced over my shoulder to see her kicking one of the men in the balls. He let out a loud groan, bending over as he staggered back.

I stomped over to Buck, kicking him in the ribs. If I could have burned a hole through him with my gaze, I would have.

"What the *fuck* are you doing on my property? I swear, if you *ever* come near Raj or me again, if you *ever* set foot on my property again, I will take a knife and I will gut you. I won't ask questions, I won't ask why you're here or what you want. I'll just take my blade and rip you open from collar to cock. Do you understand?"

"Bitch—"

"Shut up." I lifted one foot, placing the chunky heel of my boot on his balls, leaning on him just enough so that the pressure was a warning. "I suggest that you *do* understand, or you'll never father another child again. In fact, you won't even be able to *practice* fathering a child. Got it?"

The two other men were backing away, the one Ember had kicked in the nuts still bent over. They stumbled their way across the street to Buck's yard, opposite the cul-de-sac.

"I'm waiting." I held up my hand conjuring up another ball of fire, which I held out over Buck's face.

"I understand." His words were garbled, and he was snarling, but I had put the fear of the gods in him. I could see it in his eyes.

I slowly removed my foot from his genitals, and as he rolled over, trying to stand, I gave him a swift, hard kick, sending him sprawling down the sidewalk, sliding through the snow that was accumulating. He swore, but said nothing else as he stood, giving me a nervous look as he headed back to his house.

I turned. Angel was cuddling Raj.

"Raj, are you all right? Are you okay?" I glanced up at Angel, who had been looking him over.

"He'll be okay. I called the police. You can't let them get away with this. They're members of the HLA, aren't they?"

I nodded. "Buck's been having a lot of meetings over there lately. I think he's wrapped up tight in the organization. I've been doing my best to drive them out of the neighborhood, but no luck so far."

I wrapped my arm around Raj's neck, holding him tight as he whimpered and leaned against my shoulder. Angel unchained him and we took him inside while we waited for the cops. They wouldn't be able to do much except file a report, and perhaps talk to Buck. But I made myself and Raj a promise right there. Another week wouldn't go by before I ousted him and his freakshow family from the neighborhood. However I had to do it, I was getting rid of my neighbors once and for all.

CHAPTER FIVE

The cops were nice enough. Both of them were Dark Fae and neither was thrilled to hear about the meetings of the HLA. But Angel surprised us all when she held out her phone for us to look at.

"I took some video. It's only about thirty seconds, but it shows them attacking Raj." She looked sick to her stomach. "Can you use this against them?"

One of the cops—his name was Marcus Fjord—asked her to text the video to him. "We can try. Given that Raj is a gargoyle and not a dog gives us more to act on. Given he's a Crypto, I think we can consider this a hate crime. We'll do our best to get a warrant for Smith's arrest. Do you know who the other men were?"

I shook my head. "I have no idea. I probably have seen them over there, but I can't be sure. Will it go against us that we attacked them? I'm sure they'll tell you all about that. But they were on my property, and they were trespassing." At this point, I wished I'd bashed Buck's head in.

"That depends on the judge. But we can put some

pressure on him right now. Warn him to leave you alone or we'll be back out here. And we will make arrangements to have this street patrolled more often for the next few days. Unfortunately, it's hard to reason with people like Smith. They just don't *want* to get it."

I nodded. "I understand. But officers, make no mistake. If Buck comes at me or at Raj again, I *will* fight back, and I'll fight dirty. And I *will* win."

Marcus gave me a veiled smile. "You have every right to defend yourself. And you have a right to defend the gargoyle. I take it he's bound to you?"

I shrugged. "Not in so many words. He's not exactly a familiar. I'm more of his caretaker. Raj wouldn't do very well on his own, given his background."

"Understood. All right. We'll go and have a little talk with your neighbor. Based on this video, we can arrest him and he'll spend the night in jail. That is, until he or his cronies come up with bail."

"I don't expect that will take him long," Ember said, scowling. "Can't you keep him there without bail?"

"I wish we could, but unless the judge decrees that, you'd best assume that he'll be out before morning. Unfortunately, for tonight, he'll only go in on assault charges. Upgrading it to a hate crime requires taking him before the judge and we can't do that till a court date is set." They tipped their hats, then headed out into the snowy night.

I glanced outside as they left, sucking in a lungful of the chill air. It crackled with ozone and smelled like snow. How could a night that was so pristine take such an ugly turn?

Raj was curled up in his bed, still whimpering. Angel

had fixed him up a dish of cat food and we all gathered around him. I stroked his head, leaning down to kiss him on the ears.

"It's okay, Raj. Those men will never hurt you again. I promise."

Raj looked up at me, his eyes glimmering with tears. I could tell he needed to talk, but he still didn't feel comfortable in front of Ember and Angel.

"Would you like us to stay?" Ember asked. "We will, but I feel you need a little alone time."

I shook my head. "Thank you, but you're right. I think Raj and I can use some quiet time. And you should get home before the snow gets too deep."

"Will you be okay?" Angel asked.

I nodded. "I'll set some extra wards tonight. And I'm pretty sure the cops will keep a close eye on the neighborhood tonight. They seemed more concerned than I thought they would be."

"With the Tuathan Brotherhood up in arms, and the Human Liberation Army acting out, the city's becoming a war zone." Ember shook her head. "We have to do something, and soon. I love Seattle. I don't want to see it go down in flames."

"I agree," Angel said. "I suppose we better head out now. Call us if you need anything."

"Promise me you'll call Kipa after we leave?" Ember said.

"I promise." I would keep my promise, though I didn't intend to call him till tomorrow.

The last thing I needed was for Kipa to go off half cocked in the middle of the night. We would be safe until morning, and I would do what I needed to in order to make my house as much of a fortress as possible.

After they left, heading into the icy night, I retreated to my ritual room, where I found a couple charms that I hadn't set yet. They were protection talismans, and I usually kept spares around for times when someone came over who needed help. Once activated, they wouldn't last longer than twenty-four hours, but that would give us the time and the security that we needed. As I set them on the doors, then called Raj to follow me into the bedroom, it took every ounce of willpower that I had not to go across the street and torch Buck's house. But I told myself to save it for later, should everything else fail.

THE NEXT MORNING, AFTER TAKING CARE OF THE FERRETS, I made sure Raj was set with his shows and snacks, and that the wards were still working, before I headed to Llew's shop.

The snow had continued through the night and there was a good four inches piled on the sidewalk as I left the house. I could drive in snow, but a lot of people were skittish, resulting in a number of spinouts on the roads. The plows hadn't come through—the side streets weren't on the schedule to be cleared by the city. It was so slippery that, if I hadn't had the foresight to have snow tires put on my car, I wouldn't have been able to navigate the icy streets. I found a parking spot right in front of the apothecary and slammed my way through the door.

Llew took one look at me and let out a low whistle.

"Who are you ready to murder?" He pushed aside the ledger that he had been poring over.

"My neighbor." I told him what had happened. "I need stronger wards. I also need a house-clearing spell. Something to push all the mucky energy out. And while I'm at it, I need a screw-you candle."

Llew let out a long breath. "I sure as hell wouldn't want to be your neighbor right now. I just got a new batch of candles in, and they're strong. Do you need the herbs to go with them?"

I shook my head. "No, I have everything else I need at home." I lifted the scroll that he gave me, staring at it. "This is the house-clearing spell?"

"Yes. Of course, you have to do the work that goes with it, but it will set the stage." He paused, then pulled out a tall black candle. It smelled of wormwood and anise, of narcissus and black pepper. "If you need any help, call. By the way, I've been looking over everything I can find about breaking curses. So far, no results. But I'll keep looking. I won't stop until I find something that will help the ferrets."

"Thanks. I hate this shit. I know the only reason I haven't been able to drive out Buck yet is because he feels he's got the HLA on his side. But I tell you, Llew, if he so much as ever lifts his finger toward Raj or me again, I'll break his neck. I'm not joking."

"I know, sugar. I know." He handed me my package. "Did you want to read the cards here today?"

I shook my head. "No. Kipa's coming over tonight. And with what happened last night, I don't feel comfortable being away from the house very long. But thanks, and I'll see you later."

"I'll probably lock up early, anyway. With the storm, I doubt we'll see much business today." Llew waved as I left.

I stopped in at A Taste of Latte to buy a sausage muffin, a quint-shot mocha, and a dozen pastries before I headed home.

When I arrived at the house, everything looked normal, but I noticed Buck was staring at me through his front window. He'd gotten out on bail, apparently. I held up one hand, conjured a ball of fire, and launched it at his front yard where it exploded in the snow, then sizzled out. He quickly closed the curtain.

Once inside, I first boosted the existing wards with protection oil, then set the ones I'd gotten from Llew. After that, I unrolled the house-clearing scroll. Time to clean out the muck. If nothing else, I hoped that the spell would calm the disrupted energy.

As I read the scroll, though, I thought it sounded off. It was written in the arcane language of the magic-born. While I was familiar with some of the words, others escaped me. But it didn't sound like the house-clearing spells that I was used to. Llew must have updated them recently, I thought. Shrugging, I finished my magical work and called Raj over to the sofa.

"Want to curl up and watch some TV, doodlebug?"

He crawled up on the sofa next to me, resting his head on my shoulder. He had spent the night whimpering in his sleep. I was worried that the attack had spurred flashbacks to when Karjan, a demon, had owned him. Besides cutting off Raj's wings, Karjan had piled on plenty of other abuse on the young gargoyle. Even with the powerful memory-wipe I'd cast on Raj, the witch I had gotten it from had warned me there were triggers that might break through the fog.

"How did Raj sleep?"

Raj blinked, looking tired. "Raj had bad night-stories. The men who tried to hurt Raj were in them." *Night-stories* was what Raj called dreams.

I nodded, biting my lip. After a moment, I asked, "Was anybody else in Raj's night-stories?"

He shook his head. "No, just the men." Then, after a pause, he asked, "Why did those men try to hurt Raj?"

I took his hand in mine. The knuckles were calloused where he had walked on them all these years, but his palms were actually smooth, like a soft leather jacket.

With a sigh, I said, "I don't know why they did that. Raj, the truth is, some people are just spiteful and cruel. They hate others who aren't like they are. There isn't any good reason. It's just the way they are. They're entitled fucknuts and they don't want to share the world with anybody who's different. So we have to watch out for them, and try to avoid them. But if they try to hurt us, we're justified to fight back."

Raj was strong. He could probably break heads if he wanted to, though I'd never seen him even come close to trying. He *had* protected me from a spirit a couple months back, burning a hole through it with what appeared to be nothing less than laser eyes, but that was the first and only time I'd ever witnessed him doing anything like that, and he didn't remember it when I asked him about it afterward. I had a feeling Raj might have several tricks up his sleeve that I didn't know about. Maybe that *he* didn't know about, either.

He stared at the TV for a moment. "Raj no like fighting."

"Raven understands. But Raj needs to know that it's okay to fight back if someone is hurting him. It's *not okay* for anybody to try to hurt Raj."

"Or Raven," he said softly.

I nodded. "Or Raven. Raven fights back when people try to hurt her."

The conversation was clearly making him uncomfortable, so I found a TV show he liked. There was one cooking show in particular that fascinated him, though for the life of me I couldn't figure out why. Raj had never cooked a thing in his life, but he liked the hustle and bustle of *Chefs Away*—a cooking competition set on a cruise ship—so I DVR'd it for him.

I set one of the episodes to playing and, when Raj was immersed in the action, I pulled out my e-reader and returned to the mystery I was reading. I read mostly mysteries, romance, and science fiction, along with esoteric books on magic, legends, and ancient civilizations.

An hour and two episodes later, it was almost lunch time. Raj tapped me on the knee and I jumped, I'd been so engrossed in the book.

"Raj hungry. Is Raven hungry?" he asked, a hopeful note in his voice.

I set my e-reader on the coffee table and stood, stretching. "I do believe I could use a spot of lunch, Raj. What do you think about sandwiches and soup?"

He nodded, perking up. "Turkey?" Raj loved turkey sandwiches.

"Turkey it is—" I paused as a noise from the ferret's

room alerted me. "Hold on, while I check on the ferrets." I thought I'd locked their cage when I'd changed their litter and fed them, but it sounded like at least one of them had gotten out and was causing havoc.

I headed down the hall, frowning. With all the new wards, nothing should have gone awry. But as I opened the door, sure enough, I saw that I had forgotten to lock the cage. Not only that, I was confronted with a pile of litter and bedding scattered all over the floor. Elise looked up, a frantic light in her eyes, as she shoved more litter out of the open cage.

"What the hell? What's going on?" I scooped her up and walked over to the table, sitting down with her on my lap. "What are you doing, Elise?" A glance over my shoulder showed Templeton and Gordon taking her place, frantically scattering their litter everywhere.

Dirty. Dirty litter. Have to clean up. Can't have dirty litter in the cage!

"Huh? I cleaned it this morning."

Gordon peed. Can't have dirty litter in the cage! She sounded disgusted.

I frowned. What could have brought this on? They had been perfectly content this morning. "What's going on, Elise? Calm down and talk to me."

Messy, messy. Can't stand mess. Bring us clean litter?

She sounded ready to cry, if ferrets could cry.

"All right, but Elise, the litter is barely touched. Gordon couldn't have soaked all of it with one whiz unless he held it back for days." I set her down and examined the litter. Most of it was clean. Frowning, I retrieved the broom, dustpan, and a garbage bag, and cleaned up the mess on the floor. Thank gods I'd taken the carpeting out and had a durable laminate put in before I moved in. I knew the ferrets could destroy wood, so I'd found something easy to clean for their room. I replaced their litter, shook out their bedding, and replaced it in their cage, then tucked them back inside.

"There, it's clean. Don't do that again, okay? I change your litter every day." I spent a few minutes playing with them, but they all seemed distracted. In fact, Elise kept bringing me tiny bits of litter that my broom had missed.

Here's another. Must be tidy!

A little worried, I tucked them all back in the cage and made sure it was firmly locked. Whatever the hell was going on, I hoped to hell they'd get over it. Heading back to the kitchen, I washed my hands and proceeded to make lunch.

CHAPTER SIX

Kipa arrived around three P.M., snow dusting his shoulders. I glanced out behind him. The four inches had turned into six, with no sign that it was going to stop. He kissed me, but a preoccupied look in his eyes told me that he, too, was feeling a bit off.

"Something wrong?" I asked, leading him to the sofa, where we curled up together.

"Yes, actually, and I was wondering if you could help. But first, how are you doing?" He toyed with a stray curl by the side of my face, brushing it back. "I missed you."

I grinned. "We saw each other yesterday, dude." Sobering, I added, "I missed you, too. I love hanging around with you." I thought about telling him about Buck, but didn't want to spoil the mood. Besides, Buck was my problem. *My* battle to fight.

"Then let's hang more," Kipa said, gathering me to him for a kiss. His lips were warm against mine, and I felt myself stirring as he wrapped his arms around me, holding me tight against his chest. I ran my hand up his arm and through his hair, holding the back of his head as he leaned me back against the sofa cushions. But just as we were about to get hot and heavy, a loud *thump* against the front door broke the mood.

"What the hell? Today seems to be the day for interruptions." I disentangled myself and heading for the door. I opened it just in time to see Buck turning the corner off my sidewalk into the driveway. On the sidewalk, right in front of my door, the snow had been brushed away. In bright red paint, he had sprayed the word SLUTS with a circle around it and a line drawn through the circle.

"What the hell?" Kipa peeked over my shoulder. "*Who did that?* Did your neighbor do that?" He sounded dangerously perturbed.

"Yeah." I was about to explain what had gone down the night before, but Kipa pushed past me and was out the door before I could say another word. I sputtered, then grabbed my phone and followed him after taking a picture of the graffiti.

As I rounded the corner to my drive, almost slipping on the snow, Kipa had already made it across the street. Buck was waiting for him, holding a baseball bat, but Kipa took a running leap and, right in midair, turned into the most massive wolf I'd ever seen. He stood shoulder high to Buck when he landed in front of the man, and the wind rippled his gorgeous gray fur. He launched himself at Buck, knocking him down. The bat slid out of Buck's hands as Kipa's great jaws snapped at his throat. Buck screamed as he tried to grapple with Kipa.

I managed to reach them just as Minerva—Buck's wife —came racing out of the house, holding a shotgun. I conjured up a ball of fire, sending it sailing her way. She jerked to avoid it and the gun went off at the same moment that Buck managed to scramble away from Kipa. The bullet slammed into the redneck's shoulder. He shrieked again, dropping to his knees. Minerva screamed and dropped the gun, which went off a second time. This time, the bullet whizzed by and lodged in the trunk of a cedar tree. I fumbled for my phone and called the cops— Marcus Fjord had left me his number.

As I told Marcus what was going down, and that Buck would likely need an ambulance, Kipa turned back into his human form and stomped over to where Buck was writhing on the ground. He leaned down, grabbed Buck's collar, and lifted him up with one hand. Buck's feet dangled several inches off the ground. Buck was a big man, but Kipa was far stronger.

"You *ever* come near my woman's house again and I will tear your jugular out and feed it to my wolves! *Do you understand?*" Kipa's eyes blazed.

Buck, who was bleeding profusely from his shoulder wound, let out a stammered gurgle. Kipa tossed him back on the ground, like he might toss a stick or a stone. Minerva looked at me, then at Kipa, and backed away, not even bothering to pick up the shotgun.

Buck glanced at his wife. "I'm bleeding, you stupid cow. Get me a bandage."

Minerva nodded, her eyes wide, and turned back toward the house, sliding on the snow as she ran in her flip-flops. I tried not to laugh when she slipped and fell on her ass before she reached the front door.

"I don't think you answered me," Kipa said, leaning over Buck. In the distance, I could hear the wailing of sirens. Marcus in his patrol car, and a medic unit sped down the street toward us.

Buck pressed his hand against his shoulder, blood pouring through his knuckles as he tried to stanch the wound. He leaned back in the snow, cowering as Kipa loomed over him.

"All right, all right. I heard you. *What* the hell *are* you?"

"A *god*. Don't forget it." Kipa jabbed him in the chest. "I could end you with no regrets at all. But I won't—this time. Next time…"

Just then, Marcus jumped out of his cruiser as the medics raced toward Buck and Kipa. Marcus and his partner stared at the scene.

"What happened? Who shot him?"

"His wife—she's in the house right now. She was aiming for my boyfriend. I'm not sure exactly how it happened, but she ended up shooting Buck." I pulled up the picture of the graffiti on my phone. "This is what started it. You can still see it over on my sidewalk, next to the house."

"Hell in a handbasket. All right. We'll add that to his charges." He paused, glancing over at the medics, who were attending to Buck's injuries. "We'll put the pressure on the courts, Raven." A veiled look clouded his face. "We have enough problems now without having to deal with human trash."

A chill ran through me, and I had the feeling that Officer Marcus Fjord was definitely better to have on your good side. But as threatening as he sounded, I agreed with him. The world was too small to allow hate groups and their ilk to run rampant through society.

"Thanks. I appreciate it." I returned to Kipa's side.

Marcus followed me and took his information, his eyes widening when Kipa told him just exactly who he was. That cut short the interview and Marcus waved us on.

"We'll take it from here," was all he said.

As Kipa and I returned to the house, I had half a mind to pummel him for charging ahead like that. "You know, I can fight my own battles. I don't need someone else to pinch hit for me."

Kipa arched his eyebrows. "Whatever that means, though I get the gist. But Raven, it's time you accepted who I am. Be very clear about this: while I know you don't need anyone to fight your battles, I *always* protect my pack. And you're part of my pack, whether or not you realize it. I'm the Alpha wolf of all wolf packs, and you're my consort. I take my duties seriously."

"So, I'm the Alpha bitch right now?" I grinned at him, but stopped when I saw how serious he really was. This wasn't just a testosterone match like the ones he had with Herne, and I needed to accept that—just as I was true to myself, so Kipa was being true to himself as well.

"All right, I get it. But ask me from now on first. All right? Unless someone is pummeling the hell out of Raj or me, please ask before charging in. There are times when blunt force is not the way to go, and I have a number of those situations in my life."

He cleared his throat, then wrapped his arm around my shoulders. "We'll find a balance. Now, go inside while I wash this crap off your sidewalk." We were standing by the graffiti.

I shivered as the evening cooled even further. As the dusk deepened, the temperature was dropping and the snow had yet to stop, piling up in a slow, steady increase.

"All right. Thank you. I'll go make some dinner. Any requests?"

"Whatever you like," he said. "Just something hot."

I entered the house and saw Raj sitting there. "Kipa's staying for dinner," I said, glancing back at the door. I shut it, leaving it unlocked. "Macaroni and cheese all right with you, Raj?"

He nodded, then in quiet tones, added, "What is Kipa doing?"

"To the man who attacked you? He tried to... He made Raven unhappy. Kipa stopped him."

Raj paused, a contemplative look on his face. "Kipa help Raven?"

I nodded. "Yes, Kipa helped Raven."

After another pause, Raj said, "Macaroni and cheese is good. Raj go watch TV." And he lumbered off toward the living room, as though he'd settled something in his mind.

I started water boiling for the noodles, and began to grate cheddar and smoked gouda, then whisked flour and butter together to start the béchamel sauce. As the roux thickened, I added cream, some ricotta, and the grated cheese and then turned the heat down, whisking the combination. Next, I split open a baguette and brushed both sides with butter and parmesan and tucked the bread in the oven to brown. I frowned. I decided we should really have some sort of vegetable with dinner, so I tossed together a quick salad, going heavy on the cucumbers and tomatoes since lettuce wasn't my favorite food in the world.

I was almost done by the time Kipa returned. He washed his hands at the sink, then dried them on a paper towel before he wrapped his arms around my waist. He kissed my neck as I stirred the sauce into the noodles in a casserole dish, covered them with crushed potato chips, and popped the dish in the oven to broil after taking out the bread.

"It's gone," he said, breathing softly into my ear as I leaned back against him. "Your sidewalk is clean enough to eat off of. Though given the amount of water I used, the pavement will most likely ice up by morning. Temperatures are supposed to dip below freezing tonight."

"That's all right. I have rock salt in the closet in the ferrets' room." That suddenly reminded me of their peculiar behavior. "Hold on, I need to check on them. Can you watch the mac 'n cheese?"

I took off my apron—I had several retro-1950s circle aprons—and draped it over the back of a chair before heading down the hall. I hadn't heard much from the ferrets since their little cleansing frenzy.

As I peeked into the room, I groaned. While they hadn't gotten the cage door open again, they once again had shoved their litter through the cage. A tidy pile had accumulated on the floor.

"What the hell? Elise, what's going on? I want you to tell me right now." I opened the cage, scooped her out into my arms, and sat down with her at the table. "Why are you doing this?"

I peed. Templeton pooped. Dirty litter's got to go. Can't have the cage untidy. We're not filthy here.

She sounded almost drugged. I paused, glancing at the water bottle. But it couldn't be that—I had changed their water myself and I always used bottled water. Their food had come straight out of the same batch as yesterday. I hadn't brought anything poisonous into their room.

"Elise, honey, listen to me—" I stopped as Kipa peered in the door.

"Everything okay?" He froze. "What the hell? Who's been playing fast and free with magic here? I know you're a bone witch, Raven, but…" He looked around, confused.

"Magic? What are you talking about?" I asked, but stopped as the doorbell rang. I handed Elise to Kipa, who gently put her back in the cage as I went to answer the door.

Angel was standing there, a package in hand. "I should have called first, but I was on the Eastside and I wanted to drop off the material I promised to give you."

I invited her in. "You want to stay to dinner? Kipa's here." I took the bag and peeked in. Just as she had said, the material was gorgeous, a rich black velvet, embossed with plum designs, and glints of gold threads woven throughout. It would make a gorgeous dress or skirt.

She shrugged. "Sure, if I'm not intruding. I can stay for a little while. Sounds good." She followed me into the kitchen. "Need any help?"

"I was just checking on the ferrets. If you could set the table, that would be great." I hustled back to the ferrets' room, where Kipa was waiting. "Angel's staying to dinner. Did you figure out anything?"

He shook his head. "No, there's just a strong aura of magic in the room that I don't recognize. I'm surprised you don't feel it. There doesn't seem to be any malevolence behind it, but whatever it is, I'm pretty sure that it's affecting the ferrets. I'm not the best one to ask about magic, though."

I quietly shut the door, worried. One, I didn't feel much of anything—and that was unusual if there was strange magic around. Two, I didn't want anything disrupting the ferrets.

We returned to the dining room. Angel had set the table, but now she was over at my bookshelves, frantically rearranging books.

"Angel, hon, what are you doing?" I approached her. She looked confused as she pulled books out, reshelving them in other places.

"Raven, let me organize your bookcase. Look—if you're alphabetizing by author, they're out of order. If you're alphabetizing by title, they're also out of order. And the tops are dusty. Bring me a rag and I can dust them."

I cocked my head, watching her as she was getting more and more frantic with each book she found that was out of whatever order she'd gotten it into her head they should be in.

"Angel? Angel…let's eat dinner."

She allowed me to steer her away from the books, but when she served herself some food, she spent five minutes arranging it in neat piles on her plate. Angel was organized, but I'd never seen her act like this.

Glancing over at me, she said, "If you want, I can clean and rearrange your kitchen. It's not dirty, but your cupboards could be arranged better, and really, it's the time of year when you should wash every dish in the cupboard and all your silverware—"

I broke in. "Angel, *no*. First, you're thinking of spring cleaning. Second, my cupboards are organized just fine and I never put a dish away without cleaning it. What's gotten into you?"

She didn't even blush, just fidgeted through her meal. With every bite, she dabbed her lips with the napkin, and at one point, began rearranging the salt and pepper shakers, lining them up with the centerpiece. I watched her for a moment, then glanced over at Kipa, who gave me a perplexed shrug. The food was good, but the whole meal felt so off-kilter that I was relieved when it was time for her to leave. The moment she stepped outside, though, she seemed to relax.

"I had a…" she paused, blushing. "I *guess* it was fun. I'm sorry I said all those things about your house. I really don't think you're a slob, Raven. I didn't mean at all to imply that."

"You feel up to driving home?" I asked. We hadn't bothered with wine for dinner, but I was concerned about her, nonetheless.

"I'm fine. I'll text you when I get home, given the snow situation. It's still snowing and they predict almost a foot by the end of the week." She waved, then headed toward her car.

As I returned to the table, I reached for my phone and texted Ember. ANGEL SEEMED A LITTLE DISTRACTED THIS EVENING. SHE'S ON THE WAY HOME. KEEP AN EYE ON HER AND LET ME KNOW IF SHE ACTS…ODDLY.

Ember quickly returned my text. WILL DO. CAN'T THINK OF WHAT MIGHT BE GOING ON. BUT THANKS FOR THE HEADS-UP.

Trying to ignore Angel's odd behavior, I cleared the table and Kipa helped me do the dishes. After we were done, he wrapped his arm around me and walked me to the living room.

"I need your help, Raven. I'm hoping you'll be able to give me some advice," he said.

"What's going on?"

"It's one of my wolves. Gunnar's wasting away, and I think that he might be under attack by a ghost." He settled on the sofa, and I sat beside him. Raj joined us, sprawling near my feet.

I let out a long breath. Ghosts again. But that was my line of trade.

"All right," I said. "Tell me what's happening. And why you think Gunnar's being attacked." As Kipa started in with his story, I tried to tune out the odd events of the day and focus on what he was saying, but a part of me kept thinking about Buck, and just what he might try to pull next.

CHAPTER SEVEN

"Gunnar is one of my Elitvartijat, my squad of elite guards. They run beside me, four to ten of them at any time when I'm traveling, and they belong to my chosen people."

I'd never heard Kipa talk about having a chosen people. I knew he was accompanied by four wolves, at least, whenever he traveled through the woods, but I wasn't sure whether they were shifters or just massive wolves who answered to their lord.

"Elitvartijat? Who are they? Wolf shifters?"

He nodded. "Yes, but they're more than that. The SuVahta are my chosen people. They're a branch of wolf shifters who hail from the elemental realm of snow and ice. They're almost part elemental in nature, when it comes down to it. They can command storms, and they also wield earth magic to a degree. They're divine in their own right, though not gods. The SuVahta answer to me, and the Elitvartijat are chosen from them."

"So we're talking amped-up wolf shifters. What's going on with Gunnar?"

"He seems to be having hallucinations. He calls them phantoms. He's also been losing weight. He can't eat and he's not sleeping well. Whether it's due to the stress or some magical reason, I'm not certain. But the fact is, he's fading, Raven, and nothing that my healers have done seem to help him. I'd contact Tapio—the Lord of the Forest over in Finland, who's also connected with the wolves—but let's just say, last time I was there, he kicked me out with an express warning to stay away."

I narrowed my eyes. "All right, 'fess up. What did you do?"

"What do you mean—" He paused, then stopped. Laughing, he said, "Who am I kidding? You know me well enough by now to know there's usually a reason I get kicked out of places. So, the facts are…well…I may have tried to put the make on his wife—Mielikki."

I groaned, shaking my head. "Right. What did you do?"

He shrugged. "Just…grabbed her ass. Don't worry, though. I learned my lesson. Mielikki not only gave me a black eye, but for a month after that, I peed red, and boy, did that burn. But Tapio was furious and both of them ordered me to leave."

"So you can't go back to them for help?"

He shook his head. "I worked with Mielikki's Arrow, which is like the Wild Hunt. That little escapade got me kicked off the team."

"Have you tried asking Cernunnos for help?" It was just a thought, but Kipa shook his head.

"No, I'd rather wait until I've exhausted all other possibilities. But I can't wait much longer or Gunnar won't make it. Will you take a look at him? You should be able to tell if he's being haunted or possessed or whatever might be going on."

I nodded, though it didn't sound like a typical haunting to me. "All right. Come by tomorrow night. Around six?"

"Thank you, love. I can't get hold of Gunnar till tomorrow morning, anyway." He let out a long sigh, then pulled me toward him. "Until then…"

"Until then, you can come over here and kiss me." I slowly licked my lips.

Without another word, Kipa swept me up in his arms and carried me into the bedroom.

Sunday morning, I woke up to a red rose on the pillow next to me. I sat up, looking for Kipa, but he was nowhere to be seen. But Raj was sitting on the floor beside the bed, looking like he'd just inhaled some joy juice.

"Kipa fed Raj. Kipa fed Raj *three* cans of cat food." Raj grinned at me. "Maybe Kipa is okay, after all. Raj think about it." He turned and lumbered off.

"Three cans? I only feed you one!" I pushed back the covers, swinging my legs over the bed. I was naked but I didn't care. Raj never noticed whether I was clothed or not. It just didn't seem to register with him. The floor, however, was cold on my feet, and I quickly looked around for a pair of slippers.

"Kipa says Raj is a big boy and needs more food. Raj

agrees." The gargoyle gave me a salty look over his shoulder, then trundled out of the room.

Wonderful. Now, every time I gave Raj only one can, he'd remind me of the fact that my boyfriend thought he needed more food than I gave him. I wondered if Kipa realized Raj could talk. Most of the gods knew a lot about gargoyles and other Cryptos. But if Kipa did know, he wasn't pushing Raj, and for that I was grateful.

I hustled into the shower and took a quick rinse under an extremely warm pulse of water, then slipped into a cute pinup dress that had a black and white striped skirt, and a black sequined peasant top. As I buckled a wide patent leather belt around my waist, I realized that Angel hadn't texted me when she got home like she said she would. As I sat at my vanity and put on my makeup, I texted Ember.

DID ANGEL MAKE IT HOME LAST NIGHT? DID YOU NOTICE IF SHE WAS ACTING STRANGE?

SHE MADE IT HOME JUST FINE. SHE DID SEEM A LITTLE CONFUSED, AT LEAST FOR A LITTLE WHILE, BUT IT SEEMED TO CLEAR UP. WHY? WHAT ARE YOU THINKING MIGHT HAVE HAPPENED?

I DON'T KNOW. I'LL CONTACT YOU WHEN I FIND OUT. IT COULD BE NOTHING. I'VE BEEN UNDER SOME STRESS LATELY. IT MIGHT JUST BE MY IMAGINATION.

I finished with my makeup, then slid on a pair of ankle socks and my granny boots. They were black suede, with silver laces, and I'd had them resoled three times because I loved them so much. Feeling presentable, I headed for the kitchen.

Kipa was there, but thank God he wasn't trying to make breakfast this time. In fact, the kitchen smelled surprisingly fragrant with orange and cinnamon, and I looked around, trying to find out what smelled so good. There, on the counter, were freshly baked cinnamon buns, and I assumed the orange came from the glaze. Kipa was standing there, and I realized he was making mocha at the espresso machine. He glanced over his shoulder when I entered the room.

"Don't worry, I didn't mess up the kitchen. I bought some heat and serve rolls, and since I figured we'd be eating brunch, there's some ham in the oven that's almost done, and a fruit salad in the refrigerator. Will that work for breakfast for you? And do you want four or five shots in your mocha?"

"Five, please. And it sounds wonderful. Smells good too."

I pulled the plates out of the cupboard and carried them to the table, setting them on placemats. While Kipa finished making my mocha—and a latte for himself—I carried the food to the table. Then, remembering the past couple days, I warily headed for the door.

As I opened it, eight inches of pristine snow spread out on the sidewalk. That meant the yard would likely have more. I cautiously plowed through the snow to the end of the sidewalk and peered around into the driveway. At least Buck hadn't been active this morning—or if he had, I hadn't seen the results yet. But as I was about ready to turn back to the house, I noticed a large for-sale sign on Buck's lawn. I stared at it for a good two or three minutes before reality fully hit home. Trying to restrain myself, I hurried back inside, shut the door, and then let out a shout.

"I won! I won! He's moving!"

Kipa was sitting at the table. He gave me an odd look as I hurried into the dining room.

"We did it! We drove him out!" I danced around the room, wrapping my arms around Kipa's shoulders as I planted a big kiss on his forehead. "Buck and his trigger-happy family are leaving. There's a for-sale sign on their yard."

"That's wonderful!" Kipa pulled me down onto his knee. "I have to admit, I'm relieved. I really didn't like leaving you here with him so close. Now come and eat your breakfast. I'm going to go find Gunnar as soon as I finish. We'll be back around sixish tonight. That was the time, right?"

Almost too excited to eat, I slipped into my chair and dug into the rolls. "That's fine. I have some things to do today anyway." As I ate my breakfast and drank my mocha, all I could think about was that Buck was going to move. I deliberately kept my mind off who might move in in his place. I wanted to enjoy the feeling of freedom, and to take things one step at a time.

SHORTLY AFTER KIPA LEFT, I GOT A CALL FROM LLEW.

"Raven? I'm so glad you answered. Listen, there's a problem with that housekeeping scroll I sold you. If you haven't cast it yet, don't, all right?"

"*Housekeeping* spell? I bought a house-*clearing* spell. I'm not sure what you're talking about. And yes, I already cast it."

"Oops." He sounded like he had swallowed a frog.

After a moment, he asked, "Have you noticed anything unusual?"

Curious as to just what was going on, I started to shake my head, then stopped.

"Actually, yes. The ferrets have been acting up since I cast it. They keep trying to push all of their litter out of the cage even when it's clean. And my friend Angel seemed awfully strange last night when she dropped by. She tried to rearrange my books, and then offered to clean my kitchen."

Llew groaned. "Yeah, that sounds about right. The spell I sold you was mismarked. It's a housekeeping spell, specifically to...*strongly encourage* members of the household to clean up after themselves. You know, for mothers whose kids and husbands never lend a hand, or roommates who live with slobs. But I kind of think the witch who made it went a little overboard. I had two complaints this morning that it spurs on an OCD urge to constantly clean. Apparently, it affects ferrets as well."

I stared at the table for a moment. So that was what was going on.

"So instead of a house-clearing spell, I cast a spell that made my ferrets go OCD on their litter? The spell must have grazed Angel as well. So, tell me, how do I deal with this? I need to break the spell. I am not going to clean the ferrets' litter five times a day and I won't have them panicking over a drop of pee or poop. And do I need to call Angel over? Or is the spell localized to my house?"

"It was my mistake. I can come out and neutralize the spell. I'll bring an actual cleansing spell with me as well." He sounded so flustered that I took pity on him.

"It's all right, Llew. And yes, please come over. How soon can you be here?"

"Give me half an hour. I'm closing up the shop early today."

As he signed off, I breathed a sigh of relief. At least I knew what was going down with the ferrets, and with Angel. And I was still dancing a jig over the news that Buck would soon be out of my life. The thought of the neighborhood without him and his cronies made me absolutely ecstatic. I decided to celebrate with a little retail therapy and went into my office, pulling up V-Bazaar, an online artists and merchants bazaar. As I settled down for some serious shopping, it occurred to me that at the very least, my life wasn't boring. Though sometimes, boring seemed like it might be a nice change of pace.

CHAPTER EIGHT

*B*y the time Llew got there, the ferrets had managed to shove all their litter on the floor again. The fix was easier than I thought. All Llew had to do was to go through the house, using a simple hex-breaking spell, and immediately after he cleansed the ferrets' room, they settled down, looking confused and mildly hung over.

As I replaced their litter and bedding, Elise watched me carefully.

What happened? I feel like I'm drunk.

"You were under a spell. I inadvertently cast the wrong spell—it was a mistake. It turned you and your brothers into cleaning machines and you emptied your cage of litter several times."

She yawned. *I'm tired, and Gordon and Templeton are worn out.*

"Then take a nap, Elise. Everything will be all right now." I gave them a handful of their favorite treats. "Here, eat hearty and go curl up."

Thank you, Raven. I think I will have a nap.

They scarfed down the treats. Then, satiated and sleepy, they curled up in their cage for a nap.

Llew and I returned to the living room.

"Thanks," I said. "I was wondering what the hell was going on with them." I motioned to the sofa. "Want a drink or something?"

"Soda, if you have it." Llew stretched out in one of the armchairs, his long legs crossed at the ankles. "So what's going on lately?"

I handed him a cream soda and opened one for myself.

"One of Kipa's Elitvartijat has a problem."

"One of *what* has a problem?"

"His elite guards. Anyway, I'm going to see what I can do about it. The guard thinks he's being haunted. They're coming by tonight and I'll see if I can find anything to suggest a ghost or a spirit's latched onto him. I swear, the spirit world's been particularly active the past six or seven months, and it only seems to be growing."

"When *isn't* it active? I mean, given how many people have died over the eons, I'm not surprised. Hey, have you ever come across any ghosts from, oh…caveman days?" Llew's eyes lit up. He was an ancient history buff.

I blinked. "I don't think I've ever been asked that question before. When I think about it, um…*no*, actually. Though I have encountered spirits that are thousands of years old. But after a while, unless they're bound for a purpose, the spirits who hang around the Aether degrade, so to speak."

"What do you mean?"

"If a spirit doesn't eventually move into the Netherworld, they lose their sense of self. It can take hundreds—even thousands of years—but it will eventually happen."

"What happens to them at that point?" Llew asked, sitting straight. "Do they vanish?"

"Not really, because spirits can never be destroyed. Energy transforms, and spirits are energy. They either evolve and move on, or degrade and turn into creatures that move into the astral realm. That's where you get some of the demons from. Not all, because there are classes of beings who were never human to start with that are malign and want only harm. But some of the low-level demons…like the hungry ghosts…well, they come from a place of greed, rather than consciousness. They're spirits that have been trapped too long in the Aether." I shrugged. "Think of it like a bodybuilder who stops working out. His muscles don't vanish, but they lose their tone and can atrophy from lack of use."

"Ah, I get it." Llew yawned. "Speaking of which, I need to get some exercise in. I've been slacking off, working at the shop for too many hours without hitting the gym. But by the time I go home, I don't want to do much except watch TV."

I was feeling antsy myself. "Well, it's still early in the afternoon. Why don't we go for a walk? The trail at the end of the cul-de-sac here leads into UnderLake Park. Go with me?"

He frowned. "UnderLake Park has a certain reputation—"

"So do I. Come on. We'll be fine. The only trails I'm reluctant to travel are the ones that Ulstair used to go jogging on, and that's mostly because of the memories.

Also, I refuse to go anywhere near where Ember and Viktor found his body. But I won't avoid the entire park."

Llew shrugged. "All right. Let's go. You lead the way. Are you bringing Raj?"

I called to Raj. "Llew and I are going for a walk, boy. You want to come?"

Raj glanced at Llew, then at me. Then he turned toward the TV with a meaningful look.

I laughed. "Okay, you can stay home and watch TV. But you and I are going to start walking more, whether or not Captain Crushbot is on."

I turned on the TV and tuned it to the Anime Channel. Sure enough, it was time for *Captain Crushbot*—an anime about a cyborg superhero who, along with his zany side-kick, the angst-ridden ex-girlfriend, and several other tropes that never seemed to grow old, continually saved the world from destruction.

Sliding my feet into a pair of waterproof suede walking boots, I then shrugged on the jacket that I had charmed for warmth. It used my own body heat, reflecting and amping it up, to keep me warm, and it worked under freezing situations. I had enchanted several articles of clothing, but for a simple walk in the park, even on a snowy day, just the jacket should do the trick. My skirt was long enough to keep the chill air away from my legs.

I locked the door after activating the security wards, pocketed my keys along with my wallet, and grabbed a sturdy walking stick off the porch. Glancing across the street, I saw no sign of Buck or his brood, but the for-sale sign sat there, a sweet promise of peace to come.

It was snowing heavily. I'd forgotten to check the

weather report, but I had close to nine inches at this point. I wasn't complaining, though.

Seattle snowstorms, even the heavy ones, never seemed to last beyond a week or two. We enjoyed them when they came for the novelty they were. Well, except for traffic. Traffic during a snowstorm was a nightmare, even with the appearance of a mere inch or two. This was due to several reasons. One, our area didn't get much snow as a rule, so no one remembered how to drive in it. But when we did get slammed, the snow generally melted off during the day, then iced over at night. With a city built on steep hills and roads, ice was non-navigable.

Turning left, toward the greenery that covered the end of the cul-de-sac, I located the trailhead that led into the park. Motioning for Llew to follow me, I plunged into the shrubbery, onto the thickly wooded path.

UnderLake Park was a dark, shadowed tangle of vegetation that sprawled almost six hundred acres. The land had originally housed a monastery and an estate called Castle Hall, where a series of brutal murders took place. While the bodies were never found, the spirits remained, and even I was cautious in that area of the park.

Amidst old, towering trees—fir and cedar, for the most part—the park was a labyrinth of trails. There were drivable roads, and most people stuck to their cars. But since UnderLake Park was in a prime location, adjacent to so many homes, a number of brave souls weathered the darkness and the shadows to use it for jogging and even horseback riding.

The park was littered with copses of birch, their white trunks stark against the array of evergreens and conifers. Like almost all wooded areas in western Washington,

UnderLake was rife with ravines. They plunged steeply to the bottom, decked out in a thick wash of debris from autumn. Sodden leaves and branches, ankle deep in some areas, carpeted the ground, and waist-high ferns spread out, their fronds growing five to six feet long in places.

Fallen trees covered the land, the nurse logs thick with moss and mushrooms, with matted needles from the towering trees overhead. During the autumn and spring, the banana slugs showed up everywhere, and the massive gastropods slowly oozed their way along the forest floor, eating the plants and leaving trails of slime in their wake.

As we entered the park, the snow seemed to deepen—as it always does in the forest—and we slogged our way through the pristine blanket, breaking a trail as we went. It was thirty-three degrees and still snowing. Everywhere, the snow sparkled in the early afternoon light, glinting under the reflected light from the cloud cover. The sounds of the forest were muffled beneath the layers of frozen flakes, and it felt like we had the park entirely to ourselves.

"It's so beautiful," Llew said. "It's like a wonderland. I miss living in snow country. I moved out here from Maine, you know, to be with Jordan." Llew had been born in Massachusetts, to one of the older magic-born families. He had moved to Maine in the 1970s, and out to Seattle about six years ago when he and Jordan met online and immediately connected. They had gotten married the moment Llew's plane landed.

"That's right. I forgot." I paused, my breath visible in front of my face. My jacket was keeping me warm enough, at least on my chest, back, and arms, but the chill in the air was more bracing than I had expected. I glanced around. "The park looks so different with snow. It's more treacherous, you know. The glittering surface belies the energy that lives here."

"I've always been cautious around this area. Jordan won't come here. He says it sets him on edge too much."

"And well it should. He's a shifter. Shifters sense danger in a different way than you or I do. He's right, though, because a lot of things happen here. I thrive on the energy. And given I'm Ante-Fae, few things will attack me. At least, few things that live in the park."

We had been walking about twenty minutes when I spotted a side trail. "Let's see where that goes. We won't go far. I don't want to get lost out here in the cold."

Llew nodded. "You have the walking stick. Lead the way."

I plunged off to the left, making sure that it was, indeed, an actual trail. Within a few minutes, I realized we were headed into the heart of the park, descending into a ravine. I paused, wondering if we should turn back.

"What's wrong?"

"Do you notice? We're headed downhill. The trip back up the slope could be tiring. Do you want to turn around before it gets too steep?" I glanced over my shoulder at the trail behind us.

"Maybe—wait, what's that?" Llew pointed toward a spot at the bottom of the ravine. There was something sparkling below. From here, it looked like a sequined coat spread atop the snow. "Is that a person? Are they hurt?"

I squinted. I had good eyesight, but the brightness of the snow and the flurry of flakes still falling around us made it impossible to be certain what we were seeing.

"I don't know, but it could be. It looks about the size of a child."

Concerned, wondering if some kid had gotten in trouble, I began to make my way down the trail, the snow making the descent fraught with slick spots. More than once, an icy patch sent me sliding onto my ass. Llew followed me, having a harder time than I did, given his tall, lanky frame gave him a higher center of balance.

All the while, the flakes around us began to come down harder, swirling in a mist that rose from between the trees. I steadied myself using my walking stick, and turned sideways as the going grew steeper, bracing my feet into the side of the ravine as I went. The light was beginning to fade as the afternoon sped away. The last thing we needed was to be caught here after dusk. Even though we were in January and the days were starting to grow longer, it grew dark in the wooded park early.

As we neared the bottom of the ravine, my concern continued to grow. The silent figure hadn't moved, hadn't responded in any way to our calls. I prayed that the person, whoever it was, would still be alive when we reached them. I didn't sense any ghosts here, but the magic of the forest was everywhere, thick and syrupy, like crystallized honey slowly creeping out of the jar.

We finally reached the bottom of the ravine. A narrow creek, now iced over, carved its channel through the forest floor, a few yards away from where we stood. The ravine went on for some ways to the left, but to the right, it sloped upward again, where the stream gushed out of the base of the hill.

I turned to look for the jacketed form, but there was nothing there.

"What the hell? Llew, did you see whoever it was get up and leave?"

He stared at the empty spot, shaking his head. "No, I didn't. They couldn't have just stood and walked away without us noticing. No way."

I edged forward, my head cocked to the side as I listened. There was a slow, sucking sound coming from the midst of a thicket of huckleberry bushes, beneath a massive fir tree.

"There—over there. I hear something moving." I plunged into the thicket without thinking. Or rather, I was thinking that maybe if it had been a child who was hurt, they were trying to hide, afraid we were dangerous.

"Raven—stop!" Llew's call echoed behind me, but I was too busy looking for the figure among the shadow of the trees. I was so focused on the forest floor that I didn't see or hear anything until it was too late.

"Fuck!" I let out a shriek as something reached out and grabbed me. Glancing down, I saw a bristled tentacle had wound around my wrist, digging in with massive barbs. The tentacle reached out from behind one of the bushes. Whatever it was, it had an iron grip and I couldn't pull free.

"Llew!" The tentacle had hold of my left wrist, and I quickly bent to pull Venom, my short dagger, out of her boot sheath. I aimed for the fleshy arm and slashed awkwardly, reaching across my body to manage it. Venom's edge was razor sharp—I always kept her sharpened—but she bounced off at my first attempt.

Llew came charging through the brush, stopping as he took in what was happening. "Raven, fire—use fire!"

I stuck Venom through my belt, trying to avoid stabbing myself, and held out my hand, whispering to coax the flame onto my fingertips. It was hard to focus, given the creature was trying to drag me forward into the dark thicket, but I managed to summon up an orb of fire and I slammed my hand atop the tentacle near my wrist. There was a sizzle as the fire hit the creature, and a loud hiss echoed from behind one of the bushes as the tentacle released its grasp on me.

Llew grabbed hold of my other arm and pulled me back away from the thicket as another tentacle reached out, and then a second one, both waving toward me.

"Get out of here!" I shouted to Llew, not waiting to see what it was going to do next. Turning, I raced back the way I had come, Llew on my heels. We stumbled back into the main ravine and I glanced up at the waning light.

"We need to get to the top before dusk. I don't know what that thing is, or if it can follow us." I grabbed my walking stick from where I had dropped it as Llew hastened toward the trail. I followed him, forcing my legs to work harder than they had in a while.

"Hurry up," he said nervously, glancing over his shoulder. "I think I saw something moving behind us. Come on!"

Once again, he took my hand—not the one that was injured—and began half-dragging me up the hill. His long legs stood him in good stead and I stumbled along, trying to keep up. We hustled, Llew striding up the hill like he'd been born to climbing mountains. I kept glancing over my shoulder, straining to see if we were being followed. As we ascended the hill, more than once I got slapped in the face by the passing ferns and vines. But we finally stumbled out onto the main trail as the dusk began to settle in.

"We've got twenty minutes before we're back to my house, so let's get a move on."

I started down the trail, heading toward the cul-de-sac, trying to find our footprints in the snow. But they had been covered up by the fresh layer. All the way back, I kept imagining something lumbering behind us, but each time I glanced back, I couldn't see anything.

It took us only twelve minutes instead of twenty to cover the distance and, by the time we stumbled out into the street, I was beyond winded. But we were safe, and whatever it was, remained cloaked within the shadows of UnderLake Park, waiting.

CHAPTER NINE

"Gunnar and Kipa are due over soon, but before they get here, I want to find out what the hell that creature was." I stomped the snow off my boots and hustled into the house, with Llew following.

"Do you have any bestiaries around?" Llew asked. "I've got one at home, but I don't think it's all that detailed compared to some."

"Yes, actually. I have an old one, and it's very inclusive." I stripped off my jacket and boots. "Get out of those wet things. I'm going to change clothes. I'll lend you a robe, so you can dry your jeans and shirt before you head home. They're good for the dryer, right?"

He nodded. "Yeah, and thanks. I got soaked out there."

I headed into my bedroom, where I slipped out of my drenched clothes and found a comfortable tank dress with an asymmetrical hem. I slipped a belt around my waist, and then slipped on a pair of yoga socks so my feet wouldn't get cold. Opening another closet, I slowly withdrew a spare man's bathrobe. Made of microfiber, it was a dark blue. I held it for a moment, hesitating. It had been Ulstair's robe, but I couldn't bring myself to give it away. But it would fit Llew perfectly. With a sigh, I draped it over my arm.

Stopping to peek in on the ferrets—they were all asleep and the room was clean as a whistle, with no litter scattered anywhere—I headed back to the living room, where Raj was staring at Llew with a wistful look.

"Raj, are you trying to cadge a treat off of Llew?" I shook my head. "Nothing till dinner now, my friend." I handed Llew the bathrobe. "Here, go change in the bathroom and I'll toss your shirt and pants in the washer too, if you like. Or I can just dry them, if you're in a hurry."

"Dryer will be fine." He took the robe and headed toward the bathroom.

Raj came up to me, nudging my leg. "Are Llew and Raven okay?"

"Raven and Llew met a very nasty creature out in the woods today, but yes, Raven and Llew are all right, Raj." I kissed his head. "Thank you for asking. Raven has to do some research for a little bit, so why doesn't Raj go watch TV?"

"Raj want to go outside." Raj gave me that look that said *I have to go to the bathroom, lady, so open the door.* He was starting to wiggle his butt a bit and I knew what that meant.

"Come on, let's get you out there." I opened the door and hooked him to his chain. "Don't go far and if you see anybody coming up the walkway that isn't Kipa, pound on the door. I'll be listening."

Making sure he had everything he needed, I headed back inside and over to my bookcase. I sorted through the books until I found the grimoire I was looking for. *Beltan's Bestiary*—one of the most comprehensive encyclopedias in the world, and also one of the rarest. I had swiped it from my father when I left home to come out to the West Coast.

Llew returned from the bathroom, the robe belted tightly around him. "I threw my pants and shirt in the dryer. Is that *Beltan's Bestiary*?" He leaned over my shoulder, staring at the grimoire. "I've never seen an actual copy before." He glanced at me. "You do know that this is one of the rarest bestiaries in the world? It's worth a fortune. Where did you get it?"

"My father owned it. I sort of stole it when I left home. Curikan knew that I swiped it, but he never said a word. For him, it was a curiosity, rather than a tool." I motioned to the chair next to me. "Have a seat. I'm going to get a snack for us. Fritos okay? And do you want a soda?" I didn't want anything alcoholic, especially since I had work to do with Gunnar and Kipa.

"Soda's fine with me." Llew was already nose-deep in the book, cautiously turning the parchment pages on which the entries had been handwritten. "Look at these drawings! They're brilliant." He gently flipped through the pages. "Is this organized in any way? Does it have an index of any sort?" he asked as I darted into the kitchen for corn chips and two more cans of soda.

"Actually, it does. Notice the plastic tabs on the side?" I had used sticky tabs to sort out the different chapters.

Llew laughed. "Oh! I didn't notice them at first. You added these, didn't you?"

"Yes, I did." I handed him the soda and motioned for him to set it on a coaster, far away from the book. I stared at the Fritos for a moment, then looked back at the bestiary. "Maybe the corn chips weren't such a good idea. I don't want any grease marks on it."

"How about I let you turn the pages, and I just look at it. I'd rather not take a chance on ruining such a rare antiquity."

I shrugged. "Okay, that's fine with me. I keep thinking that I should take this in and get it scanned, and then tuck the original away in a humidity- and temperature-controlled environment. Then I wouldn't be so afraid every time I pulled it off the bookcase."

"I wouldn't trust anyone else to scan it, if I were you. I have a large scanner. You can borrow it and do it yourself. Then you can print out the pages and store them in a binder."

"Good idea. I think I'll do that, if you don't mind me borrowing your scanner." I opened the Fritos and pushed the bag to the center of the table. Returning my attention to the grimoire, I showed Llew the loose organization of the tome.

"Of course, it's still a mishmash because they just kept adding to it, but you'll notice that the sticky tags indicate water creatures, land creatures, air creatures, and fire creatures. Blue, green, yellow, and orange, respectively. The purple flags indicate denizens of the spirit realm, and the white flags represent sub-Fae. The black flags are things I can't really categorize."

"I think we're looking at an earth creature, unless you think it might be one of the sub-Fae. I didn't get any sense of air, fire, or water about the creature, did you?"

I held up my wrist, looking at the puncture wounds. I had almost forgotten about them by the time we got home. They stung, but I was used to bruises and bumps. I grimaced as I noticed that the wounds weren't looking all that clean and in fact, a couple of the punctures were oozing blood and pus.

"I think you'd better go clean out those wounds before we go any further," Llew said, turning a worried eye to my wrist.

"I hadn't realized they were so bad. Yeah, I guess I should. I'm not affected by a number of the poisons or venoms that other people are. But until we figure out what that creature was, I don't want to take any chances. You keep looking while I go wash my wrist."

I went to the kitchen and plugged in my electric tea kettle. As soon as the water had come to a boil, I poured it into a tall mug, carefully carrying it into the bathroom with me. I'd heard too much about people who ended up with brain-eating amoebas from using tap water in their neti pots, and I sure as hell didn't want a tapeworm or anything to take up residence in my wrist.

While waiting for the water to cool, I pulled out some antibiotic ointment—a salve that I had bought from Gowan's AFA—the Ante-Fae apothecary. It was a small shop owned by Rose Gowan, an Ante-Fae with healing powers. She had chosen to go into business because she was a natural-born healer, and one of the few who could handle the Ante-Fae. She could heal just about anything from a cold to snakebite. At least, up to a certain point. She couldn't raise people from the dead, nor could she cure terminal diseases. She had set herself up as the main healer for most of the Ante-Fae in the Seattle area.

After the water cooled, I carefully poured it over my wrist, making sure to thoroughly rinse out the wounds.

There were five of them around my wrist, where the creature had managed to get its barbs hooked into me. The warm water stung, and I winced as I flushed out a pocket of pus. The wounds were still red but looked clean enough after I finished, so I rubbed the antibiotic ointment into the punctures, then bandaged them. It looked like I had a bracelet of bandages on by the time I was done. I returned to the kitchen, holding up my arm.

"All done. Did you find anything?"

"Actually, I think I did. Look at this." Llew pushed the book over toward me as I sat down. I found myself facing the drawing of a creature that looked like a combination of a ghoul, an octopus, and a coarse-haired ape.

"What is that?" I asked, pulling the book closer.

"I don't know, I can't read the language. But those tentacles are barbed, like the one that grabbed your arm."

The text had been written in daelethi—the ancient Ante-Fae language that all Ante-Fae were taught from birth. I was reasonably conversant in it, and kept a regular practice.

I scanned the text and it fell into place. "Oh, that makes sense. This is a land wight. I've heard of them but never encountered one. They feed on death."

"What do you mean by that?" Llew looked a little queasy.

"Decomposing bodies, decomposing leaves, whatever the world is breaking down at the moment. Land wights turn decomposition into food. But they're also aggressive, and have been known to hunt out victims. They'll then break down the bodies and, as the victim decomposes, they'll eat the remains."

"Meaning...they'll kill us to get our bodies?" Llew

wrinkled his nose. "My stomach doesn't like the thought of that."

"Maybe not, but their stomachs do. Or whatever they use to digest their food." I skimmed the entry on them. "Okay, it seems that getting rid of the land wight isn't going to be easy. First, you must find their nest. They keep their souls, or essences if you will, locked within a soul stone in the nest. To destroy the wight, you have to destroy the stone. And even better, you can only destroy the stone with a magical hammer."

Llew groaned. "You don't happen to know Thor, do you?"

I shook my head. "Nope. I wish I did. The hammer has to be silver, by the way. So, even if we do go back for the wight, and I think we should, given that creature's going to lure people to their deaths, we're going to need an enchanted weapon. Venom's a magical blade, but she's not a silver hammer."

"How does it lure people in?"

"Like it nearly did us. All wights have glamour of a sort. The land wight can disguise itself as any number of things. Remember we thought we saw a child down there? That was the wight. They have some sort of telepathy, it seems." I read the rest of the entry. "They're able to project images into the minds of others. It probably sensed that we would try to rescue someone in need, and went for the jugular—a kid."

"So we were the fish, headed for the hook." Llew sat back, wrapping his arms over his stomach. He stared at the grimoire. "What if some kid goes down there?"

He had just voiced what I'd been thinking. What if, indeed, some child headed down that slope? The wight wouldn't have any compunctions about killing a kid. In fact, a wight would only realize that an easy target was on the way. Enough for a quick meal, albeit not a full-sized one. The thought nauseated me. While I had very little interaction with children—and very little desire for such —I couldn't handle the thought of something as malevolent as the land wight catching hold of a kid.

"We need to destroy it," I said. "Nobody else is going to do anything. If we tell the cops, they'll look the other way. They only respond when they deem it worth their while."

"Wait a minute!" Llew jumped up. "I think I know somebody who has a magical hammer. Let me call him." He grabbed his phone. While he put in the phone call, I went to check on Raj. I didn't trust Buck, even if he was moving.

Raj was hanging out in his house, just quietly taking in the night air. The snow had finally stopped, but by now, we had over ten inches. Seattle proper, according to the news, had five inches. As usual, the Eastside was beating them out. The air was so crisp I could have cut my lungs on it, and yet, there was a quiet beauty to the night, and the sky still had that silver-tinged shimmer that seemed so otherworldly.

"Hey, doodlebug, whatcha doing?" I crouched beside him, thinking I really should shovel my walkway.

"Raj is thinking, but mostly listening to the snow." Raj gazed up at me, his eyes luminous in the twilight.

"What's the snow saying to Raj?"

"The snow's saying it's going to stay for a while. It likes it here," he said in a dream-filled voice. "The snow makes the world slow down." Yawning, he rested his head on his feet.

"You want to stay out here for a while? You're not too cold?"

"Raj is fine. Raj take a nap now." And just like that, he was snoring away. I patted him on the muzzle, then headed back inside.

Llew was waiting for me. "I got hold of my friend. Neil's a priest of Thor. And I remembered right. He has a magical silver hammer. He said he'll come over and help us tomorrow night. He can't get away till then. He's a bouncer and works weekends."

"He's willing to help us? Did you explain what we'd be facing?" I didn't want to take anybody into that kind of danger unless they knew for sure what they were up against.

"Yeah. He said he'd be glad to. That's one thing about Thor's followers. They're usually right there when you need them. Bravery and the honor code, you know. Courage is a big thing for the Nordic crew." Llew glanced at his phone. "My pants and shirt should be dry enough now. When are Kipa and his friend coming over?"

I glanced at the clock. It was five-thirty.

"Half an hour." I retrieved Llew's pants and shirt from the dryer. They were toasty warm, and he turned his back, slipping on his jeans under the robe. Then he tossed the robe to me and pulled on his shirt, tucking the hem of the sweater into his jeans before he buttoned up. I hung the robe over a chair and walked him to the door once he had put on his socks and shoes.

"I'm sorry about the housekeeping scroll. Really, it was a mistake. I don't think I'm going to carry those anymore. Too many complaints. At least it didn't affect you."

I laughed. "True. But trust me, chasing after three

clean-freak ferrets? Not easy. By the way, on the subject of the ferrets—?"

"I'm looking. I promise you that. I'll let you know what I find, if anything." With that, he gave me a hug, slid on his coat, and headed out to his car.

CHAPTER TEN

*T*en minutes after Llew left, Kipa and Gunnar
showed up. I wasn't sure just what I had
assumed, but Gunnar didn't look anything like I thought
he would. For some reason, I'd expected him to be tall and
blond, but he was compact—about five-seven—with long
dark hair pulled back in a braid. He had the most intense
eyes I had seen in a long time, slate gray ringed with
black.

The moment he came through my door, I could feel
something enter right behind him, and immediately, I
knew that it was attached to his aura. My wards lit up,
warning me that whatever it was, I didn't want it in my
house. I couldn't very well turn Gunnar out at this point,
having invited him over in the first place, but neither did I
want to let an enemy into my territory. Uncertain of what
to do, I glanced at Kipa.

"Kipa, can I talk with you for a moment?" I jerked my
head toward the kitchen. Kipa followed me, a puzzled
look on his face. I motioned for him to follow me toward

the back of the galley kitchen and lowered my voice. "Your friend out there brought something big and nasty into my house. Whatever's attached to him set off my wards."

"Well, that's why we are here. Do you think it's his late wife?"

I started to answer, but Kipa pressed his finger to my lips. "First, a kiss." He leaned down and kissed me. Stroking my face, he kissed me again, then stepped back. "Okay. So do you think it's the ghost of his late wife?"

Snorting, I said, "How the hell should I know? I haven't had the chance to say two words to the man. But I will tell you this. He brought it in, and he's leaving with it if I can't get rid of it. I am not letting that thing loose in my house."

"Understood, loud and clear."

We returned to the dining room, where Gunnar was sitting at the table, his hands clenched together. He looked up as we entered the room.

"How do you do?" I held out my hand, striding over to him. "I'm Raven BoneTalker."

"Gunnar, of the SuVahta people. Thank you for seeing me. Kipa says you might be able to help me?" He looked ragged around the edges, too gaunt for his size, with a haunted look in his eyes.

"I'll try, but I need you to be entirely honest with me. Kipa says that you think you're being haunted by the spirit of your late wife. Why do you think that? What happened?" I settled at the table, flipping open a notebook and picking up a pen. Kipa sat down on the other side of Gunnar, waiting patiently.

"Last year, my wife Solveig and I were climbing up an

ice rock on Svínafellsjökull, a glacier in Iceland. A crevasse opened below us, and Solveig lost her footing. I tried to catch her. We were roped together, but she went over the edge and almost pulled me down with her. I was doing my best to hold her up, but I couldn't keep my traction. She must have known, because she was screaming for me to cut her loose. I refused, so she took her own knife and…" He paused, his eyes misting over.

I kept quiet, waiting for him to continue.

A moment later, he said, "The crevasse was so deep there was no way we could claim her body. She's still up there, and will be forever. I can't help but blame myself. The hike was my idea, and I had pushed her to go along. She had a headache and didn't want to go with me, but I didn't want to go alone and nobody else felt like hiking. I convinced her the hike would help her headache. Her death is on my conscience, and my shoulders."

I glanced over at Kipa, who was staring solemnly at the table.

"You do realize that it was an accident, don't you?" I said. "Your wife made the choice to sacrifice herself so that you wouldn't die along with her. It's not your fault."

"I told him that. We all did, but I think that it's a difficult thing to believe when you're in his situation." Kipa reached over and patted Gunnar's shoulder.

Gunnar shrugged him off. "Try telling that to her family. They blame me."

It struck me as odd that a woman who had voluntarily sacrificed herself to save her husband would come back to haunt him.

"Come into my office. I should be able to tell whether it's her or not." I led him back to my office, seating him at the table opposite me. I pulled out my bag of runes, holding them in my hand as they woke up.

My runes were made out of bone. For ten years I had gathered the skulls of ravens who had died from either natural or accidental causes. When I had enough, I ground them to a fine powder, using a mortar and pestle. To the powdered bone, I had stirred in powdered quartz, powdered obsidian, and powdered tourmaline. Then I added twenty-one drops of my own blood, and a sealing agent. I'd formed them into runes, and carved the sigils onto them. Then I fired them in a kiln until they were hard. They sparkled, because of the powdered gemstones, and they were each about the size of a half-dollar coin.

"Tell me more about what's going on. I know you have something attached to you—that I knew from the moment you walked into my house. But what made you think your wife was haunting you in the first place? What are your symptoms?"

Gunnar bit his lip, squinting as he thought. "I've been seeing phantoms—shadows here and there. I've seen Solveig in my dreams, which is why I thought she's the one haunting me. I can't eat, I'm losing weight, I can't sleep. I feel like a shadow of myself. It feels like I'm carrying a thousand pounds on my shoulders, and I can't shake off the gloom."

"All right. Here, take the bag of runes in hand, and focus on everything you just told me. Then reach inside and choose three runes. Don't look at them, just hand them back to me one at a time." I handed him the bag.

Gunnar did as I asked, resting the bag of runes on one hand as he lightly cupped it with the other.

I waited.

Unlike my ritual room, which was purely for magical use, my office had a desk on one side, with my computer and printer on it. Several bookshelves lined the walls, which were painted a pale silver. The table we were at held the crystal ball that I used for fortune-telling. I kept my cards and other magical tools I used for the public in a chest of drawers beneath the window. It was vital that I keep a barrier between my private practice and the practice that I used for my clients. While it was all magical in nature, I needed that sense of privacy, the space in which no one came between me and the gods.

Gunnar slowly opened the bag. Reaching in, he withdrew first one rune, then two more. He handed them to me one at a time, and I turned them facedown on the table without looking at them. Taking the bag from him, I set it to one side.

"All right, let's see what we can find out." I turned over the first rune. It was the rune of *Tears*. I glanced up at Gunnar. "This rune represents loss. It represents grief and mourning over something that has been lost to you, or an impending loss to come. In this case, I have no doubt that it represents losing Solveig, so whatever is happening to you is definitely connected to her death."

I turned over the second rune. It was the rune of *Betrayal*, upright. I blinked. On one hand, it could represent that Solveig was the force behind this, but my instinct told me it wasn't her. I didn't sense her anywhere in the room, and I was pretty sure she'd already moved on.

"This is the rune of betrayal, and in this position it means you're being betrayed from the outside. Which means that someone caused this to happen to you."

"Solveig?" he asked, an anxious look on his face.

I shook my head. "I don't think so. I'm not sure what's going on yet, but someone has cursed you in some way. Whoever—whatever—is attached to you is no accidental hitchhiker. Some demon or spirit is finding you a tasty morsel. Let me look at the third rune before making any decisions on this."

I turned over the third rune. And there it was. *Curse.* This was payback for something. Someone had set his sights on Gunnar and hexed him.

"Yes, as I thought. You've been cursed. And curses are, ninety percent of the time, cast by someone who happens to be alive. Someone has cursed you, and the attachment *is* the curse. Gunnar, is there anyone who would wish you harm? Do you have any enemies or rivals?"

Gunnar looked confused. For a moment, I thought he was going to cry, but he just leaned his elbows on the table and rested his forehead in his hands. Shaking his head, he let out a muffled, "I don't know. It's entirely possible."

As he turned to look out the window, I caught a glimpse of light from the back of his neck. *What the...*

"May I take a look at the back of your neck?" I stood, frowning.

"Sure, go ahead."

I crossed behind him, gently sweeping aside his braid. Sure enough, there was a sigil emblazoned on his neck, and a magical aura was seeping out from it. I couldn't read the rune, but I knew it was a spell, nonetheless. I placed my hand over it and a dread chill washed through me. Whatever this was, it wasn't a joke. This curse was meant to kill, in a slow, painful manner. And yet—there was still a sentient entity connected to it, though I knew down at my core it wasn't Solveig. Whatever the entity was, it must have recognized that I was trying to tune into it because a wall slammed down between me and the energy, so quickly that it jolted me as though I'd been hit. I jumped back, shaking my head.

"Are you all right?" Gunnar glanced over his shoulder at me.

"Hold on a second. I'm going to get Kipa." I poked my head out of the room, calling for Kipa to join us. He came trundling down the hall, sandwich in hand.

"You called?"

"Come in and sit down, please." I stared at the both of them. "There's an entity attached to Gunnar, and it's connected through a rune on the back of his neck."

"A rune?" Gunnar looked confused.

I lifted his hair back and took a picture of it, then showed it to him. "Have you seen this before? It's almost like a tattoo, but think of the ink as being magical in nature."

Gunnar stared at the image, then shook his head. "I had no idea that was there."

"What does it mean?" Kipa asked.

"I don't know the meaning of the rune, but I do know that Gunnar's under a curse. I'll have to do some research, though. Curses aren't usually connected to spirits or ghosts—at least not in this way. But there's definitely something feeding off of him. And before you ask, no, it's not his late wife. Solveig has moved on, I'm sure of it. She's gone to whatever awaited her in the afterlife, so you don't have to worry about her spirit being lost upon the glacier or anything of that sort."

"What will happen if you can't find out what the entity wants, or how to break the hex?" Gunnar asked.

I really didn't want to tell him what I was thinking, but he deserved to know the truth. "I'm sorry. Truly sorry. But if we can't figure out how to break this curse, I think it's going to kill you."

Both men fell silent, and I glanced out the window, where once again, the snow was beginning to fall.

CHAPTER ELEVEN

*A*ll I could really do after that was to tell Gunnar to try to rest and keep himself strong.

"I'll meet you out at the car," Kipa said, waving at Gunnar. Gunnar nodded, then headed out the door.

"I'll bring Raj in," I said, slipping out the door behind Gunnar.

When I returned, Raj trailing behind me, Kipa leaned back in his chair. "Well, what do you think we should do? I don't have much experience in things of this nature."

"I'll do what I can to research the sigil that's on the back of his neck. That might tell us something. Meanwhile, you try to find out what you can about anybody who hates him enough to curse him. I'm sure you guys make plenty of enemies in your adventures."

It occurred to me that my follow-through on promises lately hadn't been very good. I really needed to step up my game. Kipa stood, then kissed me, brushing the hair back from my face.

"I'd like to spend the night, but I promised Ember that

I'd go on the hunt with her. A pair of goblins are tearing up a neighborhood in Shoreline and she needs help. Herne's busy, so he asked me to fill in for him."

"What about Yutani? Can he go with Ember? Or maybe Viktor?"

"I'm sorry. I promised to help. Call me as soon as you find out anything. *If* you find out anything. Thank you for trying, either way. I hate the thought of losing Gunnar, especially to a curse. He's one of the most loyal guards I could ever hope for. I want to do everything I can to help him." He pulled me close, his breath warm against my ear. "Believe me, I'd rather stay here and make love to you than go hunt for sub-Fae, but I gave my word. And Herne and I are getting along better, so I'd like to keep it that way."

I ran my hand over his chest. I trembled at his touch, thirsting for him. It was as though Kipa fed every hunger I had. Pressing close, I rested my head on his shoulder.

"I don't know what this is," I whispered. "I don't know what we have, but whatever it is I can't resist it. I can't resist you." I looked up into his eyes, feeling more vulnerable than I had felt in years. I didn't like admitting my vulnerability, but I felt safe with Kipa, and each time we came together, it felt more natural to be with him.

"I believe we were destined to meet. You're beautiful, and terrifying, and you intoxicate me. I find myself thinking of you through the day, thinking about how you feel in my arms, thinking about your perfume as you press against me. About your lips against mine." He caught me up in his arms then, and pressed his lips to mine with a kiss that said, *You're mine and only mine.* A moment later, he broke away and gave me a rueful smile.

"I'd better get moving before Gunnar wonders what's keeping me. I'll talk to you tomorrow."

Before I could say a word, he was out the door, shutting it behind him. I rested my hand against the door, reeling from the passion that been left unquenched. I thought about spending some alone time in my bedroom, but then decided that I needed to clear my head.

"Hey, Raj, want to go for a ride?" I glanced out the window. The snow seemed to have stopped, though it was below freezing.

Raj came racing in from the living room, skidding to one side as he put on the brakes, his weight sending him wide like a semi making a turn on a narrow road. He wriggled, then sat back on his haunches, looking for all the world as though he were imitating a statue of Bast.

"Raj likes rides." His eyes glowed.

"I'm sorry we haven't taken many lately. This will be a short one, but I want to get out of the house for a few minutes and I thought you might like to go with me."

"Raj go with Raven!"

I pulled on my jacket and slid on my boots, zipping them up. Then, grabbing my keys and purse, I made sure the range was off, fastened a leash to Raj's collar, and we headed out into the night.

My breath immediately formed clouds in front of my face as I glanced up into the clear sky. The storm had backed away, and the stars glittered down, reflecting the sparkle of the snow. The temperature was dropping—it was already below freezing, but I had snow tires and as long as I stuck to the main roads, we should be safe.

I opened the back door of the car and Raj hopped in. As I fastened my seat belt and eased out of the driveway, I glanced over at the for-sale sign on Buck's property and did a double-take. There was already a "sold" sticker plastered across it. *Great.* I had hoped to have time to cast a spell to attract the right neighbors for our neighborhood, but it was too late.

Heading down the street, I decided we'd go to the Plum Creek Shopping Center. The mini-mall was on the border between Redmond and Kirkland and I could get there via the main roads, which had been plowed. Even though it was already icing over, the route should be clear enough. I didn't really need to do any shopping, but it was a place to go, and it also had the Downside Drive-In, one of the best dive diners in town. Raj and I could get dinner.

As I sped silently through the night, watching the lights of the houses pass by, I was lost in my thoughts. The land wight hung heavy on my mind, as did Gunnar's situation. And then there were the ferrets. I felt like everywhere I turned, somebody needed my help, and I wasn't sure how well I could help anybody right now.

I glanced in the rearview mirror at Raj, who was staring out the window, his nose pressed against the glass.

"Raj want dinner from the Downside Diner?"

He turned his gaze to the back of my head. "Raj want a Dippy Burger and a Barrel O' Fries." His eyes were bright and judging by the tone of his voice, I had just made his evening.

"You got it." I was just pulling into the shopping center when my phone jangled out the opening notes for "Journeyman" by Jethro Tull. That was the ring tone for my father. I parked in the nearest parking spot, grabbing my phone out of the dashboard holder I kept it in.

"Dad?" I hadn't heard from my father in months.

"Raven, how are you? Am I calling at a bad time?" His voice was the same as I remembered—low and gravelly.

"Never. No, you aren't. I miss you," I said. I hadn't seen him in over a year. Ulstair and I had been planning to visit for the holidays, but then he'd been killed and I'd begged off, with all that was happening.

"I miss you too, my little flame. I thought that I might come out during the spring or summer. I can drive across country then, and won't have to worry about bad weather."

My father never used public transportation, whether it was trains or planes or buses. He was too aware of the fates of those he would come into contact with, and what might happen to them through meeting him. He was terribly conscientious, more than most of the Ante-Fae would ever be.

My father was Curikan, the Black Dog of Hanging Hills, in Connecticut. The first time mortals met him in his natural form—as one of the infamous black dogs— they experienced great fortune. But if they met him again, in either his human or dog form, they would undergo a tragedy of equal proportions. My father liked people too much to put them in danger, so for the most part, he lived as a recluse, seldom having anything to do with outsiders who weren't Ante-Fae. I had gotten my love for living around mortals from him.

"Really? You'd do that? Just to see me?" My mood lifted like somebody had flipped on the light switch. "I'd love it. You could see my house, and meet Raj, and…" I was about to say "Meet my friends," but that might be pushing it. Except, of course, for the Ante-Fae I hung out with. "I'd love it, Dad."

"Then it's settled. I'll come out when the weather gets better. By the way, there's something you should know, since your mother never gives you advance notice. Phasmoria told me that she's planning on visiting you soon. As in, within the week. So be prepared."

I stared at the dashboard. I loved my mother, but we weren't nearly as close as my father and I were. Phasmoria and I had a tenuous relationship, given she had left my father and me when I was twelve, returning to the Morrígan, who had demanded she take up her duties as one of the Bean Sidhe again. Phasmoria had left me with Curikan, claiming it was best for me, though I had the feeling it was more that she had never expected to get pregnant, and when the excuse had presented itself for her to ditch being a mother, she had jumped on it.

Oh, she visited me more often than my father managed, but the meetings were always tense, and even though I looked forward to seeing her, I never felt like I measured up to her standards.

"Do you know why she's coming?" I asked after a moment.

"She says she has to talk to you about something. I'm not sure what it is." He paused. "Are you all right? Do you need money? How's Raj?"

"Raj is just fine, and no, I don't need money, but thank you." I grinned. My father was still under the assumption that I was too young to make my way in the world. Among the Ante-Fae, it was common for children to stay with their parents for several hundred years. I had branched out on my own early. But every time he asked, it made me feel that much more secure. I liked knowing he had my back.

"I'm fine. Oh, while I have you on the phone, I want to ask you something." I texted the picture of the sigil on Gunnar's neck to my father. "Have you ever seen this mark before?" I explained what was going on.

There was a pause, then my father said, "No, but you be careful. There are a lot of nasty creatures out on the Aether and the astral. Don't put yourself in danger. Now tell me, how are you doing since Ulstair died?"

I sighed. I hadn't told my father about Kipa yet. Hell, I'd barely told any of my friends about him. "All right. Better than I expected to be, to be honest. I did a Cord Cutting ceremony to let him go. I miss him, but I need to move on."

"Does that mean you're seeing someone new?"

"It might. Well, kind of."

"Tell me all about him—or her." My father laughed. "Or don't, if you don't want to. I just feel like we've been out of touch for a while, and I'd really like to reconnect."

That sobered me up. If my father was feeling pushed out of my life, then I needed to connect with him more. "I guess I've just been busy. I've had a lot going on. Of course I'll tell you about him. And yes, this time it's a *him*. His name is Kipa—Kuippana. He's from—"

"Finland. I've heard of Kuippana. You've really moved up in the world, haven't you? Isn't he the Lord of the Wolves?" My father sounded both impressed and a little afraid.

"Yes. I actually met him through Herne."

"Herne as in, *Herne the Hunter*? Oh, this is getting better and better. What *have* you been doing with yourself?"

It really *had* been a long time since we'd talked.

"Hey, listen. I'm going to hang up for the moment. I'm sitting in a freezing parking lot with Raj. We went out for a drive. I'll grab some takeout and go home and I'll call you then. We can have a long chat. So I'll talk to you in about half an hour. How does that sound?"

"That sounds delightful." Before I could say another word he had signed off.

I stuck my phone back in the holder and glanced into the backseat at Raj. "Well, let's buy dinner and go home. I'm starting to freeze my ass off."

Raj laughed. I drove through the drive-thru, placing an order for four Dippy burgers, two Barrel O' Fries, a strawberry milkshake, and dozen Downside doughnuts. I paid the cashier. When she handed me the sacks of food, I placed them on the floor in the passenger seat. I didn't dare hand them back to Raj or we wouldn't have anything left to eat by the time we got home.

Heading out again into the icy street, I drove home, feeling infinitely better than when I had started out. Talking to my father always lifted my spirits, and the thought of a cozy long chat with him in front of the fire made everything seem all right.

THE NEXT MORNING, I WOKE UP FEELING REFRESHED. THE talk with my father had done me a world of good, and spending the evening in, with Raj and the TV, had calmed me down. I had managed to sleep through the night without nightmares or any unwelcome interruptions.

After feeding the ferrets, changing their litter, and playing with them for a while, I wandered into the kitchen. Outside, the sky was overcast, and the temp was hovering barely at the freezing mark. The snow was still iced over from the low temperatures during the night, and it was the sort of day that made me not want to go anywhere. I fixed myself a cup of hot cocoa and, carrying that and the leftover doughnuts from the night before, headed into my office.

No time like the present to get a leg up on Gunnar's situation. I found a book on runes and sigils—*Drake's Compendium of Symbols*—and snuggled in the overstuffed chair in the corner, placing my cocoa and doughnuts on the side table. I tucked a lightweight throw over me and settled down to thumb through the pages.

I was looking for the symbol that had been burned onto Gunnar's neck. I wasn't sure where to start, so I flipped to the chapter on curses and began to turn the pages one by one. The book itself was a good thousand pages long, and the chapter on curses took up about one-third of the book. I had finished my cocoa and two of the doughnuts by the time I came to the symbol.

Straightening my shoulders, I pulled out my phone to compare the picture to the drawing to make certain it was the same. It was.

The fylgismadi is a specific type of curse known mostly in Northern European circles. Used by only powerful shamans and magic-born, the mark binds one of the Wandering Ghosts to the bearer of the mark, usually without their knowledge. [See Wandering Ghosts in Drake's Compendium of Spirits]

I was about to go get the companion volume when my phone rang. The ring tone was the one I had set for the Witching Hour, so it had to be a client.

"You've reached the Witching Hour. Raven speaking. How may I help you?" I had developed just the right amount of eagerness mixed in with professionalism over the years, and was told I had a lovely phone voice.

"Hi. It's Moira Ness. You read for me at the Sun & Moon Apothecary. I don't mean to bother you at home, but I have a problem with a spirit."

Moira. My lonely old lady. "Hey, Moira. What's going on?"

She sounded almost embarrassed. "I tried something and it didn't work. I was wondering if you could help me set it to rights?"

I suppressed a sigh. That could mean anything. "Why don't you tell me what's going on?"

"Well, I saw that my neighbor had a speaking board and—"

I groaned. "Don't tell me that you used it. Trying to talk to your sister?"

She whispered out a deflated "Yes" and then fell silent.

"So what's going on now? Did you talk to her?" I knew she hadn't because her sister had moved on, but there were plenty of spirits out there, ready and willing to take advantage of gullible mortals. And Moira, as sweet as she was, would be a prime target for them.

"No, I didn't. But something came through and it's tearing up my house." She sounded frantic. "I don't know if it's a ghost or what, but it's throwing things around and tipping over pots and laughing at me."

Crap. This was serious. It could be a poltergeist or

even one of the sub-Fae. They could enter this realm through the portals caused by talking boards. And Moira definitely couldn't take this on by herself.

"All right. Here, give me your address." I jotted it down as she recited it. It was in the Worchester district of Seattle—one of the most haunted, rundown places in the city. The entire district had been the scene of too many murders, attacks, and other atrocities that had settled deep within the very land that made up the ruralesque urban neighborhood. The rent was cheap, the houses were weathered, and the lots were overgrown into tangled jungles.

"Okay, Moira, I want you to listen to me." I was about to tell her to wait outside for me but then stopped. It was cold as hell out there, and little old ladies did not belong standing out on the street in subfreezing temperatures. "Try to keep out of its way. I'll be there as soon as I can, traffic allowing. Call me if anything worse happens."

I grabbed my travel bag of magical tools and headed for the door, pocketing my keys on the way. Stopping at the door to put on my boots, I called for Raj. He meandered in from the living room, a glazed look on his face. I heard the Bounce-A-Boy song in the background. He'd been watching *The Terrible Twins*, a kids' program that fascinated him because of the music, the vivid colors, and the continual action that left most adults dizzy.

"Raj, I have to run out for a while. Will you be okay here by yourself? You've had breakfast, and there's fruit on the table in case you want a snack." I had shut my office door behind me. I kept him out of there, to keep him out of trouble.

"Raj be fine. Raj watch twins."

"Yeah, Raj watch twins... Okay, I'll be back as soon as I can." I blew him a kiss and slipped out the door, locking it behind me. As I cautiously picked my way over the ice that covered the sidewalk, I hoped to hell that whatever Moira had conjured up, I'd be able to take care of.

CHAPTER TWELVE

$\mathscr{T}$he drive over to Seattle was harrowing. The temperatures over the past couple days had risen just above freezing several times before plunging into the icy range again, so that a thin layer of snow had melted, then refrozen, compacting everything into one giant ice slick. Any snow that fell over that created a sliding hazard.

Even where the plows had gone through, the danger of black ice loomed large, and the ruts and furrows through the compacted snow and ice were taking their toll on the cars. With some streets so steep they were a difficult hike at best, Seattle during a snowstorm was one big accident waiting to happen.

The Worchester district was tucked in between Lake Forest Park and a district that had once been known as Mountlake Terrace. And it was creepy as shit. Just like Beacon Hill had become a haven for streeps—the street people—with old houses turned into flops that housed twenty to thirty people in shifts around the clock, the district was the city's failed attempt at gentrification.

The city council had swept through, removing some of the worst houses, but the planners were footloose and fancy-free about how they spent the money, and when the funds ran out, only a few streets here and there had been upgraded, in a piecemeal fashion. Nobody ever figured out where the money had gone, though the word *embezzlement* hung heavy on the taxpayers' minds, and so the Worchester district was left to decay even further.

The populace of the area was mostly human, though a number of shifters had moved in during the past few years. The houses were cheap compared to most of Seattle, and the families who moved into the district barely had enough for a down payment, so even though some of the lawns were kept up, the houses themselves were still as dismal as they had been before the city's ill-planned intervention.

As I drove along 40th Place Northeast, I came to Five Acre Woods Park. Moira's house was just beyond the park, on Elspeth Way, a side street off of 40th. As I crept along the road, the houses became increasingly decrepit, their paint weathered to the point where it was almost nonexistent. The lawns, from what I could see of them, were tangled and snarled, partially hidden beneath the snow.

The entire area was one big haunted mess. I could feel it the moment I entered the district. The spirit population was high, especially the number of ghosts caught in the Aether. A high proportion of junkies died in the Worcester district, overdosing on whatever their drug of choice was. There had also been a number of suicides over the years, contributing even further to the high rate of ghostly encounters.

I kept an eye on the house numbers, finally spotting Moira's house. Pulling alongside the curb in front of the cottage, I thought it looked like a place Moira would live in. The aging cottage was trimmed with flowerboxes under the windows, and ivy trailed up one side of the house to twine around the chimney. A tidy, well-kept garden had to be Moira's handiwork. It had her gentle stamp all over it.

As I got out of the car, a blast of wind shot past me, sending a ripple of shivers from head to toe. I thought I could hear a cry on the wind, but then it was gone, as though it had been sucked away by the gusting currents. I glanced at the sky again as it began to snow, then grabbed my bag of magical goodies and hurried up the sidewalk, trying not to slip on the icy pavement. As I reached the porch, Moira opened the door. She glanced behind me, a worried look on her face.

"Do be careful. I haven't been able to get out to shovel the ice and snow off the sidewalk and I don't want anybody falling." She ushered me in and quickly shut the door behind me.

I knew she was worried about liability, and without thinking, I offered, "I can shovel the walk for you after I'm done here."

"You'd really do that for me?" The look in her eyes was payment enough.

I realized I truly enjoyed Moira's company, and I looked forward to our readings each month. "Of course I can. Now, tell me exactly what happened and where this thing—"

A gleeful cackle cut me off as a winged creature about the size of a baby flew by. It grabbed my hair and yanked hard, startling me so that I almost fell.

"What the hell? Is that it?" That was no ghost. That wasn't any sort of spirit at all.

"Yes, it's been making my life hell—pardon my language. I'm just so frustrated. It's broken four of my good vases, two teacups, and a cherub that my late husband gave me." She looked like she was about to cry, knotting her apron in her hands. Moira was wearing a cabbage rose print dress, with a pink apron over the top. It made her look like the proverbial grandmother out of some storybook fairytale, and I could almost smell the cookies from her kitchen.

"First things first. Do you still have the speaking board in your house?" The first matter of business was to get rid of that thing.

"Yes, it's in the dining room. This all started about three hours ago." She led me through the living room, which was so neat and tidy that it made my place look cluttered, into the dining room. On the table sat the speaking board. I glanced around at the heavy oak furniture, and the pictures on her walls that I assumed were her family. There was a gleeful laugh from another room and I heard a crash. Moira gave a little cry.

"I'm afraid you may lose a few more things before we're done here, but I'll try to mitigate as much damage as I can. First things first, we're getting rid of this." I held up the speaking board. "Do you know that these are portals to all sorts of dimensions? It's not just a toy or even a telephone to the dead. It's an invitation to anything that happens to be passing through. A giant 'Welcome' sign that invites them to come and play, and they always play on their own terms."

"I didn't know. I thought it was harmless." She blushed, looking guilty.

"Well, they're not. But not many people understand that, so don't fret. You're lucky that you just got an imp. That's what that creature is. It could have been much worse." I set my bag of magical tools on the table, then picked up the speaking board, staring at it. I then raised one knee and brought the board down hard across my leg. The board split, and I tossed the pieces back on the table.

"Oh, my neighbor's going to be irritated."

"Pay her back for it. She doesn't need to be messing around with this, either."

"Don't you need the board in order to send the imp back where it came from?" Moira asked.

"No, because it won't go unless it wants to or until I'm able to drive it out, and the board's not going to help either one of those things."

"Then how are you going to get it to leave?"

"I'm going to make it so damned uncomfortable that it won't want to stay. I plan on making certain that the imp *wants* to leave. It came through the board, but there are many ways to send it back to the astral plane, which is where I think it came from." I opened my bag, pulling out my war water, some Be Gone powder, and my dagger.

"Sit over there in that dining chair, please. I need you here, out of the way but safe." I glanced around the room. There were a number of things that the creature could still throw, but the imp would first have to open the heavy china hutch doors, and I could probably ward it off before it did that.

Moira hastened to obey. I stripped off my jacket, tossing it on the table, and then fastened my dagger sheath to my belt, making sure that Venom wasn't peace bound. I poured some of the war water into a small atomizer that I carried with me.

"Is that the kitchen?" I nodded toward the crashing sounds, which were coming through a swinging door on the other side of the dining room.

"Yes, that's the kitchen." Moira looked at me with wide eyes. "Please be careful. I don't want you getting hurt."

"I'll be fine. You just stay here." Grabbing the Be Gone powder in one hand, I picked up the atomizer in the other, and headed through the swinging door to the kitchen.

The place was a train wreck. The imp had overturned canisters of flour and sugar, which had spilled all over the floor. The refrigerator door was open and it looked like half the contents had been tossed around the kitchen. The counter was covered in squashed tomatoes and milk dribbled over the edge to blend with the flour on the floor, making a nasty paste. What looked to have been a lemon meringue pie had been upended over the burners on the stove. Thank gods the creature hadn't managed to turn on the burners.

The imp slowly turned toward me as I entered the room, a carton of eggs in its hands. About eighteen inches tall, the creature looked like a combination of a scrawny baby and a baby velociraptor with bat wings and bright red eyes. Imps were from the astral plane, although I wasn't sure if they were demonic or not. They weren't sub-Fae, but they often hung out with goblins and their ilk. It gave me a slow, creepy grin, and laughed.

"You need to leave this house and scram," I said. I had no idea whether it understood me — and it didn't really matter. It wouldn't listen to me if it did. I lifted the atomizer of war water and sprayed a heavy mist at it.

The imp shrieked, shooting up toward the ceiling. The damn thing was fast, that was for sure. Before I realized what it was doing, it began pelting me with the eggs, one after another. The first two missed me, but the next three hit square on my face and chest. I ignored the slime running down my face and squirted it with the war water again. The water would weaken it, kind of like a liquid version of punching it in the face. The imp dropped the eggs and headed toward the dining room. Before it could reach the door, I raced in front of it, throwing a handful of Be Gone powder on it, and began to sing.

> By hex and curse, by sun and moon,
> by the singing of this rune,
> I commend thee, leave this place,
> never return to this space.

I threw another handful of the powder on it, and the imp shrieked, turning to flee the other way. But before it could, a vortex appeared in front of it and it shot through the portal.

> By hex and curse, by sun and moon,
> by the singing of this rune,
> I close this portal forevermore,

and I seal shut this door.

I could hear the imp on the other side, cursing as it tried to get back through, but then the portal closed and the seal took effect.

I slumped against the wall. The imp wouldn't be able to return to the house now. At least, not unless it was invited back, and Moira wasn't about to extend another invitation. I'd make sure of that.

Staring at the mess in the kitchen, I shook my head. There were a few broken dishes scattered around, but the imp hadn't managed to destroy most of her good china. Realizing that I had egg running down my cheek, I gingerly made my way over to the sink, found a roll of paper towels, and wiped off as much as I could. Then I peeked back through the door. Moira was still sitting where I had told her to.

"It's gone. I got rid of it and it shouldn't be able to come back. But your kitchen is a wreck. I warn you now."

Moira grimaced. "I suppose I'd better get busy cleaning it up. I didn't mean for this to happen. I'm so sorry I involved you. But thank you so much for helping."

"That's all right. What are friends for, if not to help you evict an imp out of your kitchen?" Taking pity on her, I added, "Come on. I'll help you."

"Oh, I didn't mean for you to have to do anything like that." Moira blushed, looking chagrined.

"That's all right. I've made my share of mistakes," I said, thinking back to my ill-timed attempt to summon Jim Morrison's ghost. "We all screw up at one time or another."

As we cleaned up the kitchen, I finally broached the subject of the speaking board.

"Moira, I know you wanted to contact your sister, but I've told you a number of times that she's moved on. She's not there to talk to anymore. She's reincarnated. Why do you keep trying?"

Moira set down the sponge she was cleaning the refrigerator with and sat down on one of the kitchenette chairs. She let out a long sigh.

"Beatrice and I were twins, as you know. We were best friends. I loved her more than I loved even my late husband. There's something about having a twin… It's hard to describe."

I nodded, though I didn't fully understand.

"I was staying with her on a visit. My husband was on a business trip, and my kids were at camp. Her husband was on a trip as well, and she didn't have any children." She paused, then shuddered. "I've told you that Beatrice died in a house fire, but I've never told you the full story. We were up late one night, and we were drinking. We had a bottle of wine and both of us were lightweights. I told her to go to bed, that I would close up and make sure the doors were locked. I was just tipsy enough that I forgot to blow out the candles."

I had a horrible feeling I knew what was coming next.

Moira continued. "The guest room was on the bottom floor, but my sister's room was on the top floor. At some point during the night, the dog knocked over one of the candles or something. The smoke detectors went off, and I managed to get myself and her dog out. But by the time I realized that Beatrice was still inside, the house was engulfed in flames. I tried to run back in for her, but the firefighters stopped me. They tried to save her, but they couldn't get through the flames. I saw her standing at her window. We were yelling for her to jump, but she was terrified of heights. She waited too long, and the smoke overwhelmed her. *I'm* responsible for Beatrice's death. I can never forgive myself, and I desperately wish I could tell her I'm sorry."

"It was an accident. It wasn't intentional." I knew that wouldn't help, but I had to try. And now, I understood her drive to talk to her sister.

"You know what the horrible thing is? I never told anybody until now. The fire marshal didn't find any evidence of the candle—it burned up. They thought that the fireplace may have shot out a spark that landed on the rug. The fireplace was still burning when we went to bed. And I never said a word. I'm a horrible person." She broke down in tears, covering her face with her hands.

I slowly reached out, gently touching her shoulder. "You don't know for sure that it was the candle. It could have been the fireplace." I wanted to make her feel better. I wanted to take away her guilt. There wasn't any way of ever finding out the truth now, so many years after the fact.

"I suppose not. But I can't help but believe that I caused the fire." She raised her head. Her cheeks were flushed and tears trailed down her face. "Am I an evil person?"

I shook my head. "No, you're not. Things happen that are out of our control. Sometimes, we hurt the people we love, never meaning to. It's been thirty-five years, Moira. You need to set aside the blame. I need you to trust me when I say that your sister has gone on to another life."

She sniffled, nodding. "I just can't stand the thought that she's blamed me all these years…"

"If she blamed you, she'd be haunting you. And the only haunting she's doing is in your dreams and in your memories. I want you to stop trying to contact her. I want you to make peace with yourself. Trust me, I know spirits. If Beatrice wasn't at rest, if she was still angry at you, she would be here tearing up your house instead of that imp. Will you believe me?"

Moira slowly nodded. "I'll try. I've spent the past thirty-five years trying to make up for what I did. I've tried to help others in whatever way I can. I don't know if there's much more I can do."

"If you were an evil person, you wouldn't have told me about this. You would have kept silent. You wouldn't be trying to contact your sister to ask for forgiveness, because that's what you're trying to do. If you were a bad person, you would have gone on your merry way, and just let the entire incident die."

She nodded, mulling over my words. We went back to cleaning, and an hour later the kitchen was sparkling, and all the debris had been picked up from her house. She offered me lunch, and I accepted. We sat at the kitchen table over grilled cheese sandwiches and tomato soup, talking about the snow, talking about my neighbors, talking about life in general. When I was ready to leave, she escorted me to the door.

"I'll be seeing you next month for my reading, but this time, I'll have a different question," she said with a strained smile. "I think…I can finally accept that Beatrice is gone."

"Sometimes, silence can be as good as forgiveness. Be

grateful she's been able to move on. She wasn't trapped in the Aether. That, Moira, is a blessing."

As I left the cottage, I tucked my coat closely around me. The snow had picked up. It looked like we weren't out of the storm yet.

CHAPTER THIRTEEN

$\mathcal{I}$ stopped at the Sun & Moon Apothecary before heading home. As I stomped the snow off my boots on the rug inside the door, I could hear laughter from upstairs. Llew waved me over to the counter. He had just finished waiting on one customer and, while there were four or five other people shopping the shelves, there was nobody waiting at the register.

"This is one hell of a storm," Llew said. "They say we're due for more snow over the next week. Climate change in action. How are you today?"

"I've got egg on my face. How do you think I am?" While I had wiped off the egg as best as I could, there was still a sticky residue left in my hair and on my dress.

"Okay, tell me why you're covered in raw egg." Llew put down the catalog he had been holding and leaned his elbows on the counter, waiting.

"I got a call from Moira today." I told him the rest of the story, avoiding any discussion of about the house fire or her twin. That was a secret she had invested in me, and it would remain with me until the day she died.

"When will people learn to take things like speaking boards seriously? They ask for advice, don't believe us, then we end up going in to clean up their messes." Llew shook his head. "So I talked to Neil this morning. He's still up for the great land wight hunt tonight. What about you?"

"Yeah, though I'm not looking forward to trudging through the snow after it. Especially with as dangerous as that thing is. But at least Neil has the means to destroy it." I glanced at the calendar on the wall. "Are we in Mercury retrograde? So many glitches have been happening lately that it seems like it."

Llew studied the calendar for a moment. "No, but Mars is having a field day and that often equals aggression. So what can I do for you today?"

"I wanted to know if there's anything in particular I should have ready for tonight. You said you were going to do some study on land wights. I haven't had the chance to do much reading on them."

"They're nasty buggers. In fact, you're lucky you didn't get infected from those barbs. How's the wrist?"

I glanced down at the scabs that had formed over the puncture wounds. "Fine. I heal up fast, though. They're venomous, right?"

"I suppose you could call it venom. Venom or poison... Whatever the case, when they grab you with those tentacles, they inject a powerful toxin. It's most dangerous to humans and the magic-born. It can affect the Fae, though usually not quite so virulently as it does humans. Apparently it's a necrotic toxin, and it breaks down the tissues so the land wight can easily absorb them. So Neil and I will have to be careful. Not that you shouldn't be, but…"

"The land wight can kill you two easier than it can kill me. I know what you mean. What should we look for in terms of a nest?" I had no clue what a land wight's nest would look like.

"It's usually dug into the side of a slope or a mountain, or in a barrow of dirt. It will be covered over with a mound of decaying leaves or branches."

"Then its nest could be anywhere, and if it's a mound, there will be snow on top of it, given the weather." I frowned. UnderLake Park spanned almost six hundred acres. We could search all night and not even be close to the thing.

"Possibly, but they stay close to their nests. They don't wander far. And remember—if it has been coming in and out of its nest, the snow will be disturbed. The creature will have left some sort of footprint or trail."

I decided I'd better go home and read up on land wights before we went hunting. "What do you suggest I take with me? Neil will have the silver hammer, and that's the only thing that can destroy it. But I hurt it with fire. Do you know anything else that might keep it at bay?"

"From what I've read, fire is its most potent enemy. So I'd say stack up on the fire spells, and we might want to take a couple torches with us." Llew laughed. "I wouldn't normally recommend taking a torch into a heavily wooded park but with all the snow and moisture, I doubt if we're going to be setting any fires."

"I think we'd better leave the torches at home. They're unwieldy and my fire is plenty strong and much more controllable." I yawned. My skirmish with the imp left me tired. "I think I'm going to go home and take a quick nap before you guys come by tonight. I'll see you later. Around six thirty or seven?"

"Better figure around seven. Neil doesn't get off till six and then he'll have to drive over from Woodinville."

I glanced out the door. The snow was falling heavily now, accumulating along the sidewalk and on the tops of the cars. "Call me if you can't make it. At the rate it's coming down, I wouldn't be surprised if we were all snowed in before long. Oh, did I tell you? My neighbor is moving! His house is already sold!"

"Do you know who bought it?" Llew gave me a skeptical look. "I'd save the celebration until you find out."

"Killjoy." I sobered. "I know I should wait to celebrate until I find out who my new neighbors are, but it's such a relief knowing that Buck and his brood are going to be out of there. See you later!" I gave him a wave and headed out of the shop.

Driving home was tricky, and part of me hoped that we wouldn't be able to go after the land wight tonight. But even as I fixed Raj a snack, I knew that one way or another, it was better if we found it and destroyed it as soon as possible. The creature was dangerous, and the sooner we took it out, the less chance it would have to kill anybody else, because I was sure it had already claimed a number of victims.

I CURLED UP ON THE SOFA, WATCHING THE SNOWFALL through the window. Raj was feeling lazy too. He had stretched out in front of the fireplace and, yawning, rested his head on his "paws." I set my alarm for three P.M. and slowly nodded off, thinking about my conversation with my father the night before.

I loved my mother. I really did. But I wasn't sure how much I liked her. We had never seen eye to eye, and she didn't understand why I chose to live among humans. She kept encouraging me to move back with my father, or away from the city, out to the wilderness. More than once she had mentioned I might want to move to Annwn, but I didn't feel like living in the land of the gods. I slowly drifted to sleep, finally letting go of the turmoil of thoughts that were raging through my head. Apparently, I needed the sleep because I slept heavily, oversleeping my alarm, and it took Raj poking me with his snout in order to wake me up.

"Raven wake up? Raven feel bad? Is Raven okay?"

The flurry of questions hit me as I opened my eyes. Raj was staring me straight in the face, his nose wet. He was just about to prod me again when my eyes fluttered open, and ended up hitting my nose with his as I jerked.

"I'm awake! Let me turn off the alarm." Groggily, I reached for my phone and flipped off the alarm. Raj stepped back as I forced myself to sit up, yawning so wide that I thought I was about to break my jaw.

"Raven okay?" Raj looked at me with pleading eyes.

"I'm okay, doodlebug. I was just tired so I took a long nap." I leaned forward, resting my elbows on my knees and my chin on my hands. Raj poked his nose at me again and I gave him a quick kiss. "Everything's fine, Raj. I guess I just didn't get enough sleep last night."

"Raven takes naps like Raj takes naps. Raj is hungry

now. Food?" He wiggled slightly, looking like a giant Gothic puppy.

I raised one eyebrow, laughing. "Raj is always hungry. Raj give Raven a moment to clear her head and Raven will fix Raj a snack."

Stumbling to my feet, I headed for the bathroom. After washing my hands and splashing a little cold water on my cheeks, I returned to the kitchen where I broke open a bag of potato chips. Raj wasn't the only one who was hungry. I motioned for him to sit with me on the sofa and poured a bowl of chips for him, saving the rest of the bag for me. As we ate in comfortable silence, I watched the snow come down. We had nearly a foot, but I wondered how much longer it could actually continue. Seattle rarely had snows like this, although they were becoming more frequent as the climate shifted and changed. While parts of the world were drying up and broiling, we were getting wetter, cooler weather.

"Does Raj like snow?" I asked, breaking the silence. Raj looked up at me from his chips.

"Raj likes snow. Raj likes rain too. Raj doesn't like the sun." He nodded toward the television. "Raj watch TV?"

"All right. What do you want to watch?" I already knew the answer to that, given the time, but it was always polite to ask.

"*Acrobert and the Alphas*." Raj sounded so excited that it made me smile. *Acrobert and the Alphas* was a new cartoon. It was about a superhero named Bert, who was an incredible acrobat. He had a team of goofy friends who helped him solve crimes and save the world. And Raj absolutely loved the show.

I turned on the TV, finding the right channel.

Thinking ahead, I programmed the series to record so that if we missed it Raj wouldn't mope. Then, as he settled down to watch, I carried the empty bag and bowl back into the kitchen. I rinsed out the dishes that were in the sink and put them into the dishwasher and gathered the trash to carry out to the trash bin.

"I'll be back in a moment. I'm going to empty the garbage." But Raj didn't answer. I glanced at him. He was so wrapped up in the show that he didn't even notice me.

Carrying the garbage out the front door, I slipped and slid my way down the sidewalk to the trash bin. Moira's walk wasn't the only one that I needed to clean. I figured that since I had already shoveled one walk today, another wouldn't hurt, so I grabbed a shovel. Fifteen minutes later, my sidewalk was clean from my door down to the car and driveway.

A noise caught my attention. I looked up to see Buck and Minerva struggling to carry boxes out to their truck. As I watched, a moving van inched down the street, parking in front of the place. *That was fast.* I didn't even know you could sell a house that fast, or close on it that quickly. Although they might be moving before the actual deal went through. But still, they must be packing on the go. I thought about going over to tell them good-bye, but I decided to let sleeping dogs lie—and sleeping Bucks as well.

As the moving men jumped out of the truck and headed up the sidewalk to talk to Buck, I turned around and went back inside, propping the shovel by the door. As I entered my house, I heard my phone ring. It was Kipa's ring tone—a song called "Wolf Moon." I grabbed it and answered before the caller could hang up on me.

"Kipa? What's up?"

"You sound excited to see me," came the chuckling reply.

I snorted. "Funny man. I was just coming in from shoveling the snow and I'm out of breath."

"Oh, damn. You just broke my delusions. I thought you were happy to hear from me." Kipa laughed, then cleared his throat. "Gunnar and I need to come over and talk to you. We found out some information that may have a bearing on whatever it is that's attached to him. The fylgismadi or whatever it is."

" 'Fylgismadi' is right. I'm busy tonight. I'm heading out to fight that land wight with Llew and Neil. Can you come by tomorrow?" Even as I spoke, a wave of disappointment washed over me. I would much rather spend the evening canoodling with Kipa than tromping through a snowy forest.

"That will work. Will noon be all right? Gunnar is taking a few days off from his job."

"Noon will be fine. Can you stay afterward?" A pang of longing hit me, and I wanted nothing more than to feel his arms around me, his hands on my skin.

"So you *do* miss me?" He was laughing again, but it was gentle laughter, and I knew he was teasing me.

"I miss all of you. Every single part of you. Some parts of you more than others right now," I said in a throaty voice.

"I'm not sure what my schedule is, but I'll try to clear it. Trust me, I miss you with every inch of my body, and I mean that sincerely. It's so *hard* being away from you."

"How hard is it?" I whispered.

"So hard that I can barely keep my pants zipped." His

breathing quickened. I could hear it over the phone. "Damn, woman. Just talking to you gets me so fucking horny I can hardly stand it. You sure you have to do this land wight hunt tonight?"

Reluctantly, I said, "Yeah. Do you want to come with us?"

"No, I want to come with *you*." He sighed. "I would, honestly, but I guarantee you the wight would sense my presence, and hide itself so well you'd never find it. At least not until the next victim disappears. How many people has it claimed so far?"

"I don't know. Llew and I stumbled over it by accident. We need to find its lair tonight, and we have one of Llew's friends coming with us who has a magical silver hammer that can destroy the soul stone. I'll call you if it's not too late when we finish. If you're up for it, you can come over then."

"I'm always up for you." Still laughing, Kipa signed off.

I wandered back into the kitchen, thinking I should eat a light dinner before we headed out. But all I could think about was Kipa now, his hands on my breasts, his lips pressed hard against mine, him deep inside me. I glanced at the clock. It was four-fifteen. I set down the package of noodles that I had been going to cook, turned, and—making sure Raj was still quite occupied with his show—headed for the bedroom. Kipa might not be here right now, but there were other ways I could satisfy my hunger.

CHAPTER FOURTEEN

*B*y the time Llew and Neil arrived, I had showered to loosen the knots in my back, and dressed. For tromping in the woods, I decided on a pair of leggings and a long, black V-neck tunic that came to mid-thigh. I cinched a silver belt around my waist, then slid my feet into a pair of rubber-soled lace-up boots. The soles were a good inch thick and should hold traction on the snow and ice. I slipped on my jacket that held in body heat, and opted for a pair of cheap gloves. I'd have to remove them in order to work any magic, so I didn't want to chance losing my leather ones.

I pulled my hair into a high ponytail to keep it out of the way, and tied a brightly colored scarf around my head like a headband. I thought about wearing a pair of ski goggles, and gave in, sliding them on over my eyes. This way, falling snow wouldn't present a problem, and my eyes would be protected from any attacks. After feeling those tentacles with barbs, I wasn't keen on getting stabbed in any more vital areas than my wrist. Making sure Venom was fastened to the belt of my jacket, I hurried to the door when the bell rang.

I invited Llew and Neil in, giving Neil the once-over. He looked like a priest of Thor, all right. At least six-six, he weighed about two hundred and fifty pounds of muscle, with long brown hair pulled back in a braid, and a braided beard. He looked to be around forty, though as one of the magic-born he could easily be older, and he was wearing a heavy leather jacket, a pair of jeans that both left nothing to the imagination but yet looked like they could stretch with his movements, and a heavy sweater beneath the jacket. He was carrying a silver hammer about the size of a small sledgehammer. Whether it was silver coated or an amalgam, I didn't know, but it sparkled and looked freshly polished. It also resonated with a magical signature set on a harmonic that almost made my teeth rattle.

Llew introduced us and we shook hands. "Raven, this is Neil Johansson."

"Thank you for offering to help," I said, amazed by how gentle the man's grip was.

"Thanks for the chance to test out Helga here." He held up the hammer and gave it a shake. "In case you're wondering, she's a mixture of silver and steel, but there's enough silver in her to make a vampire weep and a werewolf run."

I blinked. Okay then, I'd never heard that one before and wondered if he was also some kind of bigot, except there had been no weight in his words. And he *was* right—neither vampires nor werewolves liked silver.

"Okay, then. We'll get started, I guess. Let me tell Raj I'm going." I wasn't about to put him in danger by taking him with us. I hurried back into the living room, where Raj had switched over to listening to an audio book. He wasn't much of a reader, but he gave it a try from time to time and he liked listening to stories, so I bought him audio books. It crossed my mind that I really needed to start getting him into a regular exercise routine, even though he never complained or seemed that interested when I wanted to take him for a walk.

"Raj, I'm headed out into the park. I may not be back for a while, but I'll try to make it as fast as possible. We're going after a land wight who's trying to hurt people." I sat down beside him, draping my arm over his back.

Raj glanced past me toward the door. In a low whisper, he said, "Raven be careful. Land wights dangerous. Raj wait up for Raven."

I smiled, leaning down to give him a kiss on the head. "Good Raj. Raven will be back as soon as she can."

With that, I made sure there were a few snacks on the table for him, grabbed a flashlight I could strap to my belt, then led Llew and Neil into the cul-de-sac and toward the entrance to UnderLake Park.

DURING THE NIGHT, UNDERLAKE PARK WAS FAR SPOOKIER than it was during the daytime. For one thing, few people hung out at the park during the twilight hours, and even fewer entered during the night, so there was an odd silence that reverberated through the acreage. For another, at night, the ghosts came out to play, and Under-Lake Park was haunted as shit.

Neil and Llew were silent as I led them onto the path

that Llew and I had traversed. We were all carrying walking sticks, given the snow was still coming down and the trail was far harder to navigate than it had been just the day before. It was amazing what a difference a mere few inches of snow could make.

We slid and slipped our way along the path as I kept a close watch out for the trail juncture. The flashlight helped, and the night sky was more silver than dark, due to the falling snow. I quickly realized that my ski goggles were getting fogged up by my breath, which was coming in puffs, so I took them off and tucked them into the lightweight backpack I was carrying.

As I turned onto the side trail, I slowed, wondering just how far the land wight's territory extended. Would it come all the way up here, to the top of the ravine? Or would we have to go down below to find it? I suddenly wished that we had something like a monster-Geiger counter.

I poked Llew's elbow. "Listen, dude. Do you have anything that can detect when we're near the wight? If it was a ghost or spirit, I'd be able to sense it, but it's not and I can't. I just realized that we could be on a wild goose chase."

"Not to worry," Neil answered for him, holding up his hammer. "My hammer senses evil and gives off a faint blue light when we're near it."

"Like Sting, in *Lord of the Rings*?" It flashed through my mind that Tolkien either had encountered goblins or other sub-Fae during his life, or he had possessed an incredibly accurate imagination.

"Kind of. Along those lines. I'm watching it, so if we get near the wight—it *is* an evil creature, isn't it?" He paused, frowning. "This wouldn't work on an alligator, for example, no matter how hungry it was."

"Land wights are malevolent, yes."

"Okay, then. It should give us a heads-up."

Comforted by the massive man's promise, I once again took the lead and began edging through the foliage, down the side of the ravine. We were approximately in the same place we'd been the day before.

Llew and Neil followed. I could hear their labored breathing behind me. Both were in fairly good shape, but the temperature was dropping and the harsh chill to the air played hell on the lungs. I was about to ask if they were okay when I stepped on a rock that was covered by snow and my foot slid out from under me. I tried to regain my balance but lost the battle, tumbling down the side of the ravine, rolling through the snow, unable to stop until I came to rest at the bottom of the gully.

Swearing loudly, I tried to ascertain if I'd broken any bones. Llew and Neil were scrambling down the hill after me. I could see them in the dim flicker of my flashlight beam. I groaned, rolling over onto my hands and knees. I was near a stand of huckleberry bushes and fern layered with a good six to seven inches of snow.

As I began to stand, I heard a rustle from the nearest bush. I tried to duck away, but my reflexes were slowed by the fall, and the next moment, a barbed tentacle lashed out, just as it had before, but this time I managed to avoid getting caught by it. I almost fell over backward trying to scramble out of reach. Neil and Llew were nearing me, and true to his word, Neil's hammer was lit up like a blue-light special at Kmart.

"The wight—it's behind the bush," I said as they pulled me away, into the open.

Neil's eyes widened. "Do wights stay near their nests?"

"I think so," Llew said. "That's where they consume their victims. And they protect their soul stones." He glanced around. "Look for any disturbance in the snow that might give away the opening, and keep well away from the bushes. I doubt if the wight's going to come out here in the open when there are several of us."

True enough, the tentacle had disappeared, and the huckleberry bush was still. The wight had probably retreated to its nest or to gain a better vantage from which to watch us.

I stared at the line of shrubbery in front of us. "Ten to one, the nest is behind all of those bushes. We're going to have to go through and hope that we don't get within its range."

"I don't like the sound of that," Llew said.

"I'll go first. It might shrink away from my hammer, and I'm bigger than both of you." Neil paused, gazing at me. "I don't know if I'm stronger, though. I've never met one of the Ante-Fae before."

I shrugged. "We can have an arm-wrestling contest later. Right now, I suggest we just get this over with because I don't want to have to come back after this thing again." I was regretting my decision to play do-gooder. All I wanted to do was head back home, curl up with Raj, and ignore the fact that there was a creepy-assed creature living so close to my house.

But reality took over and I shook off the irritation. Land wights were a danger to everybody—the wight would go after Raj, or me, or anybody near enough. We couldn't just leave it now that we knew about it.

Neil stepped in front of me, holding up his hammer. It was still glowing a pale blue, though not as bright as before.

"What's the range?"

"Ten yards, maybe," he said, keeping his voice low.

He pressed through the nearest stand of ferns. I followed him, with Llew bringing up the rear. We kept quiet, listening for any sign that we were close to the wight. Llew's hammer acted as an extra flashlight, and as we broke through the line of bushes to the other side, the hammer began to glow brighter.

I glanced to the right. There, about ten yards away, I noticed a pile of snow that seemed to be mounded up higher than the rest, and there was a dark patch in the center.

"There—that might be its nest. It would have to brush the snow away to go in and out," I said, pointing.

Neil swung to the right without a word, cautiously treading through the thick layer of detritus that covered the floor of the ravine. Covered in snow, it was dangerous, all sorts of sprained ankles waiting to happen. I followed him, watching his hammer, which was glowing brighter and brighter the closer we got to the mound of snow. I flashed my light on it, and sure enough, there to the left, in the patch of brown, we saw a hole leading back into the side of the ravine.

"That has to be the nest. Is the wight in there? Did it run home to its nest after it saw me?"

"I don't know," Neil said. "Given its soul is in the nest,

in that stone, whether the body is there or not, my hammer's going to glow."

"What happens to the wight's body if we kill its soul?" Llew asked.

"It dissolves like a number of the sub-Fae," I said, lowering my voice, though I wasn't sure what good that would do, given the wight knew we were down here and probably had picked up on the fact that we were hunting it by now.

We approached the entrance, which was about four feet high. I grimaced. It would be hard for Neil to get through, and even Llew would have difficulty.

"I can go in. If the wight's not in there, I can grab the soul stone and bring it out," I said, reluctantly offering myself up on a platter.

"I don't like the sound of that," Llew said, but Neil nodded.

"I'm not going to be much use if I try to make it through that entrance and get stuck." He looked back at me. "You're sure you want to do this?"

"Yeah, I'll do it." I drew Venom, holding her in my right hand as I held the flashlight in my left. "I'd take your hammer and smash the thing but I don't know how much effort it would take and I'd rather not find out that I don't have the swing for it. If you hear me scream, try to come in and get me, please. I don't fancy being on the dinner menu."

Llew looked irritated, but he gave in.

I ducked down, creeping into the entrance. Neil never would have made it. The passage grew narrower the farther I went and I began to feel claustrophobic, but then, about ten feet into the side of the hill, it opened up.

I broke through into a small chamber that was about ten feet wide by four feet deep. It was tall enough for me to stand in—barely—and filled with decaying debris. The stench was almost unbearable, and I grimaced as I tried to hold my breath. There was a faint green light in the center of the waste and I began to dig through the debris, grateful I'd left my good gloves at home.

I came across something hard and oval, and as I withdrew it, I saw that I was holding a gemlike stone that emanated a sickly green glow from within. As I watched, the glow pulsed with a beat that mimicked a heartbeat.

The soul stone! I had found it.

Eager to get back outside and be done with the matter, I turned and started back through the channel, but then I heard shouts and the sounds of a scuffle. I hurried, trying to push through faster. When I broke out into the night, I saw Llew entangled with the land wight. The creature had several of its barbed tentacles lashed around his waist. Neil was trying to beat the thing off, hitting it with his hammer. Blue sparks flew every time he struck a blow, but it didn't seem to be having much effect.

I stripped off my gloves, tossing them to the ground, and shoved the soul stone down the front of my jacket to hold it. Holding out my hands, I focused on conjuring a ball of flame. I whispered a chant that would coax it faster and the flames began to rise in my palm.

> *Fire to flame, flame to fire,*
> *build and burn, higher and higher.*
> *Flare to life, take form and strike,*
> *attack now, fiery spike.*

The ball coalesced in my hand, a brilliant orb of flickering orange and red flames with hints of purple tingeing the ends. I held it up, aimed carefully for the wight, and sent it flying. The fire hit the amorphous creature—it looked like a mass of steel wool and twigs with tentacles coming out of it—and the land wight screeched, letting go of Llew as it stumbled back.

Neil turned to me as I pulled the soul stone out of my jacket. I tossed it on the ground near his feet and he brought the hammer up. The wight must have realized what was going on because it rushed at Neil, flailing a hail of tentacles toward him, but the massive priest brought his hammer down, slamming it against the stone.

The air seemed to pulse, and for a moment I thought we were having an earthquake, as every nerve in my body jangled. But then, with another strike, Neil splintered the stone and it smashed into the snow, into a thousand shards of glass.

The land wight shrieked, then slowly deflated, melting into the primordial ooze that so many of the sub-Fae came from. A hiss of steam rose from the puddling mass as the heat of its body met the icy snow, and then, seeped through the blanket of white, leaching into the ground.

I ran over to Llew. "Are you okay?"

He grunted, and I could tell he was having trouble standing. I made him let me look him over, and as I pulled his jacket open, I could see the slick of blood pooling around his waist.

"No! Llew, listen to me. We have to get you back to my house." I motioned to Neil. "Can you carry him? He's losing blood."

"I can. What about the nest?"

I glanced over my shoulder. "Get him up the hill. I'll dart in and take a quick look around and then follow you."

I hurried back into the hole, cringing at the smell. I didn't relish staying any longer than I had to, but I needed to make certain we had found everything. A moment later, as I shone the flashlight around and moved debris out of the way, I suddenly froze. There, under a pile of steaming compost, were three large eggs. Land wight eggs. I stared at them for a moment, then slowly backed up. Land wights didn't eject their soul stones from their bodies until they were born, and then their mother hid it until they left the nest to build their own. If I destroyed the eggs, I'd destroy the young as well.

Finally, I gathered my wits and backed out to the edge of the tunnel leading in. Where there were three eggs, there might be more, and I didn't have the time to go through the entire nest. I could just douse it with fire, but I wasn't certain it could be contained—it might spread through roots beneath the ground and light the park on fire. No, somebody had to come down here and thoroughly destroy the entire nest.

I turned, ducking outside. The forest was silent around me, save for the falling snow. I glanced around. More snow would cover up the entrance and make it harder to find again, so I finally pulled the scarf off my head and tied it to a nearby bush to make it easier to find.

Then I turned back to the slope and hurried to the top of the ravine, slipping my way through the snow, praying that Llew hadn't been too badly hurt.

CHAPTER FIFTEEN

irst thing when we got back to the house, I stripped off Llew's jacket as Neil helped him to the sofa. Llew tried to pull away.

"Your sofa will get all bloody," he said.

I sighed. I'd just bought the sofa a couple months ago to replace one that my friends and I, along with Jim Morrison's spirit, had ruined. I didn't want to have to buy another just yet.

"All right, hold on." I raced out to the shed in my backyard and found one of the plastic camping tarps that I kept around. Slogging back through the snow, I stomped off the excess snow clinging to my boots before returning to the living room.

I spread the tarp over the sofa while Neil held Llew up so he didn't collapse. The moment the tarp was down, I threw a sheet over it—sheets were expendable—and gave Neil a hand in easing Llew down onto the seat. Neil began to unbutton Llew's shirt while I ran to my bathroom and grabbed the bandages, antibiotic ointment, and some gauze tape. I hoped that we'd be able to stop the bleeding, but if we couldn't, we'd take him into Urgent Care.

"Let's see those wounds. We already know how nasty they can be." While my wrist was healing up, Llew would be a lot more likely to succumb to the venom and we had to make certain he wasn't in danger of dying. If the blood loss didn't get to him first.

Neil examined the line of punctures that dappled Llew's torso and back. "Damn, Raven, I don't think we should be the ones treating these. They already look angry."

I leaned closer, peeking over Neil's shoulder. He was right. The wounds were bright red, looking inflamed and infected already. A couple were oozing pus, and they were all still bleeding. Llew was looking faint, and my intuition flared. He was in danger—his life was in danger. That much was clear.

"Let me make a phone call," I said, moving away. I pulled out my phone and punched in Herne's number. Herne had a direct line to one of the best healers around.

"Yo, Raven, what's up?" The husky voice of the Hunter rumbled through the phone.

"I need your help. A friend of mine needs your help. We took out a land wight, but the creature got her tentacles around Llew—I think you met him at Ember's party. He's got some nasty puncture wounds that are already inflamed and I'm afraid they're going to get infected. The land wight's venom affects the magic-born and humans a lot more than it does the Ante-Fae. I was wondering if you could ask Ferosyn to help. Whatever it costs, I'll cover it."

Herne paused, then cleared his throat. "Ferosyn's not

in the habit of making house calls, but I'll call him and get back to you as soon as I do. Did you manage to kill the wight?"

"Yeah, but there are eggs in the nest that we didn't get to."

"I'll come over and help. If there are eggs, the wight's mate might be close by." Herne signed off, promising to call back as soon as he reached Ferosyn.

I began to wash Llew's wounds the best I could, grimacing as he moaned and flinched when I touched them. I dreaded putting him through the pain. I had managed to wash out the first five punctures when my phone rang. I handed the cloth to Neil and answered it.

"Ember, Viktor, and I are on the way over, along with Ferosyn. The moment I told him about the land wight, he signed off. We'll be there as soon as we pick him up at the portal. Tell Llew to hold on." He signed off without giving me a chance to answer.

"Llew. Llew?" I knelt on the sofa beside him, the tarp crinkling under my knees. Llew's eyes were half-closed, and he was moaning. I felt his forehead.

"He's burning up," I told Neil. "Get a washcloth from the bathroom and saturate it with cold water, then fill it with ice from the kitchen."

Neil hustled to the bathroom, returning with a wet cloth. He darted by into the kitchen and I heard the sound of the ice maker. A moment later, he returned, the washcloth folded around several cubes of ice. I motioned for him to place it behind Llew's neck and we gently eased him back so his head was resting on the back of the sofa. Returning to cleaning out his wounds, I asked Neil to answer the door when Herne and the others arrived.

"Llew? Llew? Listen to me. I need you to fight the fever. Ferosyn will be here soon and he'll heal you up, but until then, don't give in. The fever's dangerous, and you need to fight against it." I stroked his hair. He was sweating now, both clammy and hot, and his eyes had taken on a glazed look. He was succumbing to the venom of the land wight quicker than I had expected. He must be hyperreactive to it, or allergic to it.

As the ice melted, I asked Neil to fill a bowl with more cubes and bring them in so we could replenish them as needed.

"Will he be okay?" the priest of Thor asked after a while, a worried look on his face.

"If he can hold on till Ferosyn gets here, yes. Damn it, I shouldn't have asked him to go with me. I can withstand the venom of that creature, but the magic-born and humans? Not so much." I glanced up at Neil, feeling horribly guilty. "Are you all right? Did it attack you?"

He shook his head. "No, it was after Llew. I don't know why, but it actually tried to avoid me, which is a good thing, I suppose. But that just meant it went after Llew with full force. I tried to stop it, but my hammer couldn't do more than damage it without the soul stone."

"It's not your fault," I said, sensing he was feeling guilty as well.

"It's nobody's fault," Neil said, staring at the bowl of melting ice. "I'll get some more ice." The doorbell rang as he was on his way to the kitchen and he hurried to answer, leading Herne, Viktor, Ember, and Ferosyn in.

Herne was gorgeous, though I preferred Kipa's swarthy looks to Herne's wheat-colored hair and fairer skin. Together, he and Ember made a striking couple.

Behind them, Ferosyn glanced around my house, frowning. The Elf was ancient, though he didn't look it, and his healing powers were the strongest I had heard of.

"Where's the patient?" he asked. Then his gaze fell on Llew and he swept over to the sofa, motioning for me to get out of the way. I started to stammer a *thank you*, but he shook his head, waving me off. "I need to concentrate."

What he lacked in manners, he made up in attentiveness to his patient. I moved over to stand by Ember and Viktor, while Herne watched Ferosyn. Neil took a seat in the overstuffed armchair. I glanced around, looking for Raj. He was staying out of the way, curled up in his bed by the dining room window. He gave me a long look, and I could tell that he was worried. He liked Llew, though he didn't let on much.

After a few moments, Ferosyn turned toward Herne. "I think I caught the venom before it reached his heart, but I should take him back to the palace. I don't want to leave him unattended for the next forty-eight hours. Where's the nearest portal?"

Herne motioned to Ember, tossing her his keys. "Take my SUV. You know where it is."

"Quest's place?" she asked, catching the keys in midair.

"Right. Get them there in one piece." He turned to Ferosyn. "Ember will go with you. The land wight apparently laid eggs, and Viktor and I will take care of them."

Viktor gathered up Llew to carry him to the car. Ferosyn followed him.

Ember turned to me. "I wish I could stay and help with the wight eggs, but I'll call you later. I hope he pulls through. I like Llew, from what I've met of him."

"Me too," I said, pressing my lips together. I was going

to have to call Jordan and explain what happened, and I wasn't looking forward to that interaction. Llew had gotten involved in this because of me, and I wasn't one to push off blame.

Ember gave me a quick hug, then turned and raced out of the house, following the others. A moment later, Viktor returned.

"They're off. Raven, while Herne and I take care of the land wight's eggs, you and your friend here should drive over to Quest's place and retrieve Herne's SUV." He paused, glancing at Neil. "You can drive, can't you?"

Neil gave him a solemn nod. "Can do."

"You're a priest of Thor, aren't you?" Viktor asked.

"Yes, I am." Neil stiffened. "But I'm no skinhead neo-Nazi punk. They're about as much true followers of Thor as I am an Elf."

"I know that," Viktor asked. "You don't have to go on the defense. We're well aware of the twisted crap people pull." He glanced at me. "You drive Herne's SUV back. Quest will have the keys for you. No speeding, either." The half-ogre grinned.

Herne snickered. "What he said. But first, where's the land wight? We should get a move on. We don't want those eggs to hatch. The wights are a danger from the moment they break out of the shell."

I explained where we had found the nest, drawing a crude map on a sheet of paper. Then, motioning for Neil to follow me, we headed out—Herne and Viktor toward UnderLake Park, and Neil and I in my sedan, toward the address that Viktor had texted to me.

Ten minutes later, I pulled into a large driveway that led into a double lot. The house at the back of the lot was modest, but neat, and I spied Herne's black Expedition in the driveway. I hopped out of the Camry, and Neil took over the driver's seat. A woman emerged from the house, glancing at us suspiciously, but then she smiled as she strode over.

"You must be Raven. Herne called and said you'd be along to pick up his car." She held out the keys to me. "I'm Quest. Quest Realto." She didn't look fully human, but I couldn't get a read on what exactly she was.

"Raven BoneTalker, and this is Neil. He's a friend of Llew's. Thank you for helping out." I glanced around the lot. There, behind the house, stood two gigantic oak trees. I could tell from where I was standing that these were the guardians of the portal, but I didn't say a word. This was one of Herne's private portal-gates, and it wasn't for me to inquire about them.

"They made it through all right." She paused, then added, "Your friend was brave, going up against a land wight. They're deadly, and even the magic-born are susceptible to them. Since you are a friend of Lord Herne's, feel free to call me if you need. I'm a coyote shifter."

I blinked. One of Herne's team—Yutani—was a coyote shifter. In fact, he was the son of the Great Coyote. But up here in the Pacific Northwest, coyote shifters weren't all that common. Most of the coyote shifter clans tended to live in the Southwest.

"Well met, Quest Realto. And the same to you. Here's my number." I fumbled in my purse and found one of my business cards. "If you need help, just call. I owe you a debt, for my friend Llewellyn."

As Neil—who had wisely kept his mouth shut—and I

left, I glanced back at the house. Quest was standing there, watching us ease down the icy road. She wasn't even wearing a jacket, and her hair was streaming back in the wind. She looked regal, reminding me of a princess. It occurred to me that Yutani should meet her, if he hadn't already. They might hit it off. Entertaining thoughts of playing matchmaker, I slowly drove home, hoping Llew would be all right.

CHAPTER SIXTEEN

y the time we got back to the house, Herne and Viktor were nowhere in sight. I parked the Expedition in the driveway and invited Neil to come in and wait.

"We haven't had a chance to really get to know one another," I said. My stomach rumbled, and I blushed. "Apparently, my stomach has a mind of its own. You hungry?"

Neil nodded, looking downcast. "I feel like a traitor, being hungry while Llew's life is in danger." He pulled the tarp off the sofa. The blood that had splattered on it had dried, and he carried it over to the sliding glass doors and dropped it out on the back porch.

"Life goes on, even during tragedy. Even when we wish the world would stop." I thought back to the days after I had found out Ulstair was dead. The errands had still been there, I'd had to take care of the ferrets and Raj. I'd had to feed and clothe myself, even though I didn't feel like budging a muscle. "Having a set routine is a saving grace. It forces us to move, to act, even when we want to curl up and hide."

"I guess you're right. I'll be right back. I need to utilize your facilities." Neil headed down the hallway.

I opened the fridge. There wasn't much that looked appetizing, so I called Smokin' Joe's Pizza and ordered four large pizzas and three sides of chicken wings. Then I decided to get things over with. I put in a call to Jordan.

"Jordan? It's Raven." I wasn't sure how to start, so I stared at the floor, hoping the words would come to me. I hated giving people bad news.

"Is Llew on his way home?" Jordan paused, then said, "What's wrong? I can feel that something's wrong. Is Llew—"

I heard the fear in his voice. "He's alive, but he was hurt. The land wight got its barbs into him. He's in Annwn now. Herne called his healer Ferosyn to take care of him, and Ferosyn wanted to take him back to Annwn for the night. Jordan, Llew's in the best hands possible at this point." I steeled myself for the recriminations, but Jordan surprised me.

"Crap. I can't… How badly was he hurt?"

I let out a slow breath. "Pretty roughed up. The land wight had a venom—a poison—something that it injected into his wounds. Right now, I don't have any other news, other than Ferosyn thinks he got to Llew in time. I'm so sorry, Jordan. If I had realized how much danger he was in, I wouldn't have let him go—" I started to say, but Jordan cut me off.

"Knock it off. Don't make me worry about consoling you. I'd rather focus on my husband, if you don't mind." His words hit like a slap, but they were right on target.

"Got it, and you're right. I'll text your number to Ember and Herne. That way, you can stay fully in the loop." I wanted to apologize again, but I slammed the lid on my personal pity party.

As I hung up, there was a sound at the door and Herne and Viktor came stomping in, their jackets covered with snow. I glanced over at them as Neil returned. He was looking refreshed, and he had sponged the blood off his shirt where Llew had bled all over him. We both turned to Herne with a questioning look.

Herne cleared his throat. "We found all the eggs and thoroughly destroyed the nest. I don't think she had a partner nearby, or the thing would have come gunning for us while we were tearing apart the nest. They can sense when their young are in danger. So either somebody already killed her mate, or he ran off. It happens."

Relieved, I sank down to the sofa. "Thank gods. I wasn't looking forward to going back in there, but I would if I had to. Have you heard anything on Llew? I just called his husband and let him know what happened."

"No, but—" Herne paused as his phone rang. "It's Ember." He took the call. I waited, my eyes glued to his face. The doorbell rang and Viktor went to answer it, returning with the pizza and the wings. He quietly set them on the coffee table, then motioned to me, mouthing, "Paper plates?"

I pointed toward the sideboard, toward the bottom drawer. Viktor returned with paper plates and napkins as Herne murmured "Okay," and then, a "Love you," and "Good-bye."

"How is he?" I leaned forward, hoping for good news. "How's Llew?"

"It's complicated. Ember's at Quest's, so I'll run over and get her. Then she can grab a bite with us and tell us what Ferosyn had to say."

Before I could say anything else, Herne was on his feet and out the door. I leaned back in my seat, sighing. "Does he always dart out before you can ask him things?" I turned to Viktor.

"Girl, you haven't seen the half of it." Viktor laughed. "Try not to worry. Meanwhile, if you don't mind, I'm going to serve myself up a couple slices of pizza and some wings. It smells so good I can't resist."

As Viktor piled his plate high and I fixed ones for Neil and me, I whispered another prayer. If Herne returned with bad news, I didn't know how I could tell Jordan. I forced myself to focus on my food. I was exhausted. First tackling Moira's imp and then the land wight and subsequent worry over Llew had left me feeling trashed. I felt like an emotional vampire, running on empty and hungry for support.

Staring at my food, I realized I barely had the energy to even lift the wing to my mouth. I set the plate on the coffee table and slumped back against the sofa, closing my eyes.

"Raven? Are you all right?" Neil's voice thrust itself in through the fog that clouded my thoughts.

Wearily, I squinted at him. "No, not really. I'm exhausted and worried. I feel guilty about involving Llew in the fight. If it hadn't been for me, his life wouldn't have been in danger. I feel horrible about what Jordan's going through, waiting for news. And I'm just...tired. I fought two battles today, one against an imp who was terrorizing a client of mine, and then, one against the land wight."

Neil stared at me for a moment. "Why don't you go take a nap?"

"Not till Ember and Herne get back. I want to hear how Llew is, so I can tell Jordan." At that moment, the door opened and Ember and Herne came trooping in. I turned, hopeful. "Speaking of… How is he? Please tell me. I can't take the suspense."

Ember immediately sat down beside me. "He's going to recover, Raven. He'll be all right. Ferosyn wants to keep him for the night, but he managed to stanch the flow of venom and he gave Llew an antidote. By tomorrow, Llew will be weak, but ready to come home. We'll pick him up and take him directly to his place."

A barricade burst inside. I had created a wall just in case it was bad news, one that would keep me on my feet through the aftershocks, but now, the bricks cascaded, landing at my feet. I slumped back in my seat, my head resting against the sofa.

"Thank the gods. I don't know what I would have done if…if…" I couldn't even say the words. "I need to call Jordan and tell him."

"You need to get some food in you, miss," Neil said, pointing at my plate. "You're sounding faint, and we don't need you collapsing on us."

I pulled out my phone and texted Jordan. LLEW WILL BE ALL RIGHT. HE'LL COME HOME TOMORROW. I'LL CALL YOU IN A BIT, BUT HE'S SAFE. Then I wearily lifted my plate and bit into the pizza.

Ember fixed herself a plate, and Herne followed suit. We all sat around the living room, eating pizza and wings in silence. After a bit, Viktor glanced at the clock.

"Not to break up a party, but I promised Sheila I'd meet her tonight."

"Yeah, and we have a long day tomorrow," Herne said. "My mother has decided she's paying us a visit and that always means there's something big coming down." He stood, stretching and yawning. "Raven, will you be all right now?"

I nodded. "Yes. As long as the land wight's eggs are gone, and Llew's going to be all right, then I'm good. Thank you again for helping." I stared at the floor. "I feel like I've been asking for a lot of help lately."

"You helped us out, too, on our trip over to the peninsula last month. It's all give and take, you know." Ember gave me a quick hug. "I'll tell Angel hi for you."

"Thanks," I said, watching as they trooped out of the house. Once they had shut the door behind them, I slumped back, trying to collect my thoughts. I glanced over at Neil, who was staring at me with a look of speculation on his face. "Yes?"

"Nothing," he said after a slow pause. "I suppose I should get a move on as well. I came with Llew, so I'll have to call an LUD." He gazed out the window, at the fresh snow that was coming down. "We haven't had a storm this bad in a while. Do they know how long it's supposed to last?"

I shrugged. "I'm not sure. It's a nasty one, out of Alaska, and sweeping down with the jet stream. A lot of frigid air and cold temps, which are, of course, leading to snow."

Neil nodded, once again glancing my way. "Raven, this may not be the time to ask, given all that's happened, but…would you consider going to dinner with me? Not tonight," he added hastily. "But in a few days?"

I froze. I had no clue whether he was trying to ask me on a date or accepting a friendzone position. "Um… I like you, Neil, but…"

"But…?"

"I'm sorry. If you're asking me out on a date, then I have to say no. I'm seeing someone and he's a god, so I don't think he'd take kindly to a rival. And…I'm happy with him. At least for now." The former was speculation, the latter, truth. I was happy with Kipa, at least for now. And while Neil was a nice guy, I was too tired to even think about whether I found him attractive. "If I'm presuming, though, and you mean going out as friends—that's different."

Llew gave me a defeated smile. "No problem," he said with a shrug. "And yes, I was asking you out on a date. So I got shot down. I took a chance, and it's fine. I like you, Raven, but there are other women in the world." He grinned. "Don't sweat it. I'm going to head home now. I'll let myself out. Be sure to lock the door after I leave."

Once he left, I dragged myself to the door and locked it. As I turned around, Raj came out of hiding. He lumbered over.

"Raven okay?"

"Raven's tired and sad, Raj. Raven's friend Llew is hurt, and while he'll get better, Raven's worried about him." I dropped back down on the sofa and stared at the uneaten food. "I'd better put everything away." I wished I could just leave it, but if I did, there was a good chance that Raj would get into it and eat himself sick. With a huge sigh, I dragged myself to my feet again and began clearing up the coffee table, tossing out debris from the wings and pizza, and boxing the rest of the food to go into the refrigerator.

I fed Raj, putting down a can of cat food for him—it was easier than cooking—and dragged myself into the bedroom. I thought about taking a long, hot bath but I could barely keep my eyes open. So, crawling into bed, I turned off the lights, and less than five minutes later, I was sound asleep.

CHAPTER SEVENTEEN

I slept hard and deep and woke up the next morning, refreshed and rested. A glance at my texts sent my mood even higher. Ember had texted that she and Herne had taken Llew home to Jordan, and that he was on the mend. She also said that Herne bought a bunch of supplies from Llew's shop, which was being watched over by Erial, one of the Water Fae. She was Light Fae, an Undine, and she had met Llew years ago when he was visiting Katmai Park in Alaska.

Feeling off the hook, and swearing I'd be more careful about bringing my friends into dangerous situations from now on, I went about cleaning out the ferrets' cage, then fed Raj and started in on housecleaning for the week. I washed out the bathtub and toilet, swept and mopped, dusted, threw a load of laundry into the washing machine, and tidied up.

Kipa and Gunnar were due to arrive at noon, and I wanted to be done with my cleaning for the week before they got here. I even played tug of war with Raj to get his favorite blanket away from him so I could wash it.

"Raven no wash blanket. Raj likes how it smells." He was using his pouty voice, which was an odd mix of belligerent and pathetic grunts.

"Raj may like how it smells, but it's dusty and muddy and Raven is going to wash the blanket whether or not Raj approves. Let go!" I tugged hard, trying to dislodge him. Raj was sitting on it. "Get *off* the blanket, Raj."

With a mournful look, he finally eased off the microfiber throw. I yanked it out of the dog bed and marched into the laundry room, where I tossed it in with the clothes that were washing. When I returned, Raj had tipped over his food bowl and beef stew was spreading all over my clean floor.

"Raj! You did that on purpose." I leaned down, narrowing my eyes. "You know better than that." Honestly, sometimes the gargoyle *did* remind me of a dog.

He gulped, then looked away. "Raven mad at Raj?"

"Raven's angry, yes. Raven loves Raj but Raj has to behave!" I hurried into the kitchen, returning with a roll of paper towels and a soapy sponge. "You made the mess. You can clean it up. Go on."

He took the towels and the sponge and slowly wiped up the saucy puddle, then tossed the paper towels in the garbage can that I held out for him. He scrubbed the spot with the sponge, and wiped it dry with clean paper towels. I took the cleaning supplies back into the kitchen and returned. With only a third of his breakfast left in the dish, Raj gave me a puppy-dog look.

"Raj hungry."

"Raj should have eaten his breakfast instead of

throwing a tantrum. Just for that, Raj can finish what's there and then wait for his midmorning snack. Which will be a banana and a roll."

"No chips? Raj likes—" he paused, gauging my expression. "Raj likes bananas," he said, before turning away to finish his breakfast.

I made sure he didn't dump the rest of it on the floor, then went back in the kitchen to unload the dishwasher. When everything was put away, I finally allowed myself to drop into a chair at the dining table with a three-shot mocha, a turkey sandwich, and a peppermint brownie. Raj turned up his nose at his snack, but ate it quietly and then went in to watch TV.

I glanced at the clock. It was nearing noon, and Kipa and Gunnar would be here soon. Pulling out my phone, I texted Jordan. LLEW IS HOME, RIGHT?

YES, HERNE BROUGHT HIM HOME AROUND TEN-THIRTY. HE'S SLEEPING RIGHT NOW. HE'S WORN OUT, BUT HE'LL SURVIVE. THAT'S THE LAST TIME I'M LETTING HIM GO TROMPING AROUND THE WOODS WITH YOU, THOUGH.

Stung by the scowling emoji he typed at the end of it, I hesitated before texting, LAST NIGHT YOU SAID YOU DIDN'T BLAME ME.

LAST NIGHT I WAS STILL SHELL-SHOCKED. SERIOUSLY, RAVEN, WHAT ON EARTH MADE YOU THINK YOU COULD TAKE ON A LAND WIGHT?

Pausing, I stared at the screen. Finally, I texted back: I'M ONE OF THE ANTE-FAE. LLEW IS ONE OF THE MAGIC-BORN. WHAT WERE WE SUPPOSED TO DO, JUST LEAVE IT OUT THERE TO KILL INNOCENT PEOPLE, INCLUDING KIDS?

OF COURSE NOT. YOU KNOW THAT'S NOT WHAT I MEANT. JUST...YOU CAN BE A DANGEROUS INFLUENCE ON LLEW AND I

DON'T TRUST HIM TO THINK THINGS THROUGH. PLEASE JUST STAY AWAY FOR A WHILE. I'LL TALK TO YOU LATER, LLEW'S CALLING ME.

Angry and hurt that Jordan was being so churlish, I tossed my phone on the table and glared at it as I finished the last bite of my sandwich. So much for his undying gratitude when I helped him out with his creepy possessed doll. I had still felt some guilt over Llew's injuries, until Jordan blamed me. Now, I just felt pissed.

I rinsed off my lunch plate and pulled out a bag of corn chips. Raj came loping into the kitchen when he heard the bag, giving me a hopeful look.

I sighed and poured some of them in a bowl and carried it into the living room for him. "Here, you can have some. Just don't get any stains on the sofa, all right?"

Raj took the bowl, staring at me for a moment. "Is Raven okay? Raven seems upset."

"Raven is upset, but not at you, Raj. Raven's upset because…" I paused, not sure just how to explain it. Raj's thought processes worked in vastly different ways than most people. Gargoyles had a totally different take on the world and while they felt similar emotions, gargoyles didn't usually entertain thoughts about ulterior motives or misplaced blame.

"Jordan is angry at Raven because he blames Raven for Llew getting hurt." I bit my lip, wondering how well this would go.

"Did Raven hurt Llew?" Raj asked, patting the cushion beside him.

I dropped down on the sofa. "No, Raven didn't hurt Llew. A land wight hurt Llew."

"Then why does Jordan blame Raven?"

"Because Llew helped me go after the land wight."

"But Raven didn't hurt Llew. The land wight hurt Llew." His confusion was evident as he cocked his head, staring at me.

I sighed, shoving a fistful of corn chips in my mouth. "Let's see if I can explain this any better. Jordan believes that Llew wouldn't have gone out into the park without Raven. If Llew hadn't gone on a walk with Raven, he never would have encountered the land wight and the land wight wouldn't have hurt Llew."

Raj shook his head. "But Raven didn't hurt Llew. The land wight hurt Llew."

I patted his head, then gave him a gentle hug. "I know, Raj. But sometimes, in the world of mortals, things get really complicated. Never mind. Everything will be all right. It will all blow over and everyone will be friends again." I hoped to hell that I was telling the truth. The thought of Jordan breaking up my friendship with Llew worried me. I didn't think he'd try, but it was hard to tell. I leaned back against the sofa, my hand deep in the bag of chips.

The doorbell rang and I sighed, heaving myself to my feet. Sure enough, it was Kipa and Gunnar. I gave Kipa a long but tired kiss and led them into the living room. Raj glanced at them, then meandered down the hall toward my bedroom.

"Hey," I said, resuming my cross-legged stance on the sofa.

Kipa gave me a worried look. "Are you all right?"

I shook my head. "Today's been the day from hell. Actually, yesterday was the day from hell and today is just a continuation of it. The whole mess with the land wight went south, Llew was hurt, and now Jordan blames me. I can't even begin to tell you how guilty I feel, even though I know it's not my fault. I didn't force Llew to go with me," I said, looking up at him. I wasn't sure whether I was trying to convince Kipa or myself.

"How badly was he hurt?" Kipa sat down next to me, motioning for Gunnar to take a seat.

"The wight got its barbs into him and poisoned him. I ended up having to call Herne, and he brought Ferosyn over. Ferosyn saved Llew's life, but it was touch-and-go for a bit. Herne and Viktor ended up going out to finish off the eggs that we found in the nest. All in all, we could have handled the situation so much better."

"Hindsight is always easiest. Sometimes you don't know which route is the best to take until you reach the end. I'm sorry your friend was hurt. And I'm sorry that his husband blames you. You know you're not to blame, right?" Kipa gave me a long look, his expression more somber than I had seen in a long time.

I shrugged. "Yeah. Logically, I know that. But I was already feeling guilty when Jordan lashed out at me. I'm afraid he may try to break up my friendship with Llew."

Gunnar cleared his throat. "If Llew is truly your friend, you should have nothing to worry about."

"Yeah, but Jordan is his husband. And family always takes precedence over friendships. I learned that years ago." I had lost a couple friends because their families didn't approve of me. It had hurt, especially when I realized they didn't even bother fighting for the friendship. "Thing is, I've always thought Jordan was my friend, too."

"I thought my wife's family were my friends," Gunnar said. "But they blame me for her death. I learned the hard way that sometimes no matter how good of a person you are, some people will think the worst of you." He looked so forlorn that I wanted to cheer him up, except I couldn't even bring myself to smile.

"Well, there's nothing I can do about it right now. So what did you find out? I've tried to do some research on the fylgismadi but it's slow going when few of the grimoires have indexes in them." I tried to push away my gloom, and focus on the matter at hand.

"Unfortunately, the news is worse than we hoped. I made some discreet inquiries, and it's come to our attention that Solveig's father is the one who attached the fylgismadi to Gunnar. I can't force him to remove it, even though he's part of the SuVahta. I may rule over their sphere, and they follow my direction, but because Solveig's father believes in his heart that Gunnar is responsible for his daughter's death, he has the right to demand blood vengeance. It's an honor code among the SuVahta that even I don't always understand. And while I am their leader, I cannot be a dictator."

Kipa looked over at Gunnar, who was staring at his feet. "It doesn't help that Gunnar accepted the blame in the beginning. They could claim that, if I were to try to force his father to call off the fylgismadi. That doesn't mean we can't take steps to break the curse. It just means that I can't order his father-in-law to stand down."

"All right then, how do we make the fylgismadi go away? How do we counter the curse?"

"Unfortunately, the easiest way is to find the fylgismadi's bones and salt them. And that's not possible because we don't know where Kristian hid them." Kipa frowned, leaning back against the sofa.

I turned to Gunnar, but he just shook his head, a hope-less look on his face. We sat for a moment in silence, each wrapped within our own thoughts. Then it occurred to me: the fylgismadi was a spirit, and therefore subject to Arawn's rule. Perhaps Annwn could possibly give me some ideas on how to cope with this.

"Arawn," I said out loud. "Here, come into my ritual room with me. Both of you." I leaned down and took off my shoes, setting them to the side. Then, pointing to both of the men's feet, I said, "Shoes off. Socks too."

"Are you sure? My feet probably stink to high hell." Gunnar grimaced.

"Yes, I'm sure. Hurry up. I'm tired and it's barely afternoon."

"All right, but don't say I didn't warn you," he said, trying to smile.

Kipa and Gunnar removed their socks and shoes, setting them to the side. Then, both men barefoot, they followed me into my ritual room. I motioned for them to take a seat on the floor, one on either side of the bench in front of my altar.

As I lowered myself onto the bench, Kipa cleared his throat.

"Is there anything we need to do in order to help? Anything we *shouldn't* do? Herne has dealt with Arawn before, but where I come from we deal with Tuoni and Tuonetar, who rule over Tuonela, our name for the Netherworld. I'm not sure if there are different protocols."

"Unless I ask you to say something, remain silent. If I ask you for information, give me exactly what I ask you for. If you don't know, say 'I don't know.' Do you understand?"

They both nodded, silent. Gunnar looked a little green around the gills. Kipa actually looked like he was taking the situation seriously for once.

I turned back to the altar. My altar was a large credenza, buttressed against the windowsill. Walnut, the wood was polished to a high sheen, and over it I had draped a black and silver cloth. In the very center was a large smoky quartz sphere, the size of a large muskmelon. It sat on a silver stand, and to either side were candle-holders shaped like skulls. One held a black taper and the other, a white taper. In front of the sphere was a votive candleholder, holding a red votive.

A brass pentacle, my ritual dagger, and my copper wand sat in front of the smoky quartz and the tapers. To the left, near the end of the altar, stood a statue of Arawn, the Lord of the Dead. And to the right end of the altar stood a statue of Cerridwen, the Lady of the Cauldron of Rebirth.

I picked up my handpan, Laralea, and settled on the bench in front of the altar. Holding the instrument on my lap, I began to tap out a slow rhythm. As the music echoed through the room, I felt myself slide into the trance that the rhythms always invoked. I didn't look at Gunnar or Kipa. I trusted them to do as I had asked.

When the energy reached a peak, I set Laralea aside, and held out my hands, palms up.

"Blessed Arawn, Lord of the Dead, guide and guard me in my journeys. Blessed Cerridwen, keeper of the sacred Cauldron of Rebirth, guard and guide me in my journeys. Teach me to walk in the shadows without fear, for I am the Daughter of Bones, Speaker for the Dead. Guide me through the Aether as I perform my duties. Strengthen me, swallow my fear, let me walk with confidence and surety. Blessed be the Guardians of the Underworld. So Mote It Be."

As my voice faded, I could feel the energy spiraling through the room, surrounding us like a whirlwind, rustling leaves blowing in the autumn wind, the chill night descending as winter kissed the earth. From a drawer in the console table, I took out a small dish carved from garnet. It was my offering dish, and I did this every time I came to talk with Arawn and Cerridwen. I picked up my ritual dagger and gently pressed my finger against the tip, piercing the flesh. I squeezed three drops of blood into the dish. Then, whispering *Spark*, I conjured fire to sizzle against the blood, evaporating it into smoke.

"Blessed Arawn, I need your guidance. *We* need your guidance. A fylgismadi has attached itself to Gunnar, and we do not know where its bones are, therefore we cannot salt them and lay the spirit to rest. Please, if you find my request worthy, tell me what I must do in order to detach the fylgismadi from Gunnar's soul."

I placed my hands palms down on the altar table, waiting. My eyes were closed, but I heard Arawn whisper, *Look into the orb.*

I pulled the orb to me, the heavy smoky quartz flashing from the rainbows caught in the fractures within the sphere. They acted like prisms, shimmering under the light of the candles. I studied the orb, letting my mind drift as I waited to see what Arawn had to show me.

A figure appeared within the orb. She was ancient, a crone beyond all crones. Her face was so deeply wrinkled it was difficult to see her mouth or her nose. But her eyes shimmered with a powerful light, glowing golden and rich. She frightened me, even though I didn't know who she was. I shivered as she turned her face to mine, and a crafty smile broke through the ridges of time that formed her countenance.

"Go to Arachana and ask for help. She is the only one who can unweave the threads that bind the fylgismadi to your friend. She will require a price and you must decide whether you can afford to pay. Do not attempt to outwit her. You will not win."

A flash of fear stabbed through me, though I didn't know why.

"Where do I find her?"

"Stand with a bloody heart in hand and call her name three times. She will come to you. But once you have clasped a deal with her, do not break your word, for she will come looking for you."

A sudden gust of wind shot through the room, blowing out the candles. I jolted, my eyes flying open as I looked around. Daylight flooded through the window, but it had seemed as dark as night, as dark as pitch during the ritual. My stomach lurched, and I felt queasy, nauseated by the energy that still flowed through my body.

I swallowed, forcing a steadiness into my voice that I did not feel.

"Blessed Arawn, blessed Cerridwen, thank you for your help. I am yours, and yours alone. So Mote It Be."

Shaking, I pushed the bench back from the altar, and glanced at Kipa, who was staring at me with a worried look on his face.

"May we talk now?" he asked softly.

"Yes, but not in here. Meet me in the living room. I need to splash some water on my face."

I stopped in the bathroom, holding the edge of the sink as I breathed deeply, trying to ease the dizziness that I felt. The ritual had left me feeling like spiderwebs were clinging to my body, like I was reeling from a ride at the carnival. My stomach lurched again, and I barely made it over to the toilet before I threw up, losing everything I'd eaten in the past couple of hours.

Clammy and shaking, I eased myself onto my vanity bench, filling a paper cup with water as I rinsed out my mouth. Then I brushed my teeth and cleaned up the toilet. Finally, feeling somewhat settled and grounded, I opened the door, heading back to the living room to talk to Gunnar and Kipa.

CHAPTER EIGHTEEN

Gunnar and I settled in at the table while Kipa popped into the kitchen to heat up some soup. I needed something to settle my stomach, a light broth with some noodles, so he heated up some soup and made toast and set the table for us. Neither Gunnar nor Kipa tried to push me into talking before I was ready.

When I had eaten half a bowl of soup and a piece of toast, I leaned back in my chair, letting out a long breath. I had tried to avoid thinking about everything that had happened and what Arawn had said while I regrouped and grounded myself. The energy had been so overwhelming that it left me reeling. But finally, with all the lights on and some soup and toast in my belly, I felt capable of talking.

I looked over at Kipa. "Have you ever heard of someone named Arachana?"

Puzzled, he thought for a moment, and then shook his head. "The name doesn't ring a bell. Male or female?"

"Female. I wondered if it was a goddess."

He frowned. "If it is, I've never heard of her. Why?"

"Because she's apparently the one who can help me dislodge the fylgismadi from Gunnar. Unless there's any chance you can get Kristian to do it." I knew even as I spoke that the answer would be no.

Gunnar cleared his throat. "Kristian would like nothing better than to see me waste away. He's not going to help. And as Kipa said, I made the mistake of blaming myself in his presence. That gives him the right of blood vengeance. I could appeal to the elders of the SuVahta, but most of them are Kristian's friends. And I'm fairly low in the ranks. I'm quite expendable, whereas Kristian's goodwill isn't." He sounded so fatalistic it made my heart ache.

"Try to hold on. Rest as much as you can, eat what you can, and try to keep your weight up. I'll do some research this evening and try to find out who Arachana is. I know how to contact her, but I'd like to know what I'm getting myself into before I knock on her door." I thought about telling them what Arawn had told me—how to contact her—but it occurred to me that Gunnar might take it on himself to do so and I had the feeling he wouldn't come out of the interaction alive. Not from the energy I had felt coming from her.

Kipa reached out and took my hand, squeezing it tightly. "And I want to know what you're getting into before you do it. Promise me you'll tell me?"

I glanced at his face. There was a concern in his eyes that I wasn't used to seeing from people. Ulstair had pretty much kept himself separate from my business, and whether he simply assumed that I was more capable than any of the creatures I had taken on, or whether he didn't care, I wasn't sure. I had the feeling it was the former rather than the latter.

"All right. I'll tell you before I do anything." I turned to Gunnar. "I'll do my best to help you. I'm sorry I don't have any better news this point. But I'll contact you as soon as I know what I'm dealing with, and as soon as I know how to go about this."

He nodded. "I have no right to expect anything from you, and I'm grateful for the work you've already done. I don't expect you to put yourself in danger for me, please know that."

He sounded desperate, in that way people have when they are facing a frightening and uncertain future. I knew that Gunnar was true to his word. He didn't expect anything from me, and that almost made me sadder than if he had been yammering at me to get busy and save him. It told me he felt hopeless, and I still had the feeling he blamed himself for his wife's death. And that only gave Kristian more ammunition.

I glanced at Kipa. "Are you coming back tonight?"

He reluctantly shook his head. "I'm afraid that I can't. I promised to help Herne again tonight. I wish I could, though."

As I showed them out, I had the sinking feeling that Gunnar didn't have much time left. Which meant I needed to get my ass in gear and find out who Arachana was, so I'd know what I was dealing with. I turned, leaning against the door after they left, wondering who to call. If Arachana wasn't a goddess—and I had the feeling she wasn't—then who was she? Heading toward my book-case, I stopped at the table to grab another piece of toast.

Raj peeked around the corner, a look of concern on his face.

"Is Raven okay? Raj feels something strange going on."

I flashed him a smile that I didn't feel. "Raven's fine, Raj. She's just worried about a friend right now." As I pulled several books off the shelf and carried them over to the table, he came over and curled up beside my feet. I reached down and scratched him behind the ears, stopping as my phone rang. I glanced at the caller ID. Great. It was Phasmoria, my mother. Just what I needed right now.

MY MOTHER'S VOICE, WHEN SHE WASN'T SHRIEKING OUT HER death knells, was throaty and sensuous, a lot like mine. It also happened to be one of the most authoritarian voices I had ever heard. Nobody ignored Phasmoria and got away with it.

"Raven, how are you?"

With my mother, no question was ever a throwaway. She wasn't one for small talk, and when she asked a question, she expected an answer. And *not* just a polite brushoff. If I tried to tell her everything was fine right now, she'd pick up on it and grill me.

"I have some serious problems to deal with right now, or rather, I'm helping friends with problems. So I'm a little worried at this point. Father said that you were going to visit me?" That was another thing about my mother, she didn't mind that I was blunt and direct.

"Your father's correct. I've been planning to come visit you for a while, but I couldn't get away until now. The

Morrígan has been running us ragged, and she promoted me to the head of the Bean Sidhe."

I could hear the tinge of pride in her voice, although Phasmoria, being who she was, would never gloat.

"What happened to old Urseala?" I had met the former head of the Bean Sidhe exactly one time, and that was one time too many. She was a terrifying creature, one of the Ante-Fae that I would go to my grave hoping never to meet again.

"She grew too chaotic. Age has not been kind to her. The Morrígan retired her, setting her up in a little house by herself in Annwn, and she created a barrier around Urseala's place so the crone can't escape and hurt anybody."

I shuddered. The thought of Urseala out on her own, without her wits about her, was a thought I could do without.

"Well, I'm grateful that the Morrígan recognized what was going on. Congratulations on taking Urseala's place. I know that's a great trust."

"Yes, well, I hope I've proved my loyalty over the years. Anyway, I'll be there by the end of the week, if not sooner. I trust that won't be a problem?" It wasn't really a question, but more of a statement.

"Of course not. I have a question for you, though."

"What is it?"

"Have you ever heard of a creature or goddess called Arachana? And if so, can you tell me about her?"

Phasmoria paused, and I almost thought I heard her catch her breath. "Why do you want to know?"

I wasn't sure I wanted my mother to know why I was asking, but caution told me to tread carefully. I was still young enough that if she ordered me to either do something or *not* do something, there would be hell to pay if I went ahead and went against her.

"I'm just curious. I'm asking for a friend." I'd never be able to pull that over on my friends, but Phasmoria wasn't used to being around humans, and human expressions didn't click with her.

"You'd best tell your friend that they're better off giving her a wide berth. And yes, to answer your question, I have heard of Arachana. I've never met her, and I hope not to." My mother sounded a little shaky. Shaky enough that it made me pause.

"Who is she?"

"She's one of the most ancient of Ante-Fae. She's older than even Urseala, and far more deadly. She also has her wits about her, and she's cunning and treacherous. To some, she's known as the spider queen."

"Like Grandmother Spider?"

"No. Grandmother Spider is reasonable and helpful to humans, even though she isn't in any remote sense humanlike. Arachana is deadly, and she lives by her own agenda. Tell your friend to walk softly and avoid her if possible."

I closed my eyes, leaning back in my chair. The last thing I needed was to make a deal with one of the ancient Ante-Fae. And the fact that I was Exosan wasn't much of a help, either.

The Exosan were all mostly younger members of the Ante-Fae who liked to hang out in the world of mortals, and that made a number of the older Ante-Fae uncomfortable. We weren't exactly considered pariah, but we weren't welcome among the others, either. My father was considered one of the Exosan as well, and my mother routinely dealt with humans as one of the Bean Sidhe, so she didn't exactly fit in with a lot of the older Ante-Fae, either.

"Thank you for the information." I paused, wanting to tell my mother what was going on, but afraid that she would forbid me to help Gunnar.

"Is there anything else you want to tell me?" Phasmoria asked in a soft voice, soft enough that I had a suspicion she was on to me.

"No, that's it. Thank you very much. I'll see you when you get here. Is there anything you'd like me to stock up on from the store?"

My mother had a big appetite like I did, and she had a particular love for a few of the more human foods—like spaghetti, mashed potatoes and gravy, and sub sandwiches.

"Just the usual. I'll see you in a few days." The line went dead, which didn't surprise me. She wasn't one for long good-byes, either.

I stared at the table, thinking that I needed to call Kipa. I would keep my promise to him, now I knew what I was dealing with. I would have to walk softly around Arachana, but I had already made up my mind. Gunnar needed help, and I seemed to be his only hope.

With a sigh, I called Kipa to fill him in on what I'd found out. I expected an argument and an argument was what I got.

"You can't do this. If your mother seems cautious of Arachana, then *you* should be afraid of her." Kipa sounded dead set against the plan.

"Then you're sentencing Gunnar to a slow, painful

death. How can you justify that? He's one of your Elitvar-tijat. You know that Kristian is wrong for what he's doing. And yet you won't force him to stop."

"*Of course* he's wrong—but I can't step in. Yes, I'm a god. I'm a force of nature, the Lord of the Wolves. But I'm not omnipotent and I'm not omniscient. And I cannot interfere in this, at least not directly. There are some wrongs in the world that we can't attack head-on, for one reason or another. If I were to negate Kristian's right to blood vengeance, the SuVahta would never trust me again. My own elite guard would be compromised. Do you understand this?"

"No," I said. "I don't understand allowing a man to be killed this way when you know that it's wrong. It was an accident, Solveig wasn't murdered. And it wasn't manslaughter or neglect, either. Sometimes things just happen and there's no way around them." The thought crossed my mind that Kristian had better hope I never met him in person. I wasn't one of the SuVahta, and I wasn't bound by their rules.

"I don't like this anymore than you do. But Raven, don't question my ethics on this. I am bound by a set of rules as much as anybody else." Kipa sounded angry now.

I paused, then said, "Then the only option is for me to deal with Arachana."

"Tell Gunnar about this and let him appeal to her."

"Gunnar wouldn't survive an interaction with her. You know that. *You* chose to involve me in this, Kipa. You're going to have to accept the consequences of your choice because I can't let him die without trying to do something."

Kipa paused, and when he spoke again, his voice was

soft. "Then I will come with you to face Arachana. I won't let you face her alone."

"Fine. But if she wants you out of the way, get out of the way. Do you understand?"

He paused, then said, "Fine. I still don't like it. When are you going to do the ritual?"

"Tonight. Gunnar's wasting away. The sooner we get this over with, the better. Now, I'm going to get off the phone, because I've got to find a bloody heart to offer up to her. Which means I need to slaughter something, because somehow I don't think she's going to accept a beef heart from the supermarket. Do you have any suggestions?"

"I'll bring you what you need. I have friends who keep livestock, and I'll have them slaughter a pig. I'll bring you the heart when I come over. See you around five." Kipa sounded about as enthusiastic as I felt.

I murmured good-bye and slumped back in my chair, staring at the table. I was jonesing for caffeine and sugar. Comfort food. I glanced down to see Raj asleep at my feet. Gently, so as not to wake him, I slid my chair back and peeked out the window. The storm had backed off for a little while. We had a good twelve inches of snow, and for a moment I thought of jumping in my car and taking off. Of trying to forget about Gunnar and his problems, but running away never solved anything. I sighed and decided to call Llew. He was always a good sounding board and he was good at helping me figure out my problems.

But Jordan picked up.

"He's sleeping right now, Raven. I'm not going to wake him. He'll be in touch with you when he's ready. Until then, just leave him alone." Jordan sounded so cold that my stomach lurched.

"Jordan, please don't be this way. You know that it was Llew's decision to go with me. He was in the wrong place at the wrong time. I would never for the world deliberately put him in danger. You know that."

Jordan paused, then mumbled, "Sorry, I can't talk right now. We'll figure this out later."

As he hung up, the gloom descended even further on my shoulders, and for the first time in a long time, I felt very much alone.

CHAPTER NINETEEN

hile I was waiting for Kipa, I made up the guest bedroom for when my mother arrived. She was never on time—always either early or late, and I preferred to be ready in case she was early. Phasmoria didn't care where she slept, but I liked making my guests comfortable, and given it was my mother, I was constantly hoping for reassurance that I was doing a good job of making it on my own. She had left me with my father, returning to the Morrígan and to her duties, and while I knew that it was her responsibility, I always felt like she chosen a life without me over having me in her life.

The whole abandonment issue was ridiculous on my part. I knew that much. There was no way she could have taken me with her into the tall towers of the Morrí- gan's Castle. It wouldn't have been a healthy life for a child anyway. Yet there was part of me that always felt like I was an afterthought in my mother's life. Given I had been an unexpected glitch in her short-lived relationship with my father, the truth was I had been an accident.

And she had given me twelve years of her life, taking as much time away from the Morrígan as the goddess had allowed. She had seen me grow up as much as she could. All of these things I knew, and yet here I was, still trying to please her—still striving to hear her say that she was proud of me. Phasmoria had never said she *wasn't*, but it crossed my mind that she never really thought that I craved her approval.

When the guest room was clean and sparkling, with fresh linens and even fresh flowers on the bedside table, I wandered back into the living room. Raj was watching *Acrobert and the Alphas*, and he glanced up as I entered the room.

"Raven want to watch TV with Raj?" He sounded so hopeful that I couldn't resist. I curled up on the sofa next to him, and he lay down with his head in my lap as we watched the show together. I wasn't able to focus on the antics of the superheroes, but I laughed when Raj laughed, and tried to let myself enjoy the down time. At least Phasmoria liked Raj. In fact, she had taken a real shine to him, and had confided in me that I had done a good thing by adopting him.

"Raven loves Raj, I hope Raj knows that." I scratched his back, my nails sliding over the leathery skin. I wasn't sure if he actually enjoyed having his back scratched, or whether it was the attention that he liked, but he never complained.

"Raj loves Raven. Raj knows Raven loves Raj." He glanced up at me, his eyes full of concern. "Raven seems sad. Raven talk to Raj?"

I bit my lip, not wanting to worry him. "My friends are going through some hard times right now, and it makes me sad."

"But Raven's okay?" Raj asked.

"Yes, Raven is fine." I glanced at the clock. I needed to check on the ferrets. I hadn't given them very much attention in the morning, and I wanted to spend a little time talking to Elise. That brought to mind another concern. Since it was Llew looking into the curse hanging over their heads, if Jordan interfered with our friendship, I didn't know who else to turn to. "I'll be right back. I'm going to check on the ferrets."

Raj shifted so I could stand up, and then immediately focused on the TV again as the commercial ended. Raj loved television. I had the sneaking suspicion that he watched too much of it, but honestly—if it made him happy, and he was healthy, I wasn't going to make a fuss about it.

I opened the door to the ferrets' room, and they poked their heads up as I peeked in. Closing the door behind me, I hurried over to the cage and made sure they had enough food and water, and that their bedding was still fine for the night. I changed it once a day, usually in the morning, clearing out the saturated litter, and spreading clean straw down for them.

Elise stood up to the cage door, blinking her beautiful wide eyes at me.

Raven, I'm glad you're here. I've missed you the past couple days.

It wasn't that I had been gone, but I knew my focus had been elsewhere and the ferrets could always tell when my attention wasn't fully engaged. I opened the door, standing back for them to race out into the room and start running around. The exercise would wear them out. I sat down on the floor next to the cage, and Elise immediately made her way into my lap.

"I'm sorry, Elise. I've been preoccupied. I was just telling Raj that a couple friends of mine are going through some difficult problems, and it's taking up a lot of my time. I don't mean to neglect you."

Oh, I understand. And we're fine. Although I was wondering, if it's nice enough, can we go out for a walk?

I pointed toward the window. "There's a foot of snow out there right now, and the storm hasn't broken yet. I don't think you'd be very comfortable. It's icy outside. I can open the window for a little while, to let some fresh air in. But I guarantee you it's cold."

Elise paused, then blinked. *An open window would be fine. Only don't do it when we're out running around unless there's a screen. Gordon might try to squeeze through the window. He's thinking more and more like a ferret nowadays. I suppose you haven't*—she paused, staring at the floor.

"No, I'm sorry. I haven't been able to find out anything. Llew's looking into matters, but I'm going to tell you right now, I'm not sure how successful we'll be. I'm doing what I can."

I know you are. And I'm ever so grateful for that. You take very good care of us, and Gordon is extremely happy, even though he's forgetting who he is. Templeton and I are happy, too. We're just hoping that someday you'll be able to free us. She paused, then asked, *What happens if we die in ferret form? Will we be free from the curse?*

"Honestly? I'm not sure, but I think you would be. So

even though you're trapped within your bodies now, at some point you should be free."

But haven't we been in ferret form longer than usual? Ferrets don't live as long as we have, not naturally.

"That's another thing I'm trying to find out. And yes, you've lived far longer than ferrets usually do." I stroked her head, smiling at the touch of her soft fur under my fingers. "Elise, I'm happy that you're with me. I hope you know that. I'm happy to take care of you as long as necessary."

I know that. So does Templeton. And as I said, Gordon's for the most part happy—he's happy doing ferret things. Now and then he has a flash where he remembers who he is, but I'm not holding out much hope that will last much longer.

I played with them for a while, bouncing balls across the floor and playing with the feather toy. Finally, I topped off their food dish and gave them clean water again before locking them back in their cage. I opened the window a little, setting my phone alarm to close it again before the room got too cold.

The doorbell rang, and I turned to go, glancing over my shoulder to see Elise staring at me through the cage. But she seemed content, and I let out a slow sigh, shutting the door to the room behind me.

Kɪᴘᴀ ᴡᴀs sᴛᴀɴᴅɪɴɢ ᴀᴛ ᴛʜᴇ ᴅᴏᴏʀ.

"I thought you had to help Herne tonight. How did you get out of it?" I asked as he pulled me into his arms and gave me a long kiss, his lips pressing against mine.

My pulse raced. I felt safe and warm when he held me,

and right now, all I wanted to do was jump into bed with him. Sex was a great way to procrastinate, especially when faced with a task I really didn't want to do. It was also a good stress reliever, and right now I was about as stressed as I had ever been.

"I told him the truth. That you needed my help tonight, and that I was putting my girlfriend's needs higher than his. He understood."

I wasn't sure how true that was, but I decided to just be grateful that Herne hadn't insisted on Kipa working. The thought of facing Arachana terrified me, and I was grateful that Kipa had offered to go through the ritual with me.

"Speaking of needs, did you bring the heart?" I grimaced. While I wasn't squeamish, the thought of playing around with a heart plucked fresh out of a pig didn't sound like a lot of fun.

Kipa held up a small cooler. "It's in here. And I'm going to have over a hundred pounds of pork in my freezer, so I hope you like bacon and ham."

I stared at him. "You really bought a whole pig just to get me a pig heart?"

He grinned. "Hey, you should feel special. I wouldn't fill my freezer for just *any* girl."

It sounded so absurd that I suddenly found myself laughing like a maniac. "That's the most romantic, ridiculous gesture I've ever heard of. My boyfriend bought me a pig heart." I couldn't stop laughing, and finally Kipa put his hand on my shoulder.

"Are you all right? It wasn't *that* funny."

I nodded, gasping as I tried to control myself. "I think I'm just a little stressed. Anyway, thank you so much. And

I love bacon and ham. So does Raj." I glanced at the clock, wondering if we had time to take a break before we went through with the ritual. After all, if Arachana was as dangerous as my mother thought she was, I wanted to go out on a good memory.

Kipa seemed to sense my mood. "Do you think we have time…?"

"We can make time. It's not like she's expecting me. I haven't called out her name and offered her the heart. I don't think an hour's going to make that much difference."

Kipa placed the heart—still in the cooler—in my refrigerator. He turned to me, his eyes glowing. Without a word, I reached out and took his hand, and led him into the bedroom.

Rather than the boisterous mood of our last assignation, we were both solemn, and silent. I began to unbutton the front of his shirt. As I slid it off of his shoulders and tossed it across my cedar trunk that held spare blankets, Kipa let out a slow hiss between his teeth. He pulled me to him, stroking my cheek as he gazed down into my eyes. His lips touched mine, warm and searching, as his tongue slid between them. Still kissing me, he lifted me up around the waist, turning toward the bed. He carried me over and lay me down gently, and I spread my legs as he knelt between them, his hands searching under my shirt.

As I came up for air, I slid back on the bed and sat up, stripping my shirt over my head and unzipping the side of my skirt. I settled back down, pushing up with my feet so that he could slide my skirt down my legs. He caught the sides of my panties with his fingers as he undressed me, stripping them off along with the skirt. I lifted my legs and he pulled them off, tossing both skirt and underwear onto the floor next to the bed.

"Pants. Take off your pants." I pointed to his jeans, where he was pressing hard against the zipper.

He unzipped, his shaft springing free as he kicked off his jeans. He was glorious, his abs strong and firm, and my head swam with desire as he knelt, once again between my legs. I wrapped my legs and feet around his waist as he kissed me, pressing his chest against my breasts.

"I want inside you. I want to own your body with mine." He whispered in my ear, his voice low and sultry.

I ached, every inch of my body craving him. Hungry for his touch, I swiveled beneath him in anticipation. My nipples hardened as his chest rubbed against mine, and he leaned down, taking one of them in his mouth, sucking so hard it almost hurt. I gasped, another jolt of desire racing through me.

"Fuck me, Kipa. Fuck me so hard I can't think."

As he sucked at my breast, he reached one hand between my thighs and began to rub gently, sending me into a spiral of need. I groaned, and he pressed harder, circling faster, before he slid two fingers inside me, stroking against the inside.

I reached down and clasped my hand around his shaft, giving him a firm squeeze as I stroked along the sides.

"You want me inside?" he teased.

"I want all of you. Fuck me as hard as you can. Drive out the darkness and help me breathe." I let go of him and wrapped my arms around his waist, trying to pull him into me.

Kipa let out a harsh laugh, teasing me. He pressed in, just the head of his shaft, then pulled out again. Then, once again, he slid inside me but withdrew.

I groaned, almost unable to bear the hunger that rolled in waves through my body. Finally, his eyes turned dark and he drove inside, penetrating my folds, thrusting as deep as he could. He held me down with his body as I reveled in the feeling of him stretching me wide. Then slowly, he began to move, little thrusts at first that set me swooning, then harder and harder, grinding against me as I welcomed every inch.

I spiraled out of my thoughts and into the moment, my awareness focused only on him, on the feeling of his body joined with mine, on the feeling of his unrelenting passion as he thrust again and again. And then, before I had time to prepare, I started to rise, letting out a series of little *ohs*, and the next moment, I capitulated, falling into the orgasm as though I might fall off a cliff, the shock waves racing through me. I let out one last cry as the wave of passion dragged me under.

Kipa stiffened, groaning so loudly at first I thought he might be hurt, but then he threw back his head and his hips beat a rhythm against mine as he came, moaning my name.

As he slowly collapsed on top of me, I wrapped my arms around him, never wanting to let go, wanting to hold on to this moment forever. I was crying, I realized, although I didn't know why. Everything felt so right, and the passion between us was so raw that it left every nerve unsettled. And yet, I was at peace. As the waves subsided, he slowly rolled off of me and I slipped into his arms, my face pressed against his chest.

"Raven, oh my Raven." He kissed my forehead, then my lips, brushing my hair back from my face.

I smiled at him through my tears, unsure of what had just happened. Something in our relationship had shifted, leaving me both nervous and yet happy.

"I've never felt anything quite like that."

He pressed his forehead against mine, smiling. "We'll have to try for it again" was all he said before he kissed me once more.

CHAPTER TWENTY

"I don't want to perform the ritual inside my house," I said. "There's no way I want Arachana coming through my front door. And it's too cold outside."

Kipa came to the rescue. He held up a set of keys. "I have a place we can go."

"Where is it? Is it far away? Your place?"

Kipa laughed. "No, it's not my house and it's not that far. Do you trust me?"

I nodded. "Do I need a coat?"

"That depends. Do you think you can make it across the street without one?"

I froze, staring at him. I was in the middle of getting dressed, and now I dropped my skirt on the bed, lowering myself to the mattress. "What did you say?"

"I'm the one who bought Buck and Minerva's house. That's why they moved so quickly. I paid them extra to get out. Actually, that's why they moved in the first place. After I saw what an asshole he was, I paid a visit to him when you were out. I made it very clear that if there was any more trouble, I would allow my wolves to use him as a chew toy. And then I offered him double what his house was worth if he'd move within one day. I told him to put up a for-sale sign, and that I'd have the contracts drawn up and we could sign off immediately. It took a little juggling, but the house is mine, and he's gone."

I shook my head, at a loss for words. "Are you planning on moving in?" While I was overjoyed that Buck and Minerva were gone, I wasn't sure exactly how I felt about having my boyfriend as a neighbor.

"I don't know what I'm going to do with it. Maybe I'll rent it out, and you can be damn sure I'll check the references of whoever moves in. Or maybe I'll keep it for other uses. I don't know yet. But I do know that it's the perfect place to hold the ritual. You don't have to tell her that you live across the street." He stared at me, a cockeyed grin on his face.

I slowly picked up my skirt again, sliding it up my hips and zipping it. The circle skirt was black with blue roses on it, and it had a built-in petticoat. I was wearing a low V-neck sweater in royal blue, and the roses matched the color perfectly. "It's going to take me a little while to process all this," I said. "But yes, we can do the ritual there."

Kipa handed me my tights and my boots and as I slid my feet into my tights and shimmied them over my hips, it occurred to me that life was getting stranger the longer it went on.

It felt odd being in Buck's house—or rather, Kipa's

house—without expecting a shotgun in my face, or some redneck yokel trying to make jokes at my expense. Buck and his family hadn't bothered to clean, and it smelled like smoke and stale beer and old peanuts. But everything was gone, and I burned an entire smudge stick to clear out some of the odors and residual energy.

Kipa had brought over a couple of folding chairs and a folding table from my shed, and he set them up while I did my best to clear out the energy. Finally, he brought over the cooler with the heart in it and set it on the kitchen counter.

"Do you need anything else?"

I shook my head. "I think we're ready. All Arawn told me was to hold a bloody heart in my hand and say her name three times. Shades of Beetlejuice, although right now, I think I'd rather have Beetlejuice standing in front of me instead of Arachana. I'm not looking forward to this. And before you start up again, I feel we owe it to Gunnar."

"He's been an excellent guard, and I'd hate to lose him." Kipa caught my gaze, shrugging. "What can I say? He's a good person, Raven, but the fact that Solveig fell through that crevasse wasn't my fault. And it wasn't Gunnar's fault, but he didn't have to tell her father that he felt he was to blame. He should have talked to me first, but his own conscience wouldn't let him go. If we do help him through this, I'm going to send him away. He won't be able to stay in the same village as the SuVahta, not with Kristian there. And I will not have a guard who second-guesses himself. Either way, Gunnar won't be around much longer."

I paused, my hand on the cooler. "Where will you send him?"

"Probably Finland. Maybe I'll petition Mielikki to take him on. She's fair. She won't let her grievances against me cloud her judgment on what's best for Gunnar. He could do a lot worse than working for Mielikki's Arrow."

That made me feel better. At least Kipa would do his best to find Gunnar a good job that he could be proud of. "All right. Let's get this show on the road. Keep the lights on, because I don't want to see her in the dark."

I opened the cooler, peeking inside. I grimaced when I saw the pig heart lying in a pool of blood. It was bloody, all right. Grimacing, I glanced down at my clothes, hoping to hell I could keep from spattering myself. I lifted out the heart, gingerly holding it in front of me over the container. Kipa stood to my left, his dagger ready. I wasn't sure exactly what good the dagger would do, although the gods were generally stronger than the Ante-Fae, but given Arachana was one of the oldest of my people, I had no doubt that her powers were honed and strong.

"Arachana. Arachana. Arachana, I need to talk to you." I almost jumped as the heart in my hand began to beat again, and the chill from being refrigerated faded away, replaced by a warmth that felt unnatural and gruesome. "What the fuck—"

"Look," Kipa said, pointing toward the center of the room.

There, in the kitchen, a black mist began to form. I forced myself to stand still, to wait as it coalesced into a figure. The lights dimmed, and then flickered out. I gasped, but felt Kipa's hand on my back, shoring me up. I was about ready to tell him to ditch the ritual when the figure took on a light, emanating stripes of gold and red from along its body. It was definitely a woman, but she had six arms, and I could barely make out her features. The light around her was a trembling, full-body halo, a nimbus that made me think of all sorts of unhealthy things.

I could hear my heart racing in my ears.

"Well, well. What have we here?" Arachana stepped forward. It was difficult to see her clearly. It was almost as though she were a smudge of ink against the air, with the chevrons of light outlining her body.

I waited, but she crossed all six of her arms and I realized I was going to have to speak first.

"I need information. Arawn told me you might be able to help." Even as the words flew out of my mouth, it felt like her gaze drove a piercing hole through me, right into the center of my core. I felt exposed and vulnerable, flayed for everyone to see.

I glanced down at the heart in my hand. It was almost as though the pulsing organ had sped up to match the beating of my own heart.

She gazed down at the heart in my hand and smacked her lips together.

"And so did the Lord of the Dead tell you how to catch my attention? Did he offer you up to me? Is he so careless with his servants that he would willingly hand you over to me, to stick on a spit and roast over an open fire? And you, young insolent child, what could you possibly give me in return for my help? What would you be *willing* to give to me?"

Momentarily confused, I glanced at the pig's heart. "I

thought this… I brought you the offering Arawn suggested."

"No, child. No, the heart is simply a way to catch my attention. Consider it a down payment." She sounded crafty and cunning, as though she were spinning a web of words around me, a web that might tighten at any moment, trussing me up.

I swallowed the fear rising in my throat. "What do you want?"

Arachana stepped forward, close enough that I should have been able to see every nuance in her face, but still she appeared like a smudge in the air, an ink drawing that was out of focus. Only her eyes were clear and ruthless, and I felt very much alone even though Kipa was near, poised to help me.

As if reading my mind, she turned to Kipa.

"And you, Lord of the Wolves. You expect to fight me? You may be a god, but you have no comprehension of how powerful I am."

I caught my breath, relieved that, for even a moment, I had escaped her attention.

"I am a *god*. And I am Lord of the Wolves. And Raven is my mate. I will *not* let you hurt her." Kipa sounded deadly serious. For a fraction of a second it seemed like Arachana pulled back, but then she stiffened.

"Stand down, Wolf. I am not going to eat up your playmate." She returned her gaze to me. "So your name is Raven? You are one of the Exosan."

I swallowed again, wishing that Kipa hadn't mentioned my name. I gave her a slow nod. "Yes, I am one of the Exosan."

"Tell me why you have called for me. Do not waste my time, child."

I stumbled over my words, but finally found my voice. "I need the spell to dislodge a fylgismadi from someone. I don't have the bones so I can't salt them. I need to know how to free it and send it on its way, so it won't bother him again."

That seemed to stop her for a moment. Arachana took a slow step back, still completely focused on my face. I wanted to look away, but I knew that wouldn't be wise. It felt like facing a cougar in the woods. Turn away from a big cat and the cat will see you as prey, and that's exactly the way it felt with Arachana.

She was silent for a moment, and then she spoke again. "I can tell you what to do, and it *will* work. But for that information I will require a favor in turn. Are you willing to make a deal?"

It was my turn to think. I scrambled, trying to decide what to do. "What kind of favor? What do you want from me? How can I help you?"

"One unconditional favor, to be called in when I choose. Will you pledge to the deal in order to save your friend?"

"No," Kipa said. "Raven, you can't give her an unconditional promise. That would give her carte blanche to ask you anything."

"Your lover is correct. The wolf speaks the truth. Your promise to me will be without conditions. What I ask of you in the future, you will do without question. I ask you once more. Are you willing to help your friend, or do I leave and take my advice with me?" And then her face cracked into a smile that was more hideous than the cold stare.

I felt a sob arise but pushed it down, I couldn't show fear even though she had to know I was terribly afraid. My words barely trickling out of my mouth, I said, "Tell me what I need to do to save my friend. But it better work."

"Oh, this will work. The deal is struck. There is no going back. Listen well, take notes if you want to. You must perform the ritual exactly the way I tell you. First, you must find a corpse newly dead, within forty-eight hours. It must be a fresh kill."

"Does the corpse have to be human?"

"Yes. And it must be the same sex as your friend." As Arachana proceeded to explain what I needed to do for the ritual, I took down notes on my phone. I could barely hear myself think, but I forced myself to pay attention. I had just promised an alliance that struck me cold to the bone. But there was no other choice. Beside me, Kipa was silent. I knew that he was angry, but he stood there with me, true to his word and true to me, as the Queen of Spiders wove her web and taught me how to weave mine.

AFTER ARACHANA LEFT, I SLID INTO THE CHAIR NEXT TO the folding table. I looked up at Kipa, shaking my head. "It seems like it would almost be easier to find the fylgismadi's bones and salt them. What she's telling me to do... I *work* with the dead, Kipa. I've worked with them since I was born. I'm a bone witch. But I'm not a grave robber."

"I know it's not the most desirable course of action, but I'll help you however I can. You've already given her your promise, so we might as well go through with this. At least we should be able to save Gunnar's life, and whoever's body we find, well, they'll already be dead and no longer using it."

I felt squeamish, which seemed odd, given my choice of professions. But Arachana had seemed all too gleeful as she explained what I needed to do.

"Thank you. I feel like I'm caught between a rock and a hard place."

Kipa reached across the table and took my hands in his. "I'm so sorry I got you into this. It's my fault. I should have been the one to promise Arachana a favor. In fact, if you want, I'll call her back now and offer to take your place. I can get another heart from somewhere, given she ate the last one." He grimaced.

"I know. What *was* that?" When she had finished telling me how to dislodge the fylgismadi, Arachana had snatched the heart from my hand and popped it in her mouth, chewing with an all too horrible delight. I had a feeling I'd never get that visual out of my mind.

"Do you want me to do that? Because I will."

I shook my head. "It was my decision. You tried to talk me out of it, but I decided it was something I needed to do. And since I'm the one she made the deal with, and I'm the only one of us who can cast spells like this, it's my responsibility. I keep my promises. Or at least, I try to keep my promises. But I will take you up on helping me find a fresh body."

I stood, trying to shake off the past hour, though I had a feeling my meeting with Arachana would haunt me for a long time. I washed my hands, declining to take the cooler back over to my house. Kipa rinsed it out, leaving it on the folding table. We headed back across the street, under the twinkling stars that had broken through the cloud cover.

"So what now? I want to get this done as soon as possible."

Kipa gnawed on his lip for a moment, then motioned for me to go in the house. "Let me make a couple phone calls. I'll follow you in a moment."

As I entered my home, I flipped on as many lights as I could. I was creeped out and wanted some light. Raj was watching a movie on TV, some old glamour girls comedy. He glanced up at me, and I shook my head.

"Don't even ask. You don't want to know. Just go on watching your show, and I'll tell you later."

"Raven knows best," he said nonchalantly.

I waited at the table until Kipa came in. He gave me a quick kiss, then sat beside me and leaned his elbows on the table.

"There's a funeral tomorrow morning. We can get the corpse then. We'll have to wait until they've buried him and cleared out of the cemetery, so we probably should go in tomorrow evening. Since the man died late yesterday, and he's being buried tomorrow, we should be within the time frame. Do you think that will be soon enough?"

Arachana said the corpse had to be freshly dead, within forty-eight hours. "We might be cutting it close, if we wait until night. What time did he die? Did you find out?"

"Eight P.M. last night. That gives us until eight tomorrow night. We'll be taking a chance, but if we get there at five, it should be dark. Here's hoping the storm continues. That would give us more cover."

I checked the weather forecast on my phone. "We're supposed to have another week of snow, and then the storm will pass and everything will melt off. Tomorrow night... Yes, snow. We should be good to go, but I want to be *at* the gates by five. We need plenty of time to not only dig him up, but transport him back here for the ritual. We'll have three hours. We don't have any room for error." I paused, then asked, "How's Gunnar doing? He looked worse this afternoon."

"He's trying to keep up appearances, but he's fading. The fylgismadi is sucking his energy at an incredible rate, and he doesn't have the strength to fight it off at this point."

I paused, thinking about peripheral matters. I didn't want the family of the corpse to realize that the grave had been plundered. "Do you have someone you can trust to come with us? I want to make sure the grave's filled in. I don't want to leave any signs that it was tampered with."

"I can do that, no problem. We don't need anybody else in on this." He paused. "Do you want me to stay the night?"

Tiredly, I looked over at him. I didn't have any energy left for more love play, but it would be nice to have someone by my side in the bed.

"If you can, I'd like that. I feel nerve wracked and shaken, and I really don't feel like being alone tonight."

"That settles it. I'll stay. Why don't you go take a long hot bath, and I'll clean up the kitchen. Should I feed Raj?"

"Yeah, please. I don't think I fed him supper yet. Give

him a can of cat food or tuna or whatever. And only give him *one* can! I think I will take a bath. I need to relax."

As I trudged toward the bathroom, all I could think about was how tired I was, and how much I wanted to sleep. I filled the tub, squirting a hefty amount of pumpkin spice bath gel in the water. As I sank into the bubbles, resting my head against the back of the tub, my muscles began to loosen. I didn't want to think about stealing the corpse out of the grave, or the ritual to come, or the promise I'd made to Arachana. All I wanted to think about was springtime, and flowers, and picnics in the park with Raj. As my breath began to come easier, I yawned. And then, before I realized what was happening, I fell asleep under the blanket of bubbles.

CHAPTER TWENTY-ONE

*M*orning dawned with a silvery tinge. I woke up, surprised to find myself in bed. The last thing I remembered was crawling into the bathtub. I glanced over at Kipa, who was still snoring beside me. I snuggled into his outstretched arm, pressing against him as he slumbered. The clock said it was half past six, and I wasn't ready to get up yet, even though Cerridwen was nudging me to visit my ritual room and meditate. An uneasiness crept over me as I thought about it, and I wasn't sure exactly why, but I only knew that I wasn't prepared to face her.

While I didn't have as close a relationship with Cerridwen as I did with Arawn, she was still my Lady, and when she pushed me, I listened. Begrudging the cold air, I pushed back the covers and swung my feet over the edge of the bed.

"Where you going, gorgeous?" Kipa said.

I jumped. "I thought you were still asleep!"

"I was, until a moment ago. But I woke up when you

pulled away from me. Come back to bed. It's too cold to get up yet." He patted the bed beside him, flashing me a lusty grin.

I glanced at the door, then back at Kipa. Surely Cerridwen would understand, considering it was so early in the morning and I didn't usually get up until later.

"Did you put me to bed last night?" I asked.

"Sure did. You were asleep in the tub. I dried you off and carried you to bed and you didn't wake up once. I guess you were exhausted." Again, he patted the mattress. "Come on."

Ignoring my inner prompting, I slipped back into bed and turned to him as he wrapped his arm around me. He pressed against me, and I could feel just how awake he was. With a laugh, I slid my hands under the covers, tracing the muscles of his thigh with my fingertips. He was warm and dusty and musty and intoxicating, and everything about him screamed sex. I pushed every *should* out of my mind and gave myself over to him, giggling as he slipped between my legs with a triumphant laugh.

AN HOUR LATER, I HAD TAKEN A SHOWER AND WAS dressing. Kipa was in the bathroom, singing through the spray of the shower in a language that I didn't understand. But he was on key and whatever he was singing was a merry tune.

I put on my makeup and dressed for the day ahead. I seldom wore jeans or pants of any kind, but I found a pair of leggings and slipped them on. I pulled on a pair of leather shorts over them, and then a turtleneck sweater.

With knee-high boots, and a duster, I would be warm enough for the time it took us to rob the grave.

I shuddered again as I thought about what we were planning to do. Some necromancers had no compunctions about robbing gravesites. I didn't mind gathering graveyard dust, but I drew the line at plundering helpless bodies in the ground. Granted, their spirits had usually moved on, but it still felt dirty. Oh, there were rare cases where ghosts haunted the graveyard, tethered to their bodies and bones, but in the vast majority of cases, the spirits had broken free of their mortal forms even if they hadn't broken free from the mortal plane yet. But their bodies seemed sacrosanct to me. There was something ghoulish about stealing what had once been the shell of a person, and it made me queasy to think about it.

I finished with my makeup and hustled into the kitchen, where I found Raj standing by the refrigerator.

"What do you want for breakfast?"

Raj glanced down the hallway. When he didn't see Kipa following me, he said in a soft voice, "Pancakes. Raj loves pancakes."

"Pancakes it is, then. Do you want some eggs with them, and bacon?"

Raj nodded, a goofy grin on his face. "Raj needs to go outside. Raj didn't get to go outside last night."

I groaned. "I'm so sorry, Raj. I wasn't in very good shape last night. Did you have an accident?"

"Raj held it. But Raj *really* has to go outside. Now."

I noticed he was squirming, doing his *I-have-to-tinkle* dance, so I put down the pan and followed him to the door, opening it against the blast of cold air. I fastened the chain to his collar.

"I'll be out to get you when breakfast is ready. You'll be okay?"

Raj nodded, looking anxious for me to leave. Even gargoyles liked their privacy. I blew him a kiss and returned to the kitchen. As I popped the bacon into the oven and then began to mix up the pancake batter, Kipa wandered out to the kitchen. He was dressed and I saw that he had brought a clean outfit for the day. He was barefoot, wearing a pair of indigo-wash jeans, and a Wonder Woman T-shirt. He had washed his hair and braided it back to dry.

"Aha! My woman's making me breakfast." He looked around, puzzled. "Where's Raj?"

"Outside. I forgot to let him out last night for his nightly toilette. In other words, he had to go and he had to go *quick*. I told him we'd bring him back in for breakfast."

Kipa looked around. "What can I do to help?"

"Why don't you cut up some strawberries and pineapple for a fruit salad?" I pointed to the fresh pineapple that was sitting on the counter, and the basket of berries. They weren't the best, given it was midwinter, but the pineapple would brighten their taste.

Kipa found a paring knife and a cutting board, and we worked in a comfortable silence. In fact, I was surprised by *how* comfortable I was with him, especially since it taken so long for Ulstair and me to find our rhythm.

I finished cooking a stack of pancakes and then cracked a dozen eggs into the pan. Between Raj's and Kipa's appetites, and my own, we'd easily polish off the entire spread.

While Kipa set the table, I retrieved Raj from the front. He was playing in the snow next to his house, tossing great pawfuls of it into the air and snapping at it with his jaws as it showered down over his head. I laughed, picking up a handful of the snow and packing it into a ball. As I closed in on him, Raj turned and I sent the snowball directly at him, landing it right on his forehead. I laughed again, as he sat back on his haunches using his great clumsy hands to form a loosely packed snowball and toss it toward me. I could have easily ducked out of the way but I let it hit me, smack in the face, and laughed again.

"Silly Raj. Raven loves you so much," I said as I knelt beside him. I gave him a big hug and then unfastened the chain from his collar.

He glanced over my shoulder and, seeing no one else in sight, said, "Raven loves Raj and Raj loves Raven. Raj loves snow. Raven take Raj for a walk later?" He sounded so hopeful that I nodded.

"Raven will take Raj for a walk later on. Raven has a busy evening, but we'll go for a walk in the early afternoon. Will that be okay?"

Raj nodded eagerly. "Raven take Raj for a walk! Breakfast? Raj hungry."

"Breakfast is ready. Come on, Raj, let's go have pancakes and eggs and bacon and fruit cup."

"No fruit cup for Raj. Pineapple gives Raj stomachache."

"That's right," I said as we headed in toward the table. "Pineapple gives Raj a stomachache."

KIPA HAD ERRANDS TO RUN BEFORE WE WERE TO MEET AT

the cemetery. He gave me a long kiss, then patted Raj on the head. "I'll see you later. Raj, take care of Raven." Raj's ears perked up, but he said nothing, just gazed at Kipa with a thoughtful look on his face.

After Kipa left, I took Raj for a short walk. After I returned home, I tended to the ferrets. I had just finished cleaning the cage and giving them breakfast when my phone rang. As they began to chow down on their food, I pulled out my phone and quietly closed the door behind me. I glanced at the caller ID. It was Llew.

"Llew! I'm so glad to hear from you. How are you doing?"

"Better. I thought I better call you and talk to you. We have a slight problem."

I knew exactly what the problem was. "Jordan?"

"I'm trying to calm him down, to make him realize that you had nothing to do with me getting hurt. Please don't blame him too much for things that he might have said. He was just worried that he was going to lose me."

I paused, then answered carefully. "I'm not going to lie. He hurt my feelings. I would *never* deliberately put you in harm's way. And that he believes I'm capable of that… I guess I thought we were better friends than that."

"I know. Just give me a little time. He'll come around. Are you coming to the shop this week?"

Even though I knew it was a low blow, I couldn't help myself. "Are you sure it's okay if I'm in your presence? What if Jordan finds out I'm there?"

"Raven, *please*. I know it's not fair, but put yourself in his shoes." Llew sounded so pained that I finally relented.

"I refuse to allow him to treat me this way…but yes, I

do understand. All right, I'll let you know by Thursday if I'm coming down to the shop."

"While I'm resting up here at home today I'm going to do some research. Look for anything I can find that might help the ferrets," Llew said, offering an olive branch.

"Thanks. I appreciate that. I guess I'll talk to you later." I hung up before he had a chance to say good-bye. While I did understand Jordan's position, he had made me feel like crap, and I needed time to process my own feelings.

I felt another tap on my shoulder—metaphorically speaking—and realized Cerridwen was trying to contact me. I groaned, because I knew that—whatever she had to say—it wasn't going to be pleasant. When you were pledged to the gods, you tended to get a read on their emotions. I couldn't put it off any longer, so I headed to the ritual room, girding my loins, so to speak.

As I lowered myself to the bench in front of the altar, I had barely started my prayer to invoke Arawn and Cerridwen when Cerridwen came blasting through loud and clear. I could see her in the orb staring at me, her eyes blazing.

"How *dare* you make an alliance without my permission?" Oh, she was pissed, all right.

" I was just trying to help Gunnar—"

"You will *break* that alliance as soon as possible. You are *not* to put yourself in that creature's debt. Do you understand me? I don't care who it's for or why you did it. And don't think Arawn will buck me on this matter. I have spoken." The words came lashing through my thoughts loud and clear.

Her anger reverberated through me and I felt like I'd

been slapped. I knew better than to argue, especially when she was this aggravated.

"I understand. I don't know how I can get out of this, though, but I'll try."

"You'll do *more* than try. You *will* break the deal. You are to tell that creature that you are no longer bound by a debt, and that you are forbidden to have any dealings with her."

"What about Gunnar? I know the spell to release him now." I knew I was taking a chance asking her when she was this angry, but I had to.

"I don't care what you do about Gunnar. But you *will* break off your alliance with Arachana or you'll face my wrath. And you do not want to face the anger of the Cauldron."

With that, she vanished as quickly as she had arrived. I reeled, nauseated from the force of her impact. I swallowed hard. How the hell was I going to do this? I had already learned the spell, there was no way I could just give information back, and even if there was, I had the feeling that wouldn't appease Arachana. I needed help, and I wasn't sure where to look for it.

CHAPTER TWENTY-TWO

*B*y the time Kipa returned, shovels in hand, I had decided to go through with the ritual anyway. I might as well, given I knew the spell to break the fylgismadi's hold. But then I would have to sever my connections with Arachana, and for that I would need *another* heart, along with a slim hope in hell that I'd make it through alive.

"Are you all right?" Kipa asked, taking one look at me and dropping the shovels on the floor.

"Not exactly. I know this sounds nuts, but I need to ask you to bring me a new heart." I sank into one of the chairs by the dining table, covering my face with my hands. "I really screwed up. I fucked up royal this time and I'm in trouble. When I made the alliance with Arachana I didn't ask for Cerridwen's permission. She just read me the riot act beyond all riot acts. I have to get out of my promise or she's going to come down hard on me."

Kipa grimaced. "I'm not even going to bother to ask if

you tried to explain. When Cerridwen makes up her mind, she makes up her mind. Even I know enough about her to know that you don't make a misstep in her presence. What do you want to do now? Are you going to go through with the ritual?"

"Yeah, I might as well. I know the spell now and there's no giving the knowledge back. Somehow I doubt that even if I promised Arachana that I wouldn't cast it that she would be willing to wipe out my debt. We'll perform the ritual before I talk to her, but I can't wait too long or Cerridwen will skin me alive."

"Then let's get it over with. You know I'll do my best to help you, and if you want, I can try to have a talk with Cerridwen. She doesn't know me very well, but maybe it will help?"

I loved that he was offering to put himself on the line for me, but I shook my head.

"I can't let you fight my battles for me, not with my goddess. I'm pledged to her and I should have thought first. When Arawn gave me the info on who to contact, I didn't even bother thinking that Cerridwen might have objections. I've worked with them both long enough that I should have known better. I should have consulted both of them at the same time. This is my mistake. I have to own up to it." Feeling jarred, I followed Kipa out the door after making sure Raj was settled in with some snacks.

The drive to the cemetery was quiet. Kipa kept his eyes on the road, trying to avoid skidding on the thick ice underneath the car tires. I stared out the window, contemplating my choices. I could try to offer Arachana something else in place of a favor. Something tangible that would wipe out my debt. I wasn't sure she'd go for it, but it was the only option I could think of.

Sunset hit as we were on the road and, because the skies were clear, the evening suddenly seemed very dark. The storm had lit up the sky for the past couple weeks, keeping it tinged with pale silver, but now that the clouds had parted, the ambient light was gone.

The cemetery that Kipa was taking us to was located out toward Woodinville, near TirNaNog. As we eased into the parking lot, I was glad to see that the gates were still open, but there were no other cars. If we were lucky, visitors would remain at home. The fewer people around, the better, especially given we were about to do something that was against the law.

We had one piece of good luck: the fresh grave was near the parking lot. It was behind a tall cedar, a hundred or so yards away from where we had parked the car. As we trudged our way through the snow, breaking a new trail, I glanced around. Sure enough, the cemetery was empty except for some of the spirits hanging out near the graves. We passed one tombstone and the spirit sitting on top of it looked up at me, a blurry vision of a skeleton dressed in clothes that had come from another century. I paused, then tapped Kipa on the arm.

"Wait for a second. I want to check something out." I headed over to that tombstone, kneeling and flashing my phone flashlight on it. Sure enough, the person buried here had died in 1892. The cemetery was one of the older ones in the area, then. I glanced up as the spirit looked at me quizzically.

"Can you hear me?" I asked.

The spirit cocked its head—I thought it was male,

given the looks of its clothing—but made no other sign that it understood me. It sat there on the headstone, seeming content. Part of me wanted to free it right here and now, to help the man go on to his other journeys. But that wasn't what we were here for tonight. I made a mental note to come back and go through the graveyard at some point, freeing the spirits who were still tied to their graves.

I rejoined Kipa, shaking my head when he started to ask why we had stopped.

"I was just checking out something. Nothing to worry about."

The newly dug grave had been covered by only a trace of snow throughout the day. If he had been buried this morning, then it looked like we'd only had about a quarter inch of snow during the day. But the deeper snow was banked to the sides, except for one flat spot where the diggers had piled the graveyard dirt so they could bury the casket. That gave us a place to put the dirt as we dug up the corpse, without anyone questioning. Kipa started to dig and I followed suit, doing my best to help him. He was a lot faster and stronger than I was, though, and before too long, we were staring down into the grave at the coffin.

"How are we going to get it open, or do we have to get the casket up here somehow?" Lifting the coffin out of the grave wouldn't be easy, that much was for sure.

Kipa twisted his lips. "Give me a moment. I'm going to jump down in there to see what we can do. I can probably open the casket if the wood's not too hard, and no one will ever be the wiser."

He handed me his bag of tools, and as I held them, he

climbed down into the grave, landing on top of the casket. He knelt, examining it under the glow of his flashlight. After a moment he stood and looked up at me.

"Hand me down my crowbar and a claw hammer, carefully."

I knelt by the side of the grave, lowering down the crowbar and hammer. He reached up and caught hold of the tools, and then knelt on top of the casket again. I could tell he was doing something, though it was hard to tell just what from where I was, but soon I heard the noise of splintering as he pried nails out from around the rim. Another moment and he scooted down lower on the coffin and opened the headpiece.

That was right, I thought. A lot of caskets had two parts to the lid.

Kipa shifted, extracting the body from the coffin. He motioned to me again.

"Rope!"

I dropped down the rope that was coiled in his bag. He tied one end of the rope around the waist of the corpse, then wrapped the other end around his own waist and scampered up and out of the grave.

"Well, this isn't so difficult. All I had to do was pry the nails up from where they had tacked them down. I'm going to pull him up, then I'll go down and close the casket, get my tools, and we'll be on our way."

He hauled up the body, stretching the man out on the dirt that we had piled to the side from the grave. Then, he jumped back in, retrieved his tools, closed the casket lid, and returned topside.

"Let's get him into the trunk, and then we'll come back and fill in the grave."

As Kipa slung the body over his shoulder, I peeked around the giant cedar to make sure we were still the only ones in the graveyard. The cemetery was still empty, so I quickly led the way back to the car and opened the trunk. We had stretched out a tarp inside the trunk, and now he lay the body on the tarp and gently covered the man with a blanket. I locked the trunk as Kipa headed back toward the grave, cautioning me to stay with the car. Fifteen minutes later, he returned, covered in loose dirt and snow.

"I filled in the grave and it looks like it did when we found it. I don't think anyone will ever notice. I made sure to cover the grave with a thin layer of snow, so it looks untouched. If we get any more snow in the next day or two, there shouldn't be any problem. And by the time it melts off, enough people will have walked around the area so no one should have any clue that we were ever here, or that the corpse isn't where he's supposed to be."

Grateful that the family wouldn't have any idea we had stolen the corpse, I started the car and we drove back to my place. Only I parked in Buck's driveway. Once again, I kept watch while Kipa quickly carried the body into what was now his house. Then, locking the trunk, I followed him in.

He had laid the body out on the floor. "We have to wait for Gunnar, so why don't you get everything ready to start with. He should be here soon. I gave him a call."

Nodding, I retrieved my bag of ritual implements from the car and set them up. The ritual wasn't difficult, though it wasn't one I would have ever thought of on my own. I would trap the fylgismadi into the corpse, and then when it took over the corpse and rose, we would destroy

the body. That would free the fylgismadi to go do whatever it wanted, but it would never be able to harm Gunnar
again.

The actual transfer wouldn't be difficult. I had brought
with me a small quartz crystal and my mandrake root. All
I would have to do was place the quartz on the sigil that
was emblazoned on Gunnar's neck and instruct my
mandrake to attack the fylgismadi. That would drive it
into the crystal. Then, I'd place the crystal on the corpse
and the spirit would attach itself to the fresh body. I'd
have to move quickly, though, so the fylgismadi wouldn't
try to return to Gunnar before the ritual was complete.
Luckily, the mandrake root I had was an old one, crafty
and cunning and powerful. I had received it from a
powerful witch when I was young, and the mandrake had
been old even then.

Once I was ready, I glanced at Kipa, who was looking
out the window into the driveway.

"Gunnar just drove up. You're ready for this?"

"I'm as ready as I'll ever be. Are you prepared to take
on the corpse?"

"Yeah, I am. I just want this over with. If only Gunnar
hadn't been so stupid as to admit fault in front of Kristian,
we wouldn't be in this mess. Solveig's father could have
taken Gunnar before the tribunal, but they wouldn't have
found him at fault. But no, he had to run off at the mouth
and cause all this havoc."

I was getting tired of beating a dead horse. "Yeah, but
he was probably feeling so much guilt that he couldn't
help it. People do, you know. Whatever the case, we're
here now, and if we play this right, he'll be free."

"Yes, I know that." He paused, then said, "I suppose

what bothers me most is that my Elitvartijat are supposed to have control over their emotions. And Gunnar didn't. One of the easiest vulnerabilities for an enemy to attack is family. And while this wasn't an enemy, so to speak, it still broke Gunnar's focus and ability to concentrate. This will be the last time I choose a family man to be on my team. All of the other members of my guard are single, and I think I'm going to institute that as a rule. When you have a family, you're vulnerable."

I jerked my head up, staring at him for a moment. I wondered if he felt that way about us. Was I a liability because he cared about me? But this was neither the time nor place to ask.

He hurried Gunnar into the house, and one look at the SuVahta told me that I was doing the right thing. I might catch hell from Cerridwen, but Gunnar was definitely on his way out unless something was done, and done quick.

"I'm ready," Gunnar said. "What do I do?"

"Lie down beside the corpse, on your stomach, but leaving some space. I know it's not pleasant, but the sooner we get this done with the better." I decided not to tell him about my encounter with Cerridwen. I didn't want him feeling guilty over this as well.

Gunnar stretched out beside the body. "What next?"

"Next, I want your promise that you will never again claim the blame for Solveig's death. I'm not going to perform this ritual a second time." Though it occurred to me that, now, I knew a powerful spell, and I knew how to deal with fylgismadi. Something I would not have known if all of this hadn't happened.

"Thank you," he said. "I promise."

I motioned for Kipa to stand next to the corpse. "Gunnar, as soon as I tell you, I need you to roll away. Be quick about it. Do you understand? You must be at least an arm's length or more away from the corpse as soon as I give you the word."

"I understand," came the muffled reply.

The ritual didn't require many accoutrements, no candles, no salt or sand. I preferred spells with few props. They were much easier to focus on, and easier to prepare for. I sat on the floor between Gunnar and the corpse, and glanced up at Kipa.

"Are you ready?"

"I'm ready. Do you need to cast a Circle?"

"Apparently not. Arachana didn't include it in the instructions. Since I wasn't told to, I'm going to leave it, so that I don't inadvertently muddy up the energy." I let out a slow breath as I moved Gunnar's braid to expose the sigil. I held out the quartz crystal. "Gunnar, I'm going to press a crystal against your neck, onto the sigil. I want you to stay very still for a moment."

"Should I think of anything in particular?"

"No. Just wait for my signal." I took a deep breath, then pressed the quartz against Gunnar's neck, directly over the symbol that linked the fylgismadi to the SuVahta. A *thrum* of energy raced through my fingers as I began the chant that Arachana had taught me.

> *Spirit that wanders, spirit that yearns,*
> *spirit that journeys, spirit that burns.*
> *Into the crystal, I evict thee,*
> *your work is done, your target free.*

There was a sudden rush, and a cold wave of energy

pulsed around my hand holding the crystal. The fylgis-madi had been sucked into the quartz. I yanked it off of Gunnar and slammed it down on the corpse next to him.

"Roll out of the way now, Gunnar. Hurry."

Gunnar rolled out of the way, and kept rolling.

I returned my attention to the corpse. I focused all of my energy into the crystal.

> *Spirit captured, wandering one,*
> *another journey you've begun.*
> *Into this body I command thee,*
> *until by death you are set free.*

The crystal shattered and the energy from the spirit—the fylgismadi—dove into the body, no doubt expecting to piggyback another living being. Instead, it found itself locked in a corpse.

Kipa pulled out his sword as the body flinched, and then lurched, rising to a sitting position.

"Now, before it stands or it will be as hard to fight as a zombie!"

Kipa thrust his sword toward the corpse, whose eyes were gleaming with a terrible light. The fylgismadi was angry and confused.

As the tip of Kipa's sword met the skull of the corpse, it cleaved smoothly through the body. Thanks to our grave robbing, there was no blood. The corpse had already been drained by the undertaker. The sword exited smoothly through the back of the skull.

I grimaced as a shriek echoed through the kitchen. The corpse dropped its head back, opening its mouth as a thin gray mist exited from its throat. The mist spun around the room shrieking again, and then darted out the nearest window, right through the glass. The window shattered as the corpse fell to the ground.

"Wow," I said, staring at the body. I had expected more of a fight, and yet, it made sense that there wasn't, given the fylgismadi hadn't had time to fully integrate itself into the corpse. If I hadn't had Kipa with me, things would have been far more difficult. I turned to Gunnar, who was pressed up against the wall, watching us with wide eyes. "How are you doing?"

Gunnar swallowed, then shrugged. "I don't know. I feel lighter, though."

I crawled over to his side, and motioned for him to lean his head forward. As I slipped his hair away, I saw that the sigil that had been against the back of his neck was gone. He was free.

"Well, that's taken care of. You should be all right now. Get lots of rest, and whatever you do, don't go near your father-in-law. As I said earlier, I'm not going to help you again if you're stupid enough to go back for more." I was too tired and worried to be tactful. I might have been able to dislodge the fylgismadi, but I still had to face Arachana and tell her I was bailing on our deal.

CHAPTER TWENTY-THREE

*B*y morning, I wasn't feeling any more hopeful. Kipa had left early, waking me only to tell me that he would return with a fresh heart as soon as he could. Cerridwen was sitting on my shoulder, her displeasure burning a hole through me. I could practically feel her tapping her nails on the top of my head. I didn't have the leeway to wait, to take my time and figure out how to approach Arachana. When the gods fiddled, you danced.

I had just finished cleaning the ferrets' room, when the doorbell rang. I hurried to answer, hoping it was Kipa. Instead, it was Gunnar. He handed me a cooler.

"Kipa got called in by Herne on an emergency. He asked me to drop by with this. He said you needed it right away." The SuVahta looked much better this morning. "I wanted to thank you again for what you did for me. I'm going to leave the country tomorrow. I fly out to Finland at dawn. But I wanted to make sure that you knew how much I appreciated your help."

I smiled. Gunnar didn't need to know about the mess

I'd gotten myself in. He didn't need any more guilt than he was already carrying.

"Just promise me that you won't blame yourself for Solveig's death anymore. And promise me you won't go back to her father. Because next time, he might not be so subtle in his attempts to kill you."

He gave me a rueful smile and nodded. "I promise you —everything you ask. I got the message finally. Kipa warned me that I would be inviting trouble if I talked to Kristian and I didn't listen. I didn't realize how angry he would be at me, but next time—if there is a next time—I'll listen to advice." He glanced at his watch. "All right, I need to go home and pack. I've got to get out of here before Kristian realizes that I'm not on my deathbed anymore." He motioned to the cooler. "I'm not sure what that's for, but Kipa asked me to tell you to be careful when you use it. He said you'd know what I mean."

I laughed. "I'll be as careful as I can. Thanks, Gunnar. Have a good trip and fly safely."

As I shut the door, my mind went back to Arachana. I should probably perform the ritual over at Buck's old house. Kipa had forgotten to leave me a key, but I could try the window that was broken during the ritual to get in. It wouldn't be safe to bring Arachana in my house, especially with Cerridwen already on my ass about her. I weighed my options, then went to find my lock picks. At one time, I'd been fairly skilled at picking locks, though I hadn't had much call to do so for a long time. Kipa wouldn't mind, as long as I didn't tear up the door.

Ten minutes later, I had managed to get into the house. It felt very different during the day, though no safer, especially since I was alone. I set the cooler down on the table, biting my lip. I had no idea how to approach Arachana, so I decided that I'd just tell the truth. When in doubt, that was usually the best direction to take. I thought about casting a Circle, but I didn't want to be trapped inside it with Arachana.

First, though, I texted Kipa: I'M ABOUT TO CONTACT ARACHANA. I'M USING YOUR HOUSE. I HOPE YOU DON'T MIND.

I WISH I COULD BE THERE. BUT HERNE HAD AN EMERGENCY AND I NEED TO HELP. LET ME KNOW WHEN YOU'RE DONE AND HOW IT WENT. IF YOU REALLY NEED ME, CALL AND I'LL DO MY BEST TO GET OUT OF WORK TODAY.

I SHOULD BE OKAY. AT LEAST, I HOPE SO. I'LL TEXT YOU WHEN I'M DONE.

To be honest, I was nervous. I wanted Kipa by my side, even though I knew that there probably wasn't a lot he could do against Arachana.

I opened the cooler and peeked in. Apparently, we were going to be eating a whole lot of ham and bacon because there was another pig's heart in a pool of blood. I had dressed for the occasion this time, wearing an old grungy tank top and a skirt that was about five years old and had seen better days. I had Venom in my boot sheath, but I wasn't convinced my blade would do any good. Arachana was a spider queen, and somehow I had the feeling that my venom wouldn't work against her.

I lifted the heart out, holding it out in front of me. With a deep breath, I tried to steady my nerves. After a moment, I closed my eyes and said, "Arachana. Arachana. Arachana."

There was a shimmer in the air. I steeled myself as a black wisp of smoke appeared, and then, the wisp grew into a cloud and a figure appeared in it. It was Arachana, all right, the ancient crone herself. Her eyes gleamed through the smoke. She waved her hand and the clouds dissipated, leaving her in full form before me. I shuddered. She was even more terrifying now that I could see all of her.

She had six arms, like I had seen the night before, her face withered and parched, a roadmap of time and trickery, a thousand wrinkles forming her features. But her eyes gleamed clear and crisp through the ravines and hills of her face, and I was more frightened of her today than I had been before. Today she was wearing a long black robe with red markings on the belly.

"And so, Raven BoneTalker, you call me forth again. Another favor, perhaps?" She sounded greedy, and she was eyeing the heart in my hand like she hadn't eaten in days.

"Not exactly. I'm not sure how to tell you this and I know you're not going to want to hear it. But I have a problem. You know that I'm pledged to Arawn and Cerridwen?"

A suspicious light filled her eyes, and she cocked her head to one side. "Arawn I knew, but Cerridwen? Cerridwen, I did not know."

The way she spat out Cerridwen's name made me think she already had an idea of what I was about to say, and *that* made me even more nervous.

"Well, it's this way. When Cerridwen found out I made a deal with you, she blew up at me. She demanded that I break off our deal and repay you some other way. Some *tangible* way. I'm not allowed to offer you unconditional favors. I'm so sorry. I didn't know that she would react this way. Truly, I didn't."

Arachana stepped forward, her face a mask of anger. Even through the wrinkles, I could see she was livid.

"Girl, you play with fire when you play with me. You expect me to let you out of our deal? Perhaps you should have thought to consult Cerridwen *before* you asked for my help, *before* you begged a favor from me. You have the knowledge that I traded to you. There's no going back from that. So what would you have me do? How would you repay me?"

"I don't know. I can bring you money. Crystals." I wasn't about to offer her food because I had the feeling she'd ask for it alive, and I wasn't going to be that cruel.

"*What do I need with money?* And I am no witch. I don't work with crystals and stones. I exist within the realm of blood and death and fear. Try again."

I stared at her helplessly, not knowing what to say. Several times I started to speak, but then caught my tongue because whatever I thought to say seemed like it would be just asking for trouble. If I offered her blood, she would probably ask for it on the vein. If I offered her death, she would probably demand that I bring her a sacrifice. As for fear, well, I was feeding her plenty of that.

"All right, then I tell you this. Money is so important in your world—the world of humans. But I prefer gems. Those I might find some use for. Sell your home. Convert every last penny you get for it into rubies. That, I claim as my price."

I caught my breath. Surely she couldn't be asking for everything I owned?

"You've got to be kidding. We needed the spell, yes.

You helped us. And for that I am ever grateful. I would have kept my promise if Cerridwen would let me. But now you are asking for every single thing I own? That's ridiculous. How can you be so greedy?" I knew it wasn't the best route to argue with her, but what else was I to do? I couldn't sell my house and give her everything. She was being petty and vindictive.

"I will give you ten thousand dollars in rubies. Even twenty thousand. That I can just manage. But to ask for every single thing I have—*no*."

She laughed, but it wasn't a pleasant laugh. "Oh, girl. You have just made the mistake of your life. I cannot refuse to let you out of the deal, given the order comes from Cerridwen. But you owe me, and by the time I'm done with you, you'll wish you *had* sold your house."

Apparently, my negotiating skills lacked refinement. "What do you mean? What are you talking about?"

"You will see, Raven my dear. *You will see*." And then, before I could stop her, she snatched the heart and stuffed it into her mouth, blood and gristle spewing out the sides of her lips as she gnashed her way through it. Queasy, I turned aside. But before I could say another word, the air shimmered around her and once again she vanished.

I knew I was in trouble. I just wasn't sure how bad it would be, but I wasn't about to place any bets.

I WAS STILL TRYING TO DECIDE WHETHER TO CANCEL MY readings at the Sun and Moon Apothecary the next day when Raj came racing into the living room. Raj seldom raced anywhere, so I put down my e-reader and turned to see what he was up to.

"What's going on? What are you doing?"

"Raj saw a big spider in the bathroom." He blinked. Raj liked to sleep in the hall bathroom sometimes, curling up on the rug in front of the bathtub.

"So? We get a lot of spiders. You know, those giant European house spiders. I'm not fond of them, but they don't hurt anything."

The giant European house spider was common in the Pacific Northwest, often racing around the house during the late summer and early autumn months during the mating season. They were the second-fastest spider in the world, and had a leg expanse up to four inches or more. But on the plus side, they ate the venomous hobo spiders, and they helped keep the bug population down. I put them outside whenever I found them, unless they startled me so much that I swatted them first.

"No. Raj has never seen a spider like this. It's big." He gave me a long look, and I realized that he really was nervous.

I followed him into the bathroom. I was expecting to see a wolf spider, given they were as large or larger than the house spiders. They were also more fractious. But there, on the bath rug, was a freaking tarantula.

My stomach lurched. I wasn't fond of tarantulas, either. Granted, they weren't terribly venomous—at least toward humans—but it shouldn't be there. We didn't have tarantulas in the area.

"You're right. That's a tarantula, Raj. We don't have those around here." I stared at the cobalt blue body. It was pretty in a creepy way, but I wasn't in the mood to deal with anything like this today. And how had it gotten in my house?

"Raven take it away?" Raj shifted from foot to foot, sitting back on his haunches and shivering.

"I'm not sure what to do with it. If I put it outside it will probably die. I wonder if it's somebody's pet." I had a sneaking suspicion where it had come from, but I didn't want to tell Raj, and I could be wrong. "I'll catch it and then make a couple calls."

I hurried back into the kitchen, Raj following close behind me. Finding a mason jar and lid, and a stiff piece of cardboard, I returned to the bathroom. As I knelt near the spider, it recoiled, showing its fangs.

"Okay, little guy, listen to me. You don't belong here. Cooperate and you'll stay alive." I set the jar in front of it, at an angle so it could crawl in. Then, using the cardboard to propel it, I herded the spider into the jar. I brought the jar up, keeping the cardboard on top until I could screw on the lid. Then I carried it into the kitchen where I found a screwdriver to punch a couple holes in the lid. Now, what to do with the creature?

I pulled out my phone, remembering that I had meant to text Kipa.

HEY, I HAD A SITUATION WITH ARACHANA. SHE'S PISSED AT ME. SHE THREATENED ME. WILL TELL YOU MORE ABOUT IT LATER BUT FIRST, CAN YOU TELL ME WHAT I SHOULD DO WITH THE TARANTULA THAT I JUST FOUND IN MY BATHROOM?

A few seconds later, Kipa texted back. TARANTULA? WHAT THE HELL WAS A TARANTULA DOING IN YOUR BATH-ROOM? DID YOU CATCH IT?

YES. I CAUGHT IT IN A JAR. I HAVE NO IDEA WHAT IT'S

DOING THERE, THOUGH I DO HAVE MY SUSPICIONS. CAN YOU CALL ME? OR CAN I CALL YOU?

UNFORTUNATELY, I'M IN THE MIDDLE OF CHASING A GOBLIN. I'VE GOT TO GO. JUST KEEP IT IN THE JAR FOR A LITTLE WHILE AND I'LL CALL BACK WHEN I CAN.

I sighed, setting my phone down on the counter. As I turned to the jar, staring at the tarantula, I had the distinct feeling that I was being watched.

"Raj, be sure you tell Raven if you see anything else like this. And don't try to eat them." Sometimes Raj caught and ate bugs around the house. Normally I'd be fine with it, but I had no idea whether this was a magical spider, or just some ordinary tarantula that had somehow gotten in my house.

It made me uncomfortable to have the creature sitting on my counter watching everything, so I found a plastic storage container that was big enough to hold the jar and set the jar inside of that, placing the lid ajar so that it could still get enough air. Then, I made quick rounds around the house, looking for anything else out of the ordinary. Satisfied that, at present, things were normal, I returned to my book, wishing Kipa would call back.

AN HOUR LATER, I HEARD A COMMOTION FROM THE ferrets' room. Usually they were pretty quiet, so whenever I heard them chattering, I knew something was up. I headed toward their room. As I got closer to the door, a sense of foreboding came over me, and I rushed ahead, throwing the door open wide.

Elise was standing up to the door of the cage,

shrieking as Templeton and Gordon hid behind her. On the floor and on the walls was what I could only describe as a swarm of spiders. They were large and hairy. Not tarantulas, but wolf spiders, and there must have been close to a hundred of them crawling around.

"Oh fuck."

I might not mind spiders but I sure as hell didn't like swarms of *anything*. And wolf spiders could land a nasty bite on a person. They wouldn't kill anybody, but their bites weren't a breeze, either. I raced back to the laundry room, where I grabbed the vacuum, lugging it back to the ferrets' room. I plugged it in and began sucking up every spider I could see. Some of them raced beneath the cage while others skittered along the walls, but I got as many as I could to clear the way to the door of the cage.

I hurried to the closet where I kept the ferrets' carriers that I used when I needed to take them to the vet. I checked inside to make sure they were clear, then quickly transferred Elise, Templeton, and Gordon into them. Then, carrying the carriers out to the dining room, I put them on the table and hustled back to their room.

I did what I could to suck up as many of the spiders that I could see, and then carried the vacuum out to the backyard to my fire pit. I slogged through the snow, opening up the vacuum and gingerly tossing the bag into the brick pit. A couple spiders skittered across my hand as they tried to escape, and I shook them onto the snow. Holding out my hand, I focused on conjuring fire, a large, substantial fireball, and sent it zooming to the bag. It caught fire, flaring up, toasting all of the spiders. I shook out the vacuum, then hurried back to the house. I wasn't worried about the firepit, since there was enough snow around that any stray sparks would be extinguished immediately.

As I entered the house, Raj was on the sofa, pointing toward the loveseat. Dreading what I might see, I turned and looked. There was another cobalt blue tarantula.

"Come on, Raj. Bring me your leash."

He raced off toward his bed and came back yelping, the leash in hand.

"Raj doesn't like spiders. There is a spider in Raj's bed like that one," he said, pointing toward the tarantula.

"I'm sorry, Raj. We'll get out of here right now." I grabbed my purse, and tossed it on the floor when another tarantula crawled out of it. I upended it, shaking it out and then scooping everything back in that wasn't a spider.

By now, I could see several more blue tarantulas milling around the room. Grateful that the carriers were soft bags with shoulder straps, I slung the ferrets over my shoulder, grabbed my purse and keys, made sure I had my phone, and took hold of Raj's leash.

We headed out the door. I knew exactly where we were going to wait. I'd gotten into Buck's house without a problem earlier. If there were no spiders over there, that was where I was headed. Crossing the street, I looked back at my house, wanting to cry. Arachana had threatened that I'd regret not selling. Now I knew what she meant. Feeling at a loss, I led Raj over to the house and jimmied the door open again. As I entered, I glanced around. There was no sign of any spiders, and the house was quiet. Setting the carriers down, I slid into one of the folding chairs by the table to text Kipa. What the fuck was I going to do now?

CHAPTER TWENTY-FOUR

I was waiting for Kipa to text me back when my phone rang. The jangle of Black Sabbath's "Lady Evil" echoed in the empty kitchen. It was my mother. I picked up immediately.

"Hey, what's up?" I wasn't sure I wanted to tell her what was going on, but if she was on her way over, I was going to have to. I had no doubt that Phasmoria would be just as happy as Cerridwen had been.

"I'm standing in your driveway. I rang the bell but there's no answer. Your car's here. When will you be home?"

I groaned, rubbing my forehead. "Come across the street, Mother. I have a few things that I have to tell you. Trust me, you don't want to go inside my house right now, not before you know what's going on." I had visions of an old William Shatner movie, *Kingdom Of The Spiders*, running through my head.

"Well, then. I'm looking forward to the story." She hung up without saying good-bye. That was par for the course. I opened the door to find Phasmoria already standing on the porch, waiting.

My mother, when she took human form, was a striking woman. Just over five-eight, she was muscled, with an hourglass figure a lot like mine. Her hair hung down to her waist, longer than mine, and it was black with silver streaks. She was wearing a pair of black jeans and a black leather jacket, and her features were chiseled and angular. In some ways she was a beautiful woman, and in other ways, she gave off a terrifying aura. I wasn't exactly frightened of her, but even in her human form, any mortals who met her would feel a sense of threat or dread when they were near her. Needless to say, she didn't hang out with humans much.

I held out my hands and she took them. I didn't kiss her—we weren't familiar like that. But I squeezed her hands and nodded over my shoulder.

"Come on into my temporary abode." I let her into the empty kitchen.

She glanced around, her gaze landing on the ferrets in their carriers, and then Raj. She liked Raj, although he tended to avoid her as much as possible. But she always brought him a special treat, and she always brought the ferrets treats as well. As odd as it seemed, my mother the Bean Sidhe was an ardent animal lover. That was how she had met my father. She met him when he was in dog form, and chased him to pet him. He had turned back into himself at that point.

Phasmoria set down her purse on the table and turned to me, her arms crossed. "All right, what's going on?"

I felt like squirming, like the little kid who knew they

were in for a scolding. "Do you remember when I asked you about Arachana?"

She dropped into the nearest chair. "Oh, Raven. You *didn't*?"

"I may have."

"Why would you call on someone like that? I told you she was dangerous."

"Believe me, I had good reasons. Good intentions, I guess. But after we made a deal, Cerridwen chewed me up one side and down the other and told me to break it. I offered Arachana what I thought would be a fair settlement. She didn't agree."

Phasmoria closed her eyes, shaking her head. "Well, that was stupid. But you've always been headstrong, to the point of being a pain in the ass. Well, then…tell me the whole thing. What did Arachana do when you told her you were breaking the deal?"

Stuttering at first and nervous as hell, I told my mother everything that had happened, ending with the spider invasion in my house.

She stared at me blankly, then shook her head and let out an impatient sigh. "Girl, you've really got yourself into trouble this time, haven't you? Honestly. Sometimes I think you should move back to Connecticut, to live with your father until you've learned more about life. I don't really believe that you're old enough to be on your own yet."

"That's not going to happen and you know it. I love Curikan, but Mother, I *can't* move back home with him. I love where I'm at. I love what I'm doing. I have a life here, and friends, and a job that I'm good at. Yes, sometimes I do make mistakes. But how else am I going to learn?"

We'd had this argument a number of times before, although never about quite such a volatile subject. Phasmoria might not be a helicopter parent in any fashion of the word, but she made her opinions known, whether or not I wanted to hear them.

Phasmoria motioned to Raj, holding out his treat. He bounced over, took it, and gave her a quick lick on the hand before returning to the spot near the heating vent.

"I suppose you need help to handle this? I mean, you aren't going to sell your house, are you? That's ridiculous and I won't stand by and see you bullied by that old freak of a crone. She's powerful, but I'm stronger."

"I don't think the offer is still on the table, to be honest. I have no idea what she wants now, except cause me as much of a headache as possible." I paused. Then, even though I didn't want to, I asked, "Can you help me?"

Those four words were incredibly difficult for me to say. I hated asking my parents for help. I always felt so young and so stupid when I did. And almost always, it was because I had leapt before I looked. And this time was no exception.

Phasmoria smiled, looking oddly pleased. "Of course. I will do everything I can. I'm not about to see my daughter homeless on the streets just because of a greedy spider queen. How do we get in touch with her?"

At that moment, the door opened and Kipa came rushing through, yet another cooler in hand. Before he noticed Phasmoria standing there, he pulled me to him and gave me a long kiss.

"I got here as quickly as I could. I brought another heart. Let's contact Arachana. I'll give her all the gold she wants if she'll leave you alone. Don't argue with me. I'm not about to let you sell your house or be driven out. I have plenty of money."

Before I could say a word, Phasmoria stepped forward, tapped Kipa on the shoulder, and held out her hand.

"And you must be Kuippana, I assume? I'm Phasmoria, Raven's mother. It's good to meet you, Lord of the Wolves."

Kipa turned around, very carefully and very slowly. He stared at my mother for a moment, and then accepted her outstretched hand.

"*Madame Valiant*, I'm honored to make your acquaintance." He gave her a subtle bow, definitely discernible as a mark of respect.

All the banshees used the title of *Madame Valiant* in public. It was an honorarium granted to them by the Morrígan, and even the gods used it.

"Lord of the Wolves, well met. So you are my daughter's beau? I would love to hear how you met, when we have more time." She glanced at the cooler. "I assume you had your part in the situation with Arachana?"

He nodded. "It was my fault from the beginning. Raven was just trying to help save the life of one of my SuVahta. I involved her, not realizing what was going to happen, and she got caught in the crossfire."

"So I understand. Collateral damage, you might say. I guarantee you this, Kuippana. If I had known she was talking about herself when she first asked me about Arachana, she would not be in this position, regardless of your friend's difficulties. I would have outright forbade her to have any dealings with the creature. The ancient Ante-Fae are treacherous, and most of them have ulterior motives and work on private agendas. You do realize that

Arachana is closer to being one of the Luo'henkah than one of my own kind."

The Luo'henkah were forces of nature, elemental beings captured in an immortal form. They were the spirits inherent within the elements, the seasons, or creatures.

I turned to my mother. "That would make sense. She seems so alien."

"When you asked about her, I had my suspicions something of this sort might happen, so I looked into her background. Arachana helped Grandmother Spider weave the world thread, but then they had a falling-out. Grandmother Spider turned her out of her service, exiling her. Arachana is nearing the place where she's almost immortal. Some of the Ante-Fae do make the transition, you know. Some of the most ancient ones. They become forces outside of the reach of mortals of any kind."

"We saw one of the Luo'henkah born last month. The Cailleach birthed her. Lady Brighid gave her the name of Isella, the Daughter of Ice." I bit my lip. Sometimes I could get myself in a shitload of trouble without meaning to. If I had done more due diligence, I would have found out the true nature of Arachana's power.

"Then you are familiar with just how strong these beings can be." Phasmoria crossed back to the table, sitting down as she stared at the cooler. "You have brought a heart to summon her?"

"Yes, as I told Raven, since this was my doing, I planned to offer the full amount of gold Arachana might ask for from your daughter. I'm so sorry that I got her involved in this." Kipa looked more remorseful than I'd ever seen him look. He knew my mother was a Bean

Sidhe and what havoc she could wreak, even when it came to the gods.

"Oh, she's *not* getting gold. Not from Raven, and not from you. She will get a fair settlement, yes. But she will get nothing more. I will warn you both, however, Kuippana—you seem just as reckless as my daughter—neither one of you will ever have anything to do with Arachana again. Do you both understand?"

The sight of my mother scolding Kipa almost made me laugh, or it would have if this hadn't been so serious.

"I understand," I said, nodding. "I give you my word."

Kipa stared at my mother for a moment, then said, "I appreciate your help, Phasmoria. I don't know if I can give you my word of honor, but I do promise I'll do my best to avoid Arachana from here on out. That's the best I can offer. We never know what the future holds."

Phasmoria considered his words for a moment. "If that is your best, it will have to do. But if you *ever* involve my daughter in anything like this again, I swear, I will shriek for you. The gods may be immortal, but I can make you *hurt*. Don't forget it."

My mother straightened her shoulders, and she was suddenly standing there in front of us, well over seven feet tall. Like all the Bean Sidhe, she had the ability to change her appearance at will, and she made use of it as necessary.

"I understand. I won't forget." Kipa gave her a solemn nod.

"Then here's what we're going to do. Prepare to call Arachana, because I'm going to have words with her."

Staring at my mother's face, I was very grateful that I wasn't the spider queen at this moment.

P<small>HASMORIA HAD US LEAVE</small> R<small>AJ AND THE FERRETS OVER AT</small>
Buck's house, and then we headed back to mine. I wasn't
looking forward to going inside because I knew what I
was going to find. I gave my mother the key and she went
first, followed by Kipa and then by me. As she unlocked
the door and swung it wide, there was a skittering sound
that echoed into the foyer. I cringed, not wanting to go
any further, but my mother insisted that we do the ritual
over in my house.

"Gods almighty, will you look at this?" Phasmoria's
voice echoed from inside the door.

I reluctantly stepped into the foyer after Kipa, cringing
as I saw spiders skittering around the walls. The walls
weren't covered, not yet, but there were enough of the
creatures to give me the creeps. There were wolf spiders
and tarantulas, and sure enough, I flashed back to
Kingdom of the Spiders again.

"I know how neat you are," Phasmoria said, glancing
over her shoulder at me. "The creatures appear to have
been busy."

As we entered the living room, I shuddered again. The
corners were filled with webs, spun by wolf spiders and
black widows, gleaming from their snares. Some of the
spiders were attacking each other. Tarantulas were
roaming around the floor, and on my furniture. They
were all the cobalt blue variety, which told me that they
must be Arachana's favorites. I'd be happy if I never saw
another spider in my life at this point.

"I can't imagine where they all came from," I said,
moving closer to Kipa. I jumped as a wolf spider scram-

bled over my foot. I kicked it off, wanting nothing more than to jump into Kipa's arms. He probably wouldn't mind, but I didn't want to seem so squeamish in front of my mother.

"They came from Arachana's realm. Remember, I told you she's almost reached the stage of transforming into one of the Luo'henkah, and that means she rules over their realm. They do her bidding."

"What about Grandmother Spider? Doesn't she rule over the spider realm?" I asked. "And I know there are other spider deities." I wasn't quite clear on how the gods worked. I'd never been interested enough to find out.

"If it's like the wolves, then trust me, there are realms aplenty with all the spiders needed to go around between the gods and the Luo'henkah," Kipa said.

"He's right. There are more realms than you can imagine, and more than enough Luo'henkah and gods to rule over them." Phasmoria crossed her arms as she surveyed the walls. They were rippling with movement. "Where's your ritual dagger?"

"In my ritual room. I forgot to grab it on the way out." I hesitantly looked down the hallway. I really didn't relish dashing beneath a ceiling covered in spiders.

"I'll get it for you." My mother stomped down the hallway, brushing the spiders off as they fell on her, giving them almost no notice at all. She knew where my ritual room was, and she returned a moment later, my dagger in one hand and the skull off of my altar table in the other. She placed the skull on the coffee table and handed me the dagger.

"Cast a Circle. Make it strong, make it tight. Cast it to keep everyone inside protected, and to repel any wayward natures from getting in." She gestured toward the skull. "Gather around the table. Hurry up now. Don't dawdle."

I took a deep breath, pointed my dagger toward the north, and began to circle around, casting the strongest invocation I could think of. I seldom used it, except for spells where I couldn't afford for the energy to run amok or uncontained.

> *Circle now, this ring of power,*
> *now I call you, burn from fire.*
> *Fly from air, rise from earth,*
> *swell from water, I give thee birth.*
> *As I circle, raise the wall,*
> *never shall thee break or fall.*
> *None shall enter, save those we call,*
> *Watchtowers, stand thee tall.*
> *Magic rise, around us flow,*
> *ancient powers I so well know.*
> *Mine the lock, and mine the key,*
> *As I Will, So Mote It Be.*

As soon as I had finished casting the Circle, a hush fell in the room, and any spiders that were within the perimeter skittered outside as if they had been blown by a great wind.

My mother wasn't one to mess around. She turned to Kipa, pointing to the cooler. "Hand me the heart. How do I summon her?"

"You hold out the heart in your hand, and say her name three times." I *so* wanted to be any place other than where I was. The thought of facing a showdown between my mother and the Queen of Spiders wasn't settling well

241

on my stomach. My mother wasn't Queen of the Bean Sidhe for nothing.

Kipa silently handed her the heart, giving me a nervous glance. I shrugged, stepping back as far as I could while still remaining in the circle. Kipa joined me. The circle itself stretched about eight feet in diameter. My mother stood near the center. She held out the heart, looking mildly disgusted at it.

"Arachana. Arachana. Arachana."

Once again, Arachana's mist rose in the circle. I stepped closer to Kipa, grateful that I wasn't the one summoning her this time, though I had to admit, a part of me felt childishly gleeful that my mother was coming to the rescue. I didn't like people fighting my battles for me, and I always took responsibility for what I did, but now and then it was nice to have somebody on my side—somebody looking after me.

While I had loved Ulstair to the core, he hadn't been strong enough to rescue me from the situations I got myself into. I hadn't expected him to, but having somebody stronger than me on my side could be a real blessing.

As Arachana took form, the spider queen pulled back when she saw Phasmoria. Only for a second, but enough to tell me that my mother made her nervous.

The two women looked at each other, both wary. They were both Ante-Fae, and yet they were both so much more. I had a sudden flash of anxiety that, perhaps, my mother *couldn't* win if it came down to a battle between the two. But then again, even though they were evenly matched, my mother did have one thing on her side. She was protected by the Morrígan, and if Arachana did anything to her, there was a good chance that the Morrígan would come down hard on the spider queen's head.

"You summoned me?" Arachana stared at my mother.

Phasmoria crossed her arms, her fist clenched around the bloody heart as she regarded Arachana with a cold stare. "We need to have a *little talk* about your demands on my daughter, as well as what you've done to her house."

This time the look of fear that crossed Arachana's face was unmistakable. "You are Raven's *mother*?"

"I'm not only Raven's mother, I'm Phasmoria, Queen of the Bean Sidhe, the Morrígan's Chosen. And you, *my friend*, you need to make a new deal with my daughter. She was foolish in promising you an unconditional favor to begin with. But when the gods negate a deal, they aren't joking. Do you really want to cross Cerridwen?"

Arachana licked her ancient lips, glancing nervously my way. "I did not realize that Cerridwen would be so upset. Nor did I think the minx would call in her mother to fight her battles for her."

"Well, Cerridwen *is* upset, and when my daughter offered you an alternative settlement, you refused to take it. Therefore, I'm here to negotiate a new payment, one that you *will* accept." She held out the heart. "It's in your best interest to work with me, rather than against me. Or perhaps you haven't heard of me and what I'm capable of."

"Oh, I've heard of you." Arachana glanced away. I had the feeling she was trying to scheme just how much she could get away with.

"I know what you love best," my mother continued. "There is a battle raging even as we speak, and there's plenty of blood on the table. I will send you there, so that you may drink your fill. You can slake your thirst on the blood that's soaking into the battlefield and have more to spare. That should be payment enough. Do we have a deal?"

My mother's voice echoed through the room. She had infused it with the power of *Command*, which told me that she was one step away from attacking Arachana with her shriek, which could shatter eardrums and shatter souls.

Arachana seemed to sense this as well, for she backed away, shooting me a furious glance.

"Very well. I will relinquish claim on your daughter this time. But mind you, Phasmoria, if she ever calls me again, things will go quite differently." Arachana turned to me, her eyes blazing. "The next time you summon me, I assure you, even your mother won't be able to protect you from my wrath and my retribution."

Phasmoria stepped between Arachana and me. "Then we shall have to make certain that Raven never again calls your name. Because should you do anything to her, I would then have to avenge my daughter, and my vengeance knows no boundaries. Take the heart to seal the deal and I will send you to the battlefront."

Arachana grabbed the heart and stuffed it in her mouth. She turned to me, spewing bits of blood and gristle as she spoke. "Do not cross my path again. Your mother may think otherwise, but not even her intervention would be enough to save you from my anger."

"Enough!" Phasmoria held out her hands, and between them a vortex opened. "You are dismissed, Arachana."

Arachana let out a hiss. "You think to dismiss me so easily, but know this, Queen of the Bean Sidhe, *even the gods fear those of us who are the true souls of the world.*" Then the spider queen stepped through the portal without another word.

I glanced out of the circle, and every spider that I could see vanished from sight as the vortex closed. The room lightened with her departure, and I slumped against Kipa's side as he wrapped his arm around me.

Phasmoria turned, her anger still engraved on her face. "You have made a powerful enemy. Arachana is cunning and treacherous. Do not rest easy, thinking she is gone for good. Perhaps she will move on to other targets, but my guess? She won't forget you soon, and while she won't initiate conflict openly because of me, never underestimate her ability to manipulate others."

A gust rushed past as the front door to my house slammed open. Outside, the wind had picked up and was howling as clouds obscured the sky, and once again, snow began to fall.

CHAPTER TWENTY-FIVE

hree Days Later...

MY MOTHER WAS OFF ON A SHOPPING TRIP, WHICH I HAD opted out of, and I was sitting with Llew at the table in the ferrets' room, grateful to see that he was up and around again and that he looked mostly healed. Llew had brought me his scanner so I could copy off *Beltan's Bestiary* and I was researching the best way to preserve the original.

Unfortunately, everything wasn't quite back to normal. Jordan was still pissed at me, but Llew said he was coming around and to give him more time.

"He really does care about you, but he was so frightened when I was hurt. He was angry at me but misdirected it at you. He knows it. I know it. He'll apologize soon enough."

"I hope so. I hate being on the outs with him. Plus, he

makes the best mochas in town and I don't want to have to find another coffee shop," I said. "So, you said you have news?"

He nodded. "I haven't been able to find a way to break the curse." Seeing my expression fall, he hurried to add, "I did, however, discover a way to make it so the ferrets can keep their memories."

"For how long?"

"Until they decide they want me to dispel the magic. It doesn't have to be permanent, and if something accidentally breaks the spell, I can always re-cast it on them. There aren't any side effects. But they have to agree. I'm not going to bewitch them unless they have given their consent." He glanced over at the ferret cage. "Unfortunately, I don't speak ferret."

"I don't either, but Elise can talk to me. Do you trust me to translate for her?" I asked hesitantly. I wondered if Llew's faith in me had been shaken since the fight with the land wight. But I needn't have worried. He answered quickly enough.

"Of course I do. How do we go about this?"

"Let's sit by the cage." I tossed a couple cushions on the floor next to the cage, and Llew and I settled ourselves by the door. Elise came up to the front of the cage and I unlocked the hutch and opened it, letting her out. Gordon and Templeton followed. Gordon took off to do laps around the room, but Templeton stayed near. I lifted Elise onto my lap and she gazed up at me with those gorgeous brown eyes of hers.

"Elise, I have to ask you and your brothers something."

Did Llew find a way to break our curse?

"No, I'm sorry. But he has found a spell that will help

you remember who you are. It won't wear off, and if it breaks by some accident, he can cast it again. But we need your permission for him to go ahead and cast it. Each one of you has to give your permission, or not, as the case may be."

Elise paused, then let out a quick dooking sound. Gordon ran over to her side. She chittered at Templeton, then at Gordon. I told all three of them what I had told her and waited. Gordon seemed a little confused.

You mean...what do you mean again?

"We can help you remember who you really are. Do you want that, Gordon?"

Elise and Templeton watched their brother as he fidgeted in my lap for a moment. Then he climbed up my chest, snuggling his head in my hair.

I don't know. I'm happy now. But...I don't know if I was unhappy before. I can't remember. What happens if I don't like it? There was something plaintive about his question, and it made me tear up.

"We can remove the spell and you can...you will forget again." I glanced over at Llew as I waited for Gordon's answer.

He turned to Elise, and they chittered away. Templeton added his voice to the conversation. A moment later, Gordon turned back to me.

All right. I'll try it, but if I'm unhappy, you can take it away?

"Yes, Gordon, and if you are unhappy, we'll do what you want."

Then, yes, I'll give it a go.

Elise immediately snuggled against her brother, obviously relieved. *Me too, but you knew I'd say that.*

"Yes, I did." I turned to Templeton. "What about you?"
I'm good to go. I'll give it a shot.

With a sigh of relief, I looked over at Llew. "They're all up for it. If Gordon's unhappy, you'll have to come back and dispel the magic on him."

"Not a problem. All right, let's get this show on the road."

As we began to prepare for the ritual, I wondered whether we were doing the right thing. But as I had promised, if they weren't happy we could break the spell. And maybe, just maybe, Llew and I would be able to find a way to break the curse as time went on. Meanwhile, I'd care for them, as I had for years now, and in my secret heart, I admitted to being happy they were still with me. I loved them all, and while I would let them go if they wanted, they were a part of my life and family.

KIPA AND I WERE SNUGGLED IN BED, THOUGH I WASN'T about to have sex with my mother in the guest room across the hall. But with all that had happened over the past week, I needed the comfort of lying in his arms. Raj was curled up at the bottom of the bed, awake and watching us, but looking comfy right where he was.

I had just finished telling Kipa about the outcome with the ferrets—so far, everything was good and the boys were happy and a lot more communicative with Elise— when I realized that I had forgotten to ask him about his plans for the house.

"So, are you moving in next door? Or…what?"

He shook his head. "No, I don't think so. I found

renters for it, though. Ones you should approve of." He
scratched his beard, then stretched, his chest muscles
rippling. I wanted to run my hands over his chest, to run
my tongue over him, but the moment I thought about it,
the image of Phasmoria peeking into my bedroom flashed
through my mind and I quashed the impulse.

"Really? Who are they?" I leaned back against the
headboard, grateful for the downtime. I needed to just sit
in bed for a while, eat cookies, and binge-watch Netflix.

"You don't know them, but their names are Trefoil and
Meadow. They're Irish, magic-born twins—a brother and
sister, and they're demon hunters. Technically, they're
investigators connected with LOCK—the Library of
Cryptic Knowledge. I'm not sure exactly *how* they're
connected, but they're part of the organization."

I'd heard of LOCK before. The brainchild of Taliesin,
the son of Cerridwen and the first bard in the Celtic
pantheon, LOCK was about two thousand years old. The
members were generally records keepers, though I knew
they had some sort of guardian branch. I had the vague
thought it might be military in nature, but wasn't sure.

"They're sane, though? And they don't belong to any
hate groups, right?"

"Right. They're just moving to the area, so they'll need
friends. I'd like you to meet them as soon as they get
settled in." He leaned down and kissed my head. "You
okay with that?"

I nodded. I was relieved that Kipa wasn't moving in.
As much as I loved the direction our relationship seemed
to be going, I wasn't ready to commit to anything long
term yet. Everything was going well and I didn't want
anything to upset the applecart at this point.

"Yeah." I paused, a flicker of uncertainty washing over me. Kipa was gorgeous. I knew he had been a player, and so… "Is Meadow pretty? I assume Meadow's the sister?"

He laughed then, shaking his head. "Yeah, she's pretty enough. But Meadow's gay, and so is her brother. I'm not her type, and Trefoil isn't my type, so you have nothing to worry about, Raven. Besides, even if she was my type, *you're* the one I want. And your mother would kill me if I hurt you. In fact, it's time for serious talk." He sat up, the smile sliding off his face. "Raven, I give you my word of honor. If for some reason I feel like I can't commit to this relationship, I'll be honest. I'll tell you upfront before anything happens. I don't want to fuck this up."

My heart swelled, and I leaned over to kiss him.

The next moment, Raj was sprawling across our laps, staring intently at Kipa.

"Kipa be good to Raven. Raj likes that."

I blinked. "Raj! You spoke to Kipa!" I turned to Kipa. "He's never spoken to anyone else!"

Raj gave an imitation of a shrug. "Raj thinks Kipa is okay. Kipa like Raj?" He looked plaintively at Kipa, who let out a belly laugh.

"Oh Raj, yes, I like you. Kipa likes Raj. Kipa thinks Raj is just dandy." He squeezed me with one arm, while he stroked Raj's back with the other. "We make a funny little team, don't we?"

I snorted. "I'm not sure *funny*'s the word for it, but we do all right."

Then, leaning my head on Kipa's shoulder, I snuggled further under the covers. Raj promptly fell asleep, stretched across our laps, setting up a loud snorefest. Kipa and I talked in low tones as, outside, the long winter's night continued.

PHASMORIA AND I WERE STANDING ATOP A TURNOUT THAT looked over TirNaNog. The great Dark Fae city spread out below us, twinkling lights shimmering against the snowy night. The storm had ended, but the snow remained. We were supposed to have rain in a week or so, and the winter would begin to melt away, but for now, everything glimmered as though bathed with a blanket of diamonds.

"There's something I must tell you," Phasmoria said. "I didn't come here just for a visit."

I glanced over at my mother. We were sitting atop the roof of my car, swinging our legs in the chill night. "What's going on?"

"You need to be prepared for a battle that's coming. Something is stirring in the depths of the Aether. An ancient evil we thought long put to rest. Typhon is rising."

I caught my breath. "Typhon?"

Typhon, the son of Gaia and Tartarus, was the primordial dragon, a hydra with a hundred heads, who had long been wed to Echidna. She had vanished, and Typhon had fallen into a death-like slumber after a battle with Zeus. Typhon was considered the father of modern occidental dragons, though thankfully, not all of them bore his poisonous nature.

"Yes, the Father of Dragons. And he brings the darkness with him. We will all be put to the test."

I blinked. "We *who*?"

"The Bean Sidhe. The Morrígan. All of those who work on the Aether. When Typhon fully wakes, he will carry the powers of Tartarus on his shoulders. The dead will walk, breaking out of their graves. The spirit world will reel, and all connected to Arawn will be called to battle the primordial evil as it plays out through the pawns of this world." She sounded so grave that any semblance of a smile died from my face.

I stared at the lights of TirNaNog. "How do you know?"

"The Morrígan returned from a council with the Triamvinate. Arawn was there as well. You know that Corra woke?" Corra was an ancient goddess, the Scottish serpent oracle for the gods. She only woke when major world-shifts were coming to play with the world.

I nodded. "Ember told me. I heard that Cernunnos and Morgana were headed to a meeting with her."

"She's held many audiences over the past few weeks. Soon, the gods will form a conclave to meet with her. And in other realms, the Fates, the Norns, they've all called in their gods. Change is coming to the world, and it comes in on the shadowed wings of Typhon, my dear. Because you are a priestess of Arawn, and Cerridwen, you will be called in to play your part in the approaching war. For there will be war, make no mistake about it. It may not play out openly, but in the shadows and dark alleys of the world, there will be blood."

I stared over the night, my heart sinking. "I don't want to be part of a war."

My mother laughed, but there was little mirth behind her voice. "Oh, Raven, my daughter. How can I put this without being too blunt?"

"Just be direct. I am." I met her gaze, straightening my shoulders. My mother expected me to be strong, and so I would be.

"Very well. Direct it is, then. War is coming, on the Aetheric realm. The Lord of Chaos is expected to join forces with Typhon. This could destroy everything the mortals of this world—human, Fae and shifters alike—have built. The humans have managed to accept the existence of those of us from their nightmares, but they will not be able to stand against Typhon's deadly forces. He won't come in guns blazing, so to speak, but he'll work through every channel he can find. You must be ready."

I stared into the night, feeling very small and very alone. After a few moments, my mother reached out and took my hand. "There will be many fighting with you. The gods, their servants, and all of those who seek to prevent the world from falling into darkness. The Wild Hunt and its sister organizations will join this fight as well. You won't be alone, but this will divide the Ante-Fae community as alliances are made and broken."

I nodded, swallowing hard. I wasn't ready for a battle. I loved my life the way it was. But as I gazed into the frozen night, I knew I didn't have any choice. At least, though, I'd have my friends with me, and Kipa and Raj, and the ferrets. And I'd do whatever I had to in order to protect them, because that was what you did with beloved family. You protected them, no matter the cost to yourself.

"Come. The battle's not on the doorstep yet," Phasmoria said, pulling me to her side and hugging me. "Let's go have burgers and fries. We'll buy Raj one, too."

Still too stunned to talk, I nodded and slipped off the

top of the car, landing gently on my feet. As my mother fastened her seat belt, I put the car in gear. In the blink of an eye, my world had changed, and for one second, I wished I could turn back time, just long enough to breathe easy again. But knowledge was always bought with a price, and I would rather know what we were in for than walk in unprepared.

I pulled out of the turnoff and headed back to town, turning on the radio. Out of the speakers came the lyrics and plaintive notes of Pati Yang's "All That Is Thirst." All the way back to town, the mournful notes echoed in my heart.

IF YOU ENJOYED THIS BOOK AND HAVEN'T READ THE OTHERS in The Wild Hunt Series, check out THE SILVER STAG, OAK & THORNS, IRON BONES, A SHADOW OF CROWS, THE HALLOWED HUNT, THE SILVER MIST, and WITCHING HOUR. Preorder Book 9 now—A SACRED MAGIC—where we return to Ember's world. There will be more to come after that.

Meanwhile, I invite you to visit Fury's world. Bound to Hecate, Fury is a minor goddess, taking care of the Abominations who come off the World Tree. Books 1-5 are available now in the Fury Unbound Series : FURY RISING, FURY'S MAGIC, FURY AWAKENED, FURY CALLING, and FURY'S MANTLE.

If you prefer a lighter-hearted but still steamy paranormal romance, meet the wild and magical residents of Bedlam in my Bewitching Bedlam Series. Fun-loving witch Maddy Gallowglass, her smoking-hot vampire lover Aegis, and their crazed cjinn Bubba (part djinn, all cat) rock it out in Bedlam, a magical town on a mystical island. BLOOD MUSIC, BEWITCHING BEDLAM, MAUDLIN'S MAYHEM, SIREN'S SONG, WITCHES WILD, CASTING CURSES, BLOOD VENGEANCE, TIGER TAILS, and Bubba's origin story THE WISH FACTOR are all available.

For a dark, gritty, steamy series, try my world of The Indigo Court , where the long winter has come, and the Vampiric Fae are on the rise. The series is complete with NIGHT MYST, NIGHT VEIL, NIGHT SEEKER, NIGHT VISION, NIGHT'S END, and NIGHT SHIVERS.

If you like cozies with teeth, try my Chintz 'n China paranormal mysteries. The series is complete with: GHOST OF A CHANCE, LEGEND OF THE JADE DRAGON, MURDER UNDER A MYSTIC MOON, A HARVEST OF BONES, ONE HEX OF A WEDDING, and a wrap-up novella: HOLIDAY SPIRITS.

The last Otherworld book—BLOOD BONDS—is available now.

For all of my work, both published and upcoming releases, see the Biography at the end of this book, or check out my website at Galenorn.com and be sure and sign up for my newsletter to receive news about all my new releases.

CAST OF CHARACTERS

Raven & the Ante-Fae:

The Ante-Fae are creatures predating the Fae. They are the wellspring from which all Fae descended, unique beings who rule their own realms. All Ante-Fae are dangerous, but some are more deadly than others.

- **Apollo:** The Golden Boy. Vixen's boytoy. Weaver of Wings. Dancer.
- **Arachana:** The Spider Queen. She has almost transformed into one of the Luo'henkah.
- **Blackthorn, the King of Thorns:** Ruler of the blackthorn trees and all thorn-bearing plants. Cunning and wily, he feeds on pain and desire.
- **Curikan, the Black Dog of Hanging Hills:** Raven's father, one of the infamous black dogs. The first time someone meets him, they find good fortune. If they should ever see him again, they meet tragedy.

- **Phasmoria:** Queen of the Bean Sidhe. Raven's mother.
- **Raven, the Daughter of Bones:** (also: Raven BoneTalker) A bone witch, Raven is young, as far as the Ante-Fae go, and she works with the dead. She's also a fortune-teller, and a necromancer.
- **Straff:** Blackthorn's son, who suffers from a wasting disease requiring him to feed off others' life energies and blood.
- **Vixen:** The Mistress/Master of Mayhem. Gender-fluid Ante-Fae who owns the Burlesque A-Go-Go nightclub.
- **The Vulture Sisters:** Triplet sisters, predatory.

Raven's Friends:

- **Elise, Gordon, & Templeton:** Raven's ferret-bound spirit friends she rescued years ago and now protects until she can find the secret to breaking the curse on them.
- **Gunnar:** One of Kipa's SuVahta Elitvartijat—elite guards.
- **Jordan Roberts:** Tiger-shifter. Llewellyn's husband. Owns *A Taste of Latte* coffee shop.
- **Llewellyn Roberts:** One of the magic-born. Owns the *Sun & Moon Apothecary*.
- **Moira Ness:** Human. One of Raven's regular clients for readings.
- **Neil Johansson:** One of the magic-born. A priest of Thor.
- **Raj:** Gargoyle companion of Raven. Wing-

clipped, he's been with Raven for a number of years.

- **Wager Chance:** Half Dark-Fae, half-human PI. Owns a PI firm found in the Catacombs. Has connections with the vampires.
- **Wendy Fierce-Womyn:** An Amazon who works at Ginty's Waystation Bar & Grill.

The Wild Hunt & Family:

- **Angel Jackson:** Ember's best friend, a human empath, Angel is the newest member of the Wild Hunt. A whiz in both the office and the kitchen, and loyal to the core, Angel is an integral part of Ember's life, and a vital member of the team.
- **Charlie Darren:** A vampire who was turned at 19. Math major, baker, and all-around gofer.
- **Ember Kearney:** Caught between the world of Light and Dark Fae, and pledged to Morgana, goddess of the Fae and the Sea, Ember Kearney was born with the mark of the Silver Stag. Rejected by both her bloodlines, she now works for the Wild Hunt as an investigator.
- **Herne the Hunter:** Herne is the son of the Lord of the Hunt, Cernunnos, and Morgana, goddess of the Fae and the Sea. A demigod—given his mother's mortal beginnings—he's a lusty, protective god and one hell of a good boss. Owner of the Wild Hunt Agency, he helps keep the squabbles between the world of Light and

Dark Fae from spilling over into the mortal
realms.

- **Talia:** A harpy who long ago lost her powers,
Talia is a top-notch researcher for the agency,
and a longtime friend of Herne's.
- **Viktor:** Viktor is half-ogre, half-human.
Rejected by his father's people (the ogres), he
came to work for Herne some decades back.
- **Yutani:** A coyote shifter who is dogged by the
Great Coyote, Yutani was driven out of his
village over two hundred years before. He walks
in the shadow of the trickster, and is the IT
specialist for the Wild Hunt.

Ember's Friends, Family, & Enemies:

- **Aoife:** A priestess of Morgana who guards the
Seattle portal to the goddess's realm.
- **Celia:** Yutani's aunt.
- **Danielle:** Herne's daughter, born to an Amazon
named Myrna.
- **DJ Jackson:** Angel's little stepbrother, DJ is half
Wulfine—wolf shifter. He now lives with a
foster family for his own protection.
- **Erica:** A Dark Fae police officer, friend of
Viktor's.
- **Elatha:** Fomorian King; enemy of the Fae race.
- **Ginty McClintlock:** A dwarf. Owner of Ginty's
Waystation Bar & Grill
- **Marilee:** A priestess of Morgana, Ember's
mentor. Possibly human—unknown.
- **Myrna:** An Amazon who had a fling with

Herne many years back, resulting in their daughter Danielle.

- **Rafé Forrester:** Brother to Ulstair, Raven's late fiancé; Angel's boyfriend. Actor/Fast-food worker. Dark Fae.
- **Sheila:** Viktor's girlfriend. A kitchen witch; one of the magic-born. Geology teacher who volunteers at the Chapel Hill Homeless Shelter.

The Gods, the Luo'henkah, the Elemental Spirits, & Their Courts:

- **Arawn:** Lord of the Dead. Lord of the Underworld.
- **Brighid:** Goddess of Healing, Inspiration, and Smithery. The Lady of the Fiery Arrows, "Exalted One."
- **The Cailleach:** One of the Luo'henkah, the heart and spirit of winter.
- **Cerridwen:** Goddess of the Cauldron of Rebirth. Dark harvest mother goddess.
- **Cernunnos:** Lord of the Hunt, god of the Forest and King Stag of the Woods. Together with Morgana, Cernunnos originated the Wild Hunt and negotiated the covenant treaty with both the Light and the Dark Fae. Herne's father.
- **Corra:** Ancient Scottish serpent goddess. Oracle to the gods.
- **Coyote (also: Great Coyote):** Native American trickster spirit/god.
- **Danu:** Mother of the Pantheon. Leader of the Tuatha de Dannan.

- **Ferosyn:** Chief healer in Cernunnos's Court.
- **Herne:** (see The Wild Hunt)
- **Isella:** One of the Luo'henkah. The Daughter of Ice (daughter of the Cailleach).
- **Kuippana (also: Kipa):** Lord of the Wolves. Elemental forest spirit; Herne's distant cousin. Trickster. Leader of the SuVahta, a group of divine elemental wolf shifters.
- **Morgana:** Goddess of the Fae and the Sea, she was originally human but Cernunnos lifted her to deityhood. She agreed to watch over the Fae who did not return across the Great Sea. Torn by her loyalty to her people, and her loyalty to Cernunnos, she at times finds herself conflicted about the Wild Hunt. Herne's mother.
- **The Morrígan:** Goddess of Death and Phantoms. Goddess of the battlefield.

The Fae Courts:

- **Navane:** The court of the Light Fae, both across the Great Sea and on the east side of Seattle, the latter ruled by **Névé**.
- **TirNaNog:** The court of the Dark Fae, both across the Great Sea and on the east side of Seattle, the latter ruled by **Saílle**.

The Force Majeure:
A group of legendary magicians, sorcerers, and witches. They are not human, but magic-born. There are twenty-one at any given time and the only way into the

group is to be hand chosen, and the only exit from the group is death.

- **Merlin:** Morgana's father. Magician of ancient Celtic fame.
- **Taliesin:** The first Celtic bard. Son of Cerridwen, originally a servant who underwent magical transformation and finally was reborn through Cerridwen as the first bard.
- **Ranna:** Powerful sorceress. Elatha's mistress.
- **Rasputin:** The Russian sorcerer and mystic.
- **Väinämöinen:** The most famous Finnish bard.

TIMELINE OF SERIES

Year 1:

- May/Beltane: **The Silver Stag** (Ember)
- June/Litha: **Oak & Thorns** (Ember)
- August/Lughnasadh: **Iron Bones** (Ember)
- September/Mabon: **A Shadow of Crows** (Ember)
- Mid October: **Witching Hour** (Raven)
- Late October/Samhain: **The Hallowed Hunt** (Ember)
- Dec/Yule: **The Silver Mist** (Ember)

Year 2:

- January: **Witching Bones** (Raven)
- Late January/Imbolc: **A Sacred Magic** (Ember)

PLAYLIST

I often write to music, and WITCHING BONES was no exception. Here's the playlist I used for this book.

- **Android Lust:** Here and Now; Saint Over
- **Beck:** Farewell Ride; Emergency Exit
- **The Black Angels:** Currency; Don't Play With Guns; Love Me Forever; Always Maybe; Young Men Dead
- **Black Mountain:** Queens Will Play
- **Boney M:** Rasputin
- **Broken Bells:** The Ghost Inside
- **Cher:** The Beat Goes On
- **Colin Foulke:** Emergence
- **Crazy Town:** Butterfly
- **Cream:** Strange Brew; Sunshine of Your Love
- **Damh the Bard:** Land, Sky and Sea; Green and Grey; The Cauldron Born; Tomb of the King; Obsession; Cloak of Feathers; Gently Johnny; The Hills They Are Hollow; Lady of the Silver

Wheel; The Wicker Man; Scarborough Faire;
Lady in Black
- **Dizzi:** Dizzi Jig; Dance of the Unicorns
- **Donovan:** Sunshine Superman; Season of the Witch
- **Dragon Ritual Drummers:** Black Queen; The Fall; Dance of the Roma
- **Eastern Sun:** Beautiful Being (Original Edit)
- **Eivør:** Trøllbundin
- **Everlast:** Black Jesus; I Can't Move; Ends; We're All Gonna Die; One, Two
- **Faun:** Hymn to Pan; Iduna; Oyneng Yar
- **FC Kahuna:** Hayling
- **The Feeling:** Sewn
- **Fleetwood Mac:** The Chain; Gold Dust Woman
- **Flight of the Hawk:** Bones
- **Gary Numan:** Cars (Remix); Ghost Nation; My Name Is Ruin; Hybrid; Petals; I Am Dust; Here in the Black
- **Godsmack:** Voodoo
- **Gorillaz:** Last Living Souls; Kids with Guns; Dare; Hongkongaton; Rockit; Clint Eastwood; Stylo
- **The Gospel Whisky Runners:** Muddy Waters
- **The Hang Drum Project:** Shaken Oak; St. Chartier
- **The Heathen Kings:** Rambling Sailor; Rolling of the Stones; The Blacksmith
- **Hedningarna:** Chicago; Ukkonen; Fulvalsen; Juolle Joutunut; Gorrlaus; Grodan/Widergrenen; Räven; Drafur & Gildur; Dufwa; Tuuli

- **The Hu:** Wolf Totem; Yuve Yuve Yu
- **Ian Melrose & Kirsten Blodig:** Kråka; Kelpie
- **Jay Price:** The Devil's Bride; Coming for You Baby; Boneshaker
- **Jessica Bates:** The Hanging Tree
- **Jethro Tull:** Jack Frost and the Hooded Crow; I'm Your Gun; Down at the End of Your Road; Rhythm in Gold; Part of the Machine; Overhang; Witch's Promise; Bungle in the Jungle; Cross-Eyed Mary; Locomotive Breath; And the Mouse Police Never Sleeps; Journeyman; Weathercock; North Sea Oil; Something's On the Move; Old Ghosts; Dun Ringill
- **John Fogerty:** The Old Man Down the Road
- **Lorde:** Yellow Flicker Beat; Royals
- **Loreena McKennitt:** The Mummer's Dance; The Mystic's Dream; All Souls Night
- **Low and tomandandy:** Half Light
- **Marconi Union:** First Light; Alone Together; Flying; Time Lapse; On Reflection; Broken Colours; We Travel; Weightless; Weightless, Pt 2; Weightless, Pt 3; Weightless, Pt 4; Weightless, Pt 5; Weightless, Pt 6
- **Motherdrum:** Big Stomp
- **Nick Cave:** Right Red Hand
- **Oingo Boingo:** Elevator Man; Dead Man's Party
- **Pati Yang:** All That Is Thirst
- **Robin Schulz:** Sugar
- **Rolling Stones:** Miss You; Sympathy for the Devil

- **SJ Tucker:** Firebird's Child; Hymn to Herne
- **Sharon Knight:** Ravaged Ruins; Mother of the World; Bewitched; Crimson Masquerade; Let the Waters Rise; Star of the Sea; May Morning Dew
- **Shriekback:** The Shining Path; Underwaterboys; This Big Hush; Now These Days Are Gone; The King in the Tree; And the Rain; Church of the Louder Light; Wriggle and Drone
- **Spiral Dance:** The Goddess and the Weaver; Boys of Bedlam; Rise Up; Fae Dance; Asgard's Chase
- **Tamaryn:** While You're Sleeping, I'm Dreaming; Violet's in a Pool
- **Tempest:** Iron Lady; Same Side of the Fence; Hangman' Buffalo Jump; Dark Lover; Queen of Argyll; Nottamun Town
- **Thievery Corporation:** Water Under the Bridge; Voyage Libre
- **Tingstad & Rumbel:** Chaco
- **Tom Petty:** Mary Jane's Last Dance
- **Traffic:** Rainmaker; The Low Spark of High Heeled Boys
- **Tuatha Dea:** Irish Handfasting; Tuatha De Danaan; The Hum and the Shiver; Wisp of a Thing (Part 1); Long Black Curl
- **Wendy Rule:** Let the Wind Blow; The Circle Song; Elemental Chant
- **Woodland:** Blood of the Moon; Roots; First Melt; Witch's Cross; I Remember; Will O' The Wisp; The Dragon; Into the Twilight

BIOGRAPHY

New York Times, Publishers Weekly, and USA Today bestselling author Yasmine Galenorn writes urban fantasy and paranormal romance, and is the author of over sixty books, including the Wild Hunt Series, the Fury Unbound Series, the Bewitching Bedlam Series, the Indigo Court Series, and the Otherworld Series, among others. She's also written nonfiction metaphysical books. She is the 2011 Career Achievement Award Winner in Urban Fantasy, given by RT Magazine.

Yasmine has been in the Craft since 1980, is a shamanic witch and High Priestess. She describes her life as a blend of teacups and tattoos. She lives in Kirkland, WA, with her husband Samwise and their cats. Yasmine can be reached via her website at Galenorn.com.

Indie Releases Currently Available:

The Wild Hunt Series:
    The Silver Stag

Oak & Thorns
Iron Bones
A Shadow of Crows
The Hallowed Hunt
The Silver Mist
Witching Hour
Witching Bones
A Sacred Magic
The Eternal Return

Bewitching Bedlam Series:
Bewitching Bedlam
Maudlin's Mayhem
Siren's Song
Witches Wild
Casting Curses
Blood Music
Blood Vengeance
Tiger Tails
The Wish Factor

Fury Unbound Series:
Fury Rising
Fury's Magic
Fury Awakened
Fury Calling
Fury's Mantle

Indigo Court Series:
Night Myst
Night Veil
Night Seeker

Night Vision
Night's End
Night Shivers
Indigo Court Books, 1-3: Night Myst, Night Veil, Night Seeker (Boxed Set)
Indigo Court Books, 4-6: Night Vision, Night's End, Night Shivers (Boxed Set)

Otherworld Series:

Moon Shimmers
Harvest Song
Blood Bonds
Earthbound
Knight Magic
Otherworld Tales: Volume One
Tales From Otherworld: Collection One
Men of Otherworld: Collection One
Men of Otherworld: Collection Two
Moon Swept: Otherworld Tales of First Love
For the rest of the Otherworld Series, see website at Galenorn.com.

Chintz 'n China Series:

Ghost of a Chance
Legend of the Jade Dragon
Murder Under a Mystic Moon
A Harvest of Bones
One Hex of a Wedding
Holiday Spirits
Chintz 'n China Books, 1 – 3: Ghost of a Chance, Legend of the Jade Dragon, Murder Under A Mystic Moon

Chintz 'n China Books, 4-6: A Harvest of Bones, One Hex of a Wedding, Holiday Spirits

Bath and Body Series (originally under the name India Ink):
Scent to Her Grave
A Blush With Death
Glossed and Found

Misc. Short Stories/Anthologies:
The Longest Night: A Starwood Novella
Mist and Shadows: Tales From Dark Haunts
Once Upon a Kiss (short story: Princess Charming)
Once Upon a Curse (short story: Bones)

Magickal Nonfiction:
Embracing the Moon
Tarot Journeys

CPSIA information can be obtained
at www.ICGtesting.com
Printed in the USA
LVHW031521260919
632369LV00003B/579/P

9 781687 369024